At Wits' End

A Doyle Cozy Mystery

Kirsten Weiss

Cover artist: Wicked Smart Designs

Flying Saucer on Last Page from ClipArtLord.com - http://www.clipartlord.com/category/space-clip-art/flying-saucer-clip-art/

Visit the author website: www.kirstenweiss.com

Misterio Press third mass market paperback edition / April, 2019 http://Misteriopress.com

ISBN-13: 978-1-944767-26-6
ISBN-10: 1-944767-26-6

Sign up for a free e-copy of the urban fantasy novel, *The Alchemical Detective,* exclusive content, and author updates at
kirstenweiss.com

Books by Kirsten Weiss

The Witches of Doyle Series

Bound (Book 1) | Ground (Book 2) | Down (Book 3) | Spirit on Fire | Tales of the Rose Rabbit

The Doyle Cozy Mysteries

At Wits' End | Planet of the Grapes (Coming September, 2018)

Perfectly Proper Paranormal Museum Series

The Perfectly Proper Paranormal Museum | Pressed to Death

The Pie Town Series

The Quiche and the Dead | Bleeding Tarts (Coming April, 2018)

The Riga Hayworth Paranormal Mystery Novels

The Metaphysical Detective | The Alchemical Detective | The Shamanic Detective | The Infernal Detective | The Elemental Detective | The Hoodoo Detective | The Hermetic Detective

The Mannequin Offensive

Sensibility Grey Steampunk Suspense

Steam and Sensibility | Of Mice and Mechanicals | A Midsummer Night's Mechanical

Chapter 1

All I had to do was pick up the phone and make the call.

Weak, blue sunlight slanted through the foyer's stained-glass window and knifed across the reception desk. It pointed accusingly at the old-fashioned desk phone, its rotary dial stretching in a rictus grin. Outside, late afternoon thunder rumbled, echoing off the mountains and rattling the Victorian B&B.

My finger hesitated over the dial, my shoulders tightening.

The dry thunder had been near constant for the last hour. The slowly rotating ceiling fan made no difference in the oppressive heat. I just wished it would rain, that *something* would break loose.

Wisps of my blond hair stuck to my neck, and I plucked at the collar of my neat white blouse.

Was it any surprise I was flustered, aggravated and perturbed? Flustered because my cousin Dixie had failed to show for work *again*. Aggravated I could never fire her, because... family! Perturbed by the man upstairs in room seven.

But maybe room seven was a misunderstanding? Maybe I hadn't been clear enough that the room bill was due yesterday? Or the day before. Or the day before that.

Bailey, my grandmother's beagle, whuffed from his dog bed. His tail whipped back and forth, tickling my ankle.

"I know, I know," I muttered and bent to scratch his head.

Bailey's tongue lolled, his eyes closing, and in spite of myself, I smiled.

Okay. I'd just call the room and tell Tanner McCourt he needed to pay today or vacate the premises.

But I didn't.

Instead, I studied my day planner and the command I'd circled in green highlighter: *Get Payment!!!* If it was in my planner, I had to do it. Even if I didn't want to.

I blew out a slow breath. And I'd thought the week had started out so well. The mantra at the top of this week's page was: *I am in control.* It also happens to be my personal mantra (second only to: *Never argue with a fool. Onlookers may not be able to tell the difference*).

I added an extra exclamation point to my note and sighed.

Tanner McCourt had checked into my grandmother's — now my — UFO-themed B&B two weeks ago for a one-week stay. He hadn't paid up front, because I never ask anyone to. And he hadn't paid when his week was up, asking to stay a few more days to clear up some business.

If this was one of those fancy hotels, I might be able to change the key card when he left his room upstairs. But he never left the room, not even to eat. He ordered takeout, the delivery boys somehow knowing to slink up the back stairs, so I'd be less inclined to notice.

My hand hovered over the phone. The ceiling fan hummed overhead.

A trickle of sweat dripped down my spine.

This was the limit. If Tanner didn't march downstairs with cash, check, or credit card in hand, I'd call the police.

I'd really do it this time.

The screen door banged open. My best friend, Arsen Holiday, trooped into the B&B's foyer, and warmth spread through my chest.

He was tanned, tough, and sinewy, and dressed in hiking pants with lots of pockets. A long-sleeved tee stretched heroically across his broad chest. "Afternoon, Sue. We made it back alive." He brushed back the wavy brown hair clinging damply to his head.

He held the screen door open. A middle-aged woman and her twenty-something son — both guests of Wits' End — staggered inside.

Unlike Arsen, who looked energized by their tramp through the mountains, my two guests drooped. Well, Professor Green drooped. Her son's brunette head had been in a slump since we'd met, two days ago, his gaze locked on his phone. But he looked fairly fit — lanky, even if his jaw seemed soft, his skin too smooth from a life indoors.

The thunder grumbled again, and I flinched.

"UFO weather." Arsen laid his outdoor-roughened hands on the ancient wooden desk.

"There's no such—" I shook my head. And there's no such thing as earthquake weather either, but there was little point arguing. "Find any bear tracks?"

Beneath her sheen of sweat, Professor Green's face lit. "We did! From a mother bear and two cubs." She reached behind her and flapped the back of her blue, microfiber hiking shirt to cool herself. The shirts were supposed to wick the sweat away, but this one had obviously failed. The summer Sierras could do that.

"It might be a good thing tracks were all you found," I said. Mama bears were notoriously defensive when cubs were nearby.

She chuckled, removing her khaki hat and ruffling her short, graying hair. "Indeed. And I need a shower." She looked up the green-carpeted stairs, grimaced, and began her ascent. Pausing on the third step, she turned. "Ethan?"

Without taking his eyes from his phone, her son grunted and followed her upstairs.

Above us, two doors slammed.

Arsen jerked his thumb toward the stairs. "It was all I could do to keep that guy from wandering off a cliff," he said in a low, rumbly voice. "He whined all the way up the mountain and all the way down."

I grinned. "You should be an expert at hiker management by now." Small-town Doyle was a UFO hot spot, and Wit's End was a UFO-themed B&B, thanks to my enterprising grandmother. Arsen made a business for himself as a guide, taking them on UFO-spotting night hikes. I wasn't sure how lucrative being a pathfinder was, but at least it was *something*, and Arsen came from money.

He wiped away the drops of moisture clinging to his forehead, and his handsome face creased with annoyance. "That kid's not going to make it to thirty if he doesn't start paying attention to the real world."

"Thanks for getting them back before the storm hits."

Arsen shrugged. "It's not going to." He brightened. "Hey, did you hear the news? Xavier Ultra is coming to Doyle."

"Who?" My gaze flicked to my day planner, open on the desk.

"He's that TV survivalist – the Amazon, the Sahara, those reality shows. Remember? Last year they dropped him in Ethiopia's Danakil Depression for a week without any food or water. He had to survive drinking his own—"

I shot him a look.

He cleared his throat. "Anyway, the guy's amazing. He's signing books in Doyle next Tuesday."

"You're excited about a reality TV star?" Arsen was the real deal when it came to mountain survival. Why would he care about some faked TV show?

"Why wouldn't I be psyched? Xavier Ultra is so tough, he can strangle you with a cordless phone. He's so tough, he can kill your imaginary friends. Death once had a near-Xavier-Ultra experience."

"I think you mean Chuck Norris."

"Who's he? Listen, I gotta go," he said. "Some tourists want me to take them paddle boarding."

I raised a brow but refrained from comment. Arsen and I had been friends since childhood, and for that I loved him. But his family money and good looks had made his life too easy. At seventeen, he'd run off to join the circus. I'd received postcards from him every now and again — from a Caribbean resort where he'd worked as a dive instructor, an island in the Pacific where he'd taught surfing. He'd gone where his whims and the wind had taken him. All he'd gained from the experience were fun memories and an impressive collection of airplane barf bags. But I guess people living in UFO-themed B&Bs shouldn't throw stones.

I had a good idea of what today's "tourists" looked like. Young. Sexy. Female. Not that I was jealous or anything. Arsen and I had always been and would always be friends.

His smile broadened, as if he'd read my mind, and he sauntered out the door. The screen banged behind him.

Bailey woofed gently, reminding me of my duties.

I bent and scratched behind his floppy brown and white ears. "I know. I'll do it." Because what did I have to be afraid of? Either Tanner McCourt would pay me, or he wouldn't. And if he didn't, I'd do what Gran did on those rare occasions she'd had a deadbeat guest — call the cops and have him removed.

My stomach twisted into a knot. *I was in control.*

More importantly, I couldn't fail Gran, who'd left me this B&B. I couldn't fail my cousin Dixie, who worked here and loved Wits' End like I did. I couldn't fail, period.

Swallowing, I dialed room seven.

He picked up halfway through the first ring.

I hesitated, waiting for him to speak.

He didn't.

Had we been cut off? The house line was old and didn't always work right.

Faint breathing drifted over the line, and my scalp prickled.

"Mr. McCourt, this is Susan Witsend. Your bill is a week past due." Silence.

"Like I said," I rushed on, "it's a week past due, and I have guests coming tomorrow who'll need your room." This was a lie. The guests wouldn't be arriving until Friday, and it was only Tuesday, but he didn't need to know that. I cleared my throat. "So, I'm afraid I'm going to have to ask you to leave," I squeaked. "Today. This afternoon."

A click. A dial tone.

Outraged, I stared at the receiver. The jerk had hung up on me!

"That does it," I told the beagle and dialed the sheriff's Department. Tanner McCourt might think I'm a pushover, but he was about to learn B&B owners had the law on their side.

"Doyle Sheriff's Department," a brisk, feminine voice said. "How can I help you?"

I explained the situation.

She sighed. "All right. We'll send someone over."

"Thanks." We said our goodbyes and hung up.

Fueled by righteous adrenaline, I drummed my fingers on the scarred wooden desk. It would serve Tanner McCourt right if two deputies dragged him from the room. Though more likely they'd escort rather than drag. It wasn't as if he was a violent criminal, just a deadbeat. "And that's bad enough," I told Bailey.

He yawned, looking away.

"You don't think I was too hard on him by calling the cops, do you?"

Bailey had definite opinions about uniforms. Except for the postman, who, for some reason, he adored. But California hotel law was clear. I had every right to call in the police at this stage in the game. And Tanner had hung up on me!

Booted feet clunked on the front porch steps. A screen door bammed shut. The interior screen door swung open, and a female sheriff's deputy strode into the foyer. She looked about my height — five-six — though she was probably fifteen years older – I guessed mid-forties. Her blue eyes crackled with annoyance.

Bailey growled and lumbered to his feet.

"Wow." I bent and grasped the dog's collar. "You got here fast."

She frowned, her tanned brow creasing beneath her broad-brimmed hat. Whipping it off, she ran up the stairs, taking them two at a time.

So, that was service in a small town.

Bailey snorted.

Except the deputy didn't know what room Tanner was in. "Wait!"

Rolling my chair back, I stood and hurried after her. I didn't want her banging on the wrong door. Professor Green was probably still taking her shower, and her son was so plugged in he wouldn't hear her knocking.

At the top of the stairway, I paused. The long, narrow corridor was empty. At the opposite end of the hall, the door to the rear, exterior stairs hung open. My brow creased. It was letting all the heat in, thank-you-very-much.

I walked past sepia-tinted photos of old-time Doyle. Grinning, gap-toothed miners. Women in long gowns walking down a dusty Main Street, figures ever-so-slightly blurred. It was like walking past a parade of ghosts.

The door to room seven also stood open.

Weird. I'd swear I hadn't told the dispatcher what room Tanner was inside.

I hesitated on the hallway's thin, green carpet. What was the etiquette once the police were involved? I'd never had to throw someone out before, but I hadn't owned the B&B long.

My heart squeezed, and I pushed thoughts of my grandmother aside. This was business, and I couldn't get emotional, not with the police here.

I cocked my head, listening.

And heard nothing.

And that was weird too. Shouldn't she be ordering him out or listening to his excuses or something?

I stepped through the open door.

Gun drawn, the deputy stood over Tanner McCourt.

The room tilt-a-whirled. A chill rippled the skin between my shoulders, as if I'd been touched by a gray shadow. Any sense of control slithered from my limp fingers.

Tanner sprawled flat on his stomach on my grandmother's rag rug at the foot of the brass bed. Eyes open. Blank. Dead.

Chapter 2

I gasped. "I didn't want you to kill him!" My face warmed, and I clapped my hands to my mouth. Of course, she hadn't killed him. I hadn't heard a shot. No blood stained the colorful rag rug or the hardwood floor. The room was a mess, the end table and desk drawers open, papers scattered.

All my grandmother's framed UFO photos lay upside down on the unmade bed, its quilt puddled on the floor on the side by the window. Faded squares, where the photos had once hung, marked the antique floral wallpaper.

The deputy's expression hardened. She slid the gun into the holster on her complicated-looking belt. Her sleeves were rolled to the elbow, ready for business. "I didn't shoot him. Calm down."

Moving on. "Sorry," I stammered. "I know you didn't. I'm just... Is he dead?" His upper half lay across the blue-and-green rag rug. His face was turned away from the open window. The blue-checked curtains breathed gently. Tanner breathed not at all, but I'd found denial an excellent coping mechanism. *Please tell me he isn't dead.*

"He's dead."

"But he was just..." I trailed off. We'd been on the phone moments before the deputy had arrived.

Unless we hadn't been.

"This doesn't make sense," I said. "I called his room to ask him to pay his bill not five minutes ago. He picked up."

Her blue-eyed gaze sharpened. "You spoke to him?"

"I told him he had to pay today, and then he just hung up. He didn't say a word." The puzzle pieces clicked into place. Someone had picked up the phone. Someone who wasn't Tanner?

His killer.

A killer in my B&B. I gripped the brass footboard for balance. The realization shouldn't have taken so long to strike. But in my defense, small-town Doyle wasn't exactly a high-crime area. The town's greatest villains were a teenage hacky sack gang, and they weren't violent. Just super irritating.

"You're Harriet's granddaughter," she said. It was more statement than question, and I nodded. "All right. Go downstairs. I'll call this in, and we'll talk more later. Don't say anything to anyone. Got it?"

I nodded, backing from the room.

A determined expression on his doggy face, Bailey huffed down the green-carpeted hall.

I scooped up the beagle before he could reach the deputy or the open door to the exterior stairs. Had a killer come and left through that upstairs door?

Stomach burning with worry, I lugged the dog downstairs. Was Tanner's death my fault for leaving the door unlocked?

Two thirty-something deputies strolled into the foyer. The men wore white shirts with badges pinned to their broad chests and gear belts low on their hips.

The smooth-faced blond smiled. "You got a guest who won't leave?" he asked, his voice surprisingly deep.

"You haven't..." I whipped around, confused, and looked up the stairs. If they were here to eject McCourt, why had the other cop showed up out of the blue? The gears in my brain disengaged, whirring uselessly. "Room seven. There's another officer with him now, and he's dead. Murdered, I think. And his name is Tanner, Tanner McCourt." Bailey wriggled in my arms and strained toward the deputies. I squeezed the beagle to my chest.

They stared at me, looked at each other.

The taller man, dark-haired and handsome, shook himself. "Tanner McCourt's dead?"

"Yes. That's what the other police officer said." Tanner could have just slipped and fell and hit his head on the brass bed on the way down. I gnawed my bottom lip. But then who had picked up the phone? Or maybe he'd slipped, fallen, and died in those few minutes between my phone call and the deputy's arrival? Was I jumping to conclusions there'd been foul play at work?

"Stay here," the dark-haired man commanded.

The two deputies pounded up the stairs.

Bailey wriggled in my arms, and I set him on the Persian-ish rug. He trotted to the screen door, whined, and looked over his shoulder at me.

I plucked my thick day planner off the desk and opened the door for Bailey to the sunroom-slash-porch. He trotted past the white wicker furniture and sat, panting, beside the second screen door to the front yard.

I opened that as well, and he picked his way down the three steps. The beagle was fine going up stairs, but he wasn't a fan of down. He bounded around the corner of the old Victorian. Bailey never left the yard without me, so I wasn't worried about him running off.

Puffy thunderheads rimmed blood orange clotted the sky. Two sheriff's department SUVs sat in the gravel driveway.

Planner clutched to my chest, I sat on the porch steps and breathed deeply.

Tanner McCourt. Dead. I stared sightlessly at the picket fence encircling the lawn. Its borders overflowed with my Gran's rose bushes. Gran. What would she do in this situation?

She'd stay calm and figure it out. All right, so would I. Logically. Step-by-step. My insides jittered. I was in con—Oh, who was I kidding? I was not in control. There was nothing about a dead body in my upstairs bedroom that was under control!

I got a grip on myself. If it hadn't been Tanner who'd answered the phone, why on earth had the killer picked up? If I'd just killed someone, I'd hardly take a message for them. So, I'd been wrong, it couldn't have been murder, and it wasn't my fault the upstairs door was open.

What if he'd tripped over the rug and hit his head? Guilt twisted my gut at the thought.

I rose and walked around the side of the two-story Victorian. Sun glinted off the UFO embedded in the peaked, shingled roof. I shielded my eyes against the glare.

I almost preferred the idea of murder to accident. How many other people had Tanner McCourt owed money to? He'd been proficient at putting off my requests for payment. That sort of dodgy skill didn't blossom overnight, and it left a trail of enemies.

A curtain fluttered through Tanner's open window above the porch's sloped overhang.

Someone *could* have climbed out the window. Then they might have slithered down one of the posts to the garden. Arsen and I had done it plenty of times when we were kids, before my grandmother had caught us.

But the rear door would have been an easier means of access. The odds of running into another guest during the day were low.

I straightened. It *had* to be murder. Why else had someone searched Tanner's room? And it had definitely been searched. Sure, he could have made the mess days ago, and I'd never have been the wiser. But he wouldn't have been able to sleep with the framed photos on the bed. And why remove them from the wall in the first place?

Shifting my weight, I shook my head. Maybe I didn't need to know. The police would figure this out, and Tanner McCourt would no longer be my problem.

"What's going on?" A male voice said in my ear.

"Gagh!" I rocketed into the air.

Arsen cocked his head and stared at Tanner's open window. "So, you finally called the cops on that guest?" Still watching the window, he jerked his chin toward the two sheriff's SUVs in the driveway.

"No. I mean yes." I worked to steady my breathing. "There's been a murder." That sounded overly dramatic, and I cleared my throat. "At least, I think it was murder. His room looked like it had been searched." My fingers whitened on the planner.

His bronzed brow creased. "His?" Arsen turned his head and looked down at me. "Slow down. Start from the beginning."

"I called the police because of my deadbeat guest. He's the one who died. They discovered the body."

He whistled. The sunlight caught his eyes, and something seemed to light behind them. "Who was he?"

"Some guy named Tanner McCourt. I think he used to live in Doyle and then moved away and came back—"

"Tanner Mc— Sheriff McCourt's husband?"

I gaped. "Who? You know him? Knew him, I mean?"

He shook his head. "I know you haven't been back long—"

"I came to Doyle every summer to be with Gran." Except for the last three. I'd had a job with my parents' accounting firm then.

"Didn't you hear about it? It was a huge scandal. The sheriff's husband got arrested a few years back for welfare fraud. He was running a scam from his job with the county."

"Arrested?" I squeaked. I'd been hosting an ex-con? I grabbed his arm and dragged him away from the open window and to the front of the Victorian. "Please tell me he was released and hadn't escaped."

"He was released."

"I knew they had the same last names, but I've never met the sheriff, and lots of people have the same last names. You're sure it's the same person?"

"How many Tanner McCourts can there be?"

"And the sheriff – the Doyle sheriff – kept her job in spite of being married to a crook?" I asked, disbelieving. People *must* have wondered if she'd been in on the scam. I know I did.

"Sheriff McCourt had a tough reelection campaign, but she won. I think they're going through a divorce. Maybe it's already happened."

Two more sheriff's cars rolled to a halt in front of my B&B. Officers exited, doors slamming. Uniformed men strode purposefully into the Victorian. I clutched the top of my head. This was terrible. A murder. Here. In my house.

Thunder rumbled, and a chill wind whipped down from the mountains. The pines in the yard next door whispered, its branches tossing.

My heart sank. And now Tanner would never pay me. I know it was a horrible thing to think under the circumstances. But I was barely squeaking out a living from the B&B.

"You are a fount of useful gossip," I said, depressed.

He shrugged. "I like to know the score when I land somewhere."

"What are you doing back here anyway?"

"I saw the police cars heading in your direction, and thought I'd check up on you, just in case."

The female deputy walked down the front steps, her boots thunking on the wood. She glanced at us. Her face hardened, and she strode to the waiting SUV.

"Wowza," he said. "That's her."

"Her? Who? You mean that's Sheriff McCourt?"

He nodded.

"But she's the one who discovered the body." How awful for her. I folded my other arm across the planner and clutched my elbow. The sheriff had less reason to like her husband than I did. That gave her a motive. Should she be investigating?

Inside the SUV, she adjusted her seatbelt.

"When I found her standing over him," I whispered, "I'd thought she'd killed him." Had my first instinct been right?

The SUV started up and backed from my driveway. It drove to the cul-de-sac's inlet and turned, vanishing behind a stand of pines.

"She's taking herself off the case," he said. "That's why she's leaving."

The blond sheriff's deputy walked onto the porch. He pushed open the screen door and leaned out, motioned to us. "Hey, Arsen. What are you doing here?"

"I just dropped off some hikers," he said. "Susan's a friend."

I glanced between the two of them. Of course, they knew each other. Arsen knew everyone.

"Then stick around," the deputy said. "I'll have questions for you too. Why don't you wait over there?" He pointed to a grouping of Adirondack chairs on the lawn.

"Susan Witsend?" the deputy asked, clicking a button on the radio clipped to his collar. "I need to ask you some questions. This will be recorded."

My mouth went dry. Recorded? But it wasn't like I was a suspect. He wasn't mirandizing me. Being recorded was no big deal. Who wouldn't want to use modern technology to record an interview? It beat having to write everything down and potentially miss a critical word. "Sure."

Arsen lounged in the wooden chair facing us, his ankles crossed, his expression inscrutable.

The deputy, whose badge said DENTON, ran me through my call with Tanner.

He nodded. "When did he check in?"

I flipped open my planner and doublechecked, though I already knew the answer. "Two weeks ago, on a Monday." Mondays were terrible days for tourism and usually my day off, which I enjoyed. But when Tanner had arrived on my doorstep, I couldn't turn away weekday business. Not when I needed it so badly.

"What were his habits?"

"His habits?" I parroted.

"Did he have visitors? Was he loud?"

"He was quiet, and he never left the room." Which was why I hadn't been able to clean it - something I hadn't minded until now. "And he did have visitors." I flipped through the planner, searching. "Restaurant delivery guys mostly, but there was a man, a big guy. He didn't give me his name, but he looked like a bear."

"A bear?"

My face heated. "Dark and hairy. He had rough hands with grease under the nails, like a mechanic."

"How tall was he? My height? Taller? Shorter?"

"About your height, maybe a little shorter."

"How tall do you think I am?"

"Five-eleven?"

He smiled. "Exactly. Okay, when was this visit?"

"Two days ago, in the afternoon, sometime after my shopping." I pointed to the spot on the page.

"Did this man say anything to you?"

"He asked where McCourt's room was. I made him call up to Tanner rather than giving him the number myself."

Bailey trotted to us and whuffed, exposing rows of unthreatening teeth.

Denton bent to scratch behind his ears. "Did he give you any trouble?"

Offended, the dog shook his head. In his mind, he was ferocious, a predator, defender against squirrels and uniformed men.

"No," I said, "Tanner was always polite." Especially when he was putting me off.

I glanced over my shoulder and tensed. My cousin Dixie ambled down the court, her slim figure casting a long shadow. Her head was bent to her cellphone. And of course, she didn't see the police cars. How could she? An obscuring, thundercloud of chaos followed wherever she went.

I turned to face the deputy and made shooing motions behind my back. Dixie'd had some youthful run-ins with the law. My cousin was on the straight and narrow now, but she got stiff and defensive and guilty-looking around police. I didn't think it was a good idea she and Officer Denton meet.

The deputy made a note. "Anyone else?"

Arsen coughed, drawing Denton's attention.

Dixie looked up. Her eyes widened, and she dove like a leopard seal behind a rose bush.

My shoulder muscles released. I could always count on Dixie's sixth sense to avoid a hassle.

"Anyone else?" Denton prompted again.

"There was a woman, who came to see Tanner," I said. "I recognized her. She works at the coffee shop, Ground."

He looked up sharply. "Not the owner?"

"No, one of the baristas. She's older, mid-forties, and blond. Her name's French sounding. Charis?"

His face cleared. "Cherie?"

"That's the one. She came by last week — I'm sorry, I can't remember what day. It was in the late afternoon, and she didn't stay long."

"Okay, why don't you run me through your day?"

I handed him the planner. "It's all here. Prepare breakfast at six. Clean up breakfast at ten. Clean rooms at eleven..."

When I finished, he let me go and went to speak to Arsen. My friend rose from the Adirondack chair and stretched, unconcerned.

Casually, Bailey and I walked around the corner to the side yard. I picked up speed when the deputy was out of sight.

Dixie, sleek in denim shorts and a tank top, balanced warily on the gazebo steps. "What's going on?" Her shoulder-length, near-black hair was tipped with violet. "Why's Wits' End crawling with cops?" She scratched the side of her nose, carefully avoiding her piercing.

"One of the guests was, um, killed. I think."

"You think?" She folded her arms. "Who was it?"

I blew out a noisy breath. "That guy who wouldn't leave."

"Tanner?" She wrinkled her pert nose. "Figures. He was creepy." She paused, considering. "Do I still have to come to work tomorrow?"

My face tightened. Ah yes, the truly important question. "Yes, you do. And where were you today?" Dixie usually helped out from eleven to three, cleaning and manning the desk so I could take a break. It was now nearly six o'clock, the sun slanting across the nearby mountains. Thunder cracked, and I twitched.

"It's Tuesday. I thought you might have bundt cake."

"I don't, and you were supposed to help clean today. Where were you?"

"Around. Gotta go." Lithely, she hopped the low fence and vanished into old Mr. Fitzgerald's yard. If he caught her trespassing, she was in for it. Part of me wished he *would* catch her.

Put out, I wandered to the front yard. Dixie stopping by to bogart a bundt cake was par for the course. So was looking for a reason not to come to work tomorrow. But I couldn't worry about Dixie. I was too rattled by my guest's death. I didn't have any policies or procedures that covered a murder in a guest room.

Out of the corner of my eye, I saw the deputy slap Arsen on the shoulder.

Bailey growled a warning, and I grabbed his collar before he could rush to Arsen's defense.

Oblivious, Denton returned inside the B&B.

Arsen strolled to me. "What did you tell him?" he asked.

Releasing the dog, I relayed our conversation.

Arsen rubbed his chin.

"What?" I asked.

"If the sheriff's involved, things could get sticky."

"But Sheriff McCourt's not involved. She's taken herself off the case. You said so yourself."

"But there's a lot of loyalty in the department."

"How do you know so much about the department?" I asked.

Bailey whuffed.

He grinned. "It's a small town. Guys talk."

"I'm sure the police will figure it out." I tried to inject confidence into my voice. "Like you said, it's a small town. They probably already know who did it."

"Maybe, but I don't like that it happened in your place. You need better security."

"It's a B&B, not a fortress."

"You're right though, it shouldn't be too hard to figure this out. Not in a town this size." His eyes gleamed. "I've always wanted to be a private investigator."

So had I until age seven, when my parents had made it clear being a girl detective wasn't practical. "There's no reason to play amateur detective," I said sharply, worried about where this was headed. "The police have all sorts of resources you don't."

"But no one wants to open up to the cops. For example, I bet there are all sorts of things you didn't tell them."

"No, there weren't." I crossed my arms over my chest. Prickles of heat swept my neck. The thing was, flirtation had been one of

Tanner's techniques for putting me off. It had been super embarrassing and not at all relevant to the police investigation. I wasn't about to tell the cops Tanner had hit on me.

Arsen jabbed a finger at me. "There *was* something. I can always tell when you're lying."

"I don't lie."

"But you're holding something back. What is it?"

"Nothing. I told the police everything I know about Tanner, and I told you everything I told them."

"You *are* holding out," he said. "What are you afraid of telling me?"

"Only of you sticking your nose into police business. Leave it alone, Arsen Holiday, or I'll tell your aunts that you broke their Ming vase playing football in the house and blamed the cat."

He paled. "You wouldn't."

"In a red-hot minute."

"That was ages ago."

"It was last week."

"Water under the bridge." He gripped my shoulder. "Don't worry. I'll take care of this."

"There's nothing to take care of."

His bronzed face turned serious. "I've spent my share of time in villages—"

"Villages? You lived in resorts."

"And one thing is constant."

"Oh?"

"When things go wrong, they blame the outsider."

"You mean — one of my guests? Like the Greens?"

In the waning light, his eyes darkened to cobalt. "I mean like you."

Chapter 3

The storm broke, rain pounding the Victorian's peaked roof, thunder breaking my sleep. But the real storm was in my own house. Someone had been killed in my B&B. A murderer had been right upstairs.

The shadow clutched at me. Breath speeding, I rolled over, as if I could ever escape it, and twisted the covers tighter.

When I finally did sleep, I dreamt a tidal wave was bearing down on me. I'd wake up, roll over, fall asleep, and return to the same dream, different setting.

Stupid thunder storm.

At five AM, I gave up on sleep and surfed the Internet for information on Tanner. He hadn't been the only one arrested for his welfare fraud. He'd fingered two other county employees — Davin Markarian and Cherie Cavalier. That might explain why Cherie had come to the boarding house last week. Had Tanner's male visitor been Davin?

The sky outside my sitting room window lightened, clouds parting.

Bleary-eyed, I stumbled to the kitchen. I prided myself on my breakfasts. So in spite of my exhaustion, I baked coffee cake and a mushroom, egg and potato casserole. Shredded swiss cheese over the finished casserole. Lit tea lights beneath the chafing dishes.

Savory and sweet scents filled the octagonal breakfast room. Morning sunlight streamed past the drawn curtains and made angular shapes across my grandmother's blue toile wallpaper and the hardwood floor.

I floated a white cloth over the oval-shaped dining table, flicking the base of the hanging brass lamp. When I had the cash, I'd replace the lamp with something more Victorian, less old west. If I ever had the cash.

A stellar jay leapt onto the windowsill. It cocked its head, as if sniffing the coffeecake. It was shaped like a duck and something I usually made on weekends, but I wanted comfort. I couldn't stop replaying the moment I'd seen Tanner McCourt's body.

"I don't much like the idea of staying in a hotel where someone was murdered right down the hall."

I started.

Professor Green stood in the entry to the breakfast room. She jammed her hands on the hips of her hiking trousers.

Her son, eyes glued to his phone, edged past her.

"I don't much like it either." I smoothed the front of my loose, khaki slacks. "A death in the house, I mean," I added hastily, adjusting a chair at the oval table. "But I don't think it was a random killing or a robbery. If it matters, he was targeted." Tanner had let the killer inside his room, which meant he'd known him. Or her.

"It doesn't," she said tartly, the fine lines around her brown eyes deepening.

"Did you hear or see anything?"

"The police interrogated us quite thoroughly." She studied the sideboard, laden with plates and glasses and chafing dishes. "We'd prefer not to go through that again."

"Of course. Sorry."

Her son wandered to the sideboard and snitched three pieces of bacon from the warming tray. He folded the bacon in half and crammed it all into his mouth. Since it was thick-cut bacon, it was quite a feat. He loaded his plate.

"But why do the police think he was targeted?" the professor asked in a lowered voice.

"I don't know what the police think." I stared at the hardwood floor. I could come up with at least one motive for killing Tanner. He'd owed me money. Maybe he owed others. But why would the killer have removed my UFO pictures from the walls?

Ethan pulled out an antique chair and sat. "About time something interesting happened," he mumbled through a mouthful of coffee cake. He chased it with a gulp of orange juice. Freckles had sprouted on his pale nose and cheeks – a souvenir of yesterday's hike. His brown hair stuck up modishly at the front.

"It is not interesting," she said.

"If it upsets you to stay," I said, crossing my fingers, "I'd be happy to call the Historic Doyle Hotel. They may have rooms available." I didn't want to lose a night's income, especially now that Tanner's debt to me was out of reach. Two week's room and board, up in smoke.

Gran's first mortgage had been long repaid. But she'd taken out a second to repair the roof and upgrade the plumbing and install the UFO. The monthly payment was due next week, and my bank account was woefully low.

Professor Green sighed. "No. We're leaving tomorrow for the watch tower anyway. There's no use switching hotels."

"Do I have to go into the mountains?" her son whined. "There's no connectivity."

"There's no electricity either," she said, "but you're coming, and that's that."

"How am I going to get wi-fi?" he asked.

"You won't," she said, "and that's the point. It's time for you to unplug."

His brow lowered threateningly. "I don't want to unplug."

"That's not—" She puffed out her cheeks. "We'll discuss this later."

"Whatever. But I don't see why I can't stay here. I'm not a little kid." He folded another piece of bacon and crammed it into his mouth.

Arsen, in brown hiking pants and a matching tee with an outdoor company's logo on the front, breezed into the breakfast room. Grabbing a plate, he thunked into a wooden chair. "Hey Professor. Ethan. Suzy-Q."

I frowned. I hated that nickname. "Hey. Are you taking the Greens out this morning?"

Slicing into the coffee cake, he glanced up at them. Crumbs scattered across the white table cloth. "Didn't have any plans to, but if you two need something—"

"No," the Professor said. "We've decided to spend the day at the lake and get some R&R in before we head up into the mountains."

"What brings you here at this hour?" I asked Arsen.

He reached across the table and stabbed three slices of bacon with his fork. "Where else would I be? You make the best breakfast in Doyle."

Like I'd fall for that. "Moocher."

He grinned and bit into the coffee cake.

I rolled my eyes and marched upstairs. The police had told me I could clean room seven, which seemed kind of fast since Tanner had only died last night. They'd taken the rag rug and bedding as evidence, and a strangely eager young CSI type had vacuumed the room for stray bits of evidence.

From the small upstairs closet, I grabbed my bucket of cleaning supplies, a mop and a broom. I fumbled the keys from my pocket, unlocked room seven, and pushed open the door. But in the doorway, I paused, uncertain.

With the rug and Tanner's possessions gone, the only unusual part of the cleanup would be returning the grainy UFO photos to the walls. So why was I hesitating in the doorway and holding my bucket in a death grip?

I swallowed. I wasn't afraid of ghosts. The room had to be cleaned, and Dixie wasn't here yet.

Edging inside, I wedged the door open with a rubber stopper. I scraped open the window and returned the photographs to the walls. I snapped on yellow rubber gloves and wiped the windows and mirror over the bureau, then moved into the small bathroom.

The new faucets looked like old-timey water pumps. Gran had also installed a bowl sink and a soaking tub with jets and a heater. The bath wasn't in bad shape, considering I hadn't cleaned the room for two weeks. I should have known something was wrong when Tanner had refused to let me inside.

This being a crime scene, I scrubbed like a madwoman, using bleach everywhere. Then I mopped the floors, using Gran's vinegar mixture in the cleaning water. Tanner might not be haunting the room, but I definitely felt some bad juju.

I wrung out the mop and set it aside. The curtains fluttered at the window. Yanking off my yellow gloves, I rubbed my forearm across my damp brow and inhaled the smell of clean. No one would guess a man had been murdered here. I bit the inside of my lip. But they'd hear about it. Would anyone want to stay in this room again?

I was tucking fresh sheets beneath the mattress when the bell over the front door jingled. That was weird. It was a Wednesday, and I wasn't expecting new guests.

I hurried down the stairs.

A tall woman with dark skin and silky black hair cropped at her jawline stood in the hallway and looked up at me. She carried a leather attaché case rather than a suitcase, so maybe she was here to see the Greens or...

My stomach plunged. Or she was here about Tanner McCourt. "Hi," I said. "Can I help you?"

She reached inside her black blazer and drew a slim, black leather case from the inside pocket. Impassive, she flipped it open, displaying a badge. "I'm Agent Manaj, FBI. I'm here to see the owner."

I stumbled on the last step and grabbed the wooden railing for balance. "FBI?"

"Are you Susan Witsend?"

I nodded.

"I'd like to see the crime scene."

"Sure... I just finished cleaning it. The deputies told me I could," I said, quick and defensive.

"I'd still like to see it, if you don't mind." But her tone said it didn't matter if I minded or not.

I rubbed my palms on the thighs of my white jeans. "Okay. The room's upstairs." I turned and walked up the steps.

Behind me, the agent's footsteps were silent, but her presence pressed against me. The spot between my shoulders heated.

I stood aside at the open door to room seven. "This is it."

She walked inside and drew the attaché case from beneath her arm. Opening it, she pulled out an eight-by-ten, black-and-white photo of the room. "The photos that were removed," she said, voice flat. "Did you return them to the same places they'd hung before?"

"Yes." From the doorway, I motioned to the wall over the desk and opposite the bed. The quilt spilled over the desk chair. "I went by the fade lines in the wallpaper. The photos are all different sizes."

She set her attaché on the wooden desk and peered at each framed UFO photo in turn, taking her time.

"Do you think the photos have something to do with his murder?" I didn't see how they could, but I had a fake UFO in my roof and a crime scene on my second floor. And Doyle did have a history of, well, odd events.

Her expression didn't change. "I can't discuss an ongoing investigation." She turned to study the partially-made brass bed.

"The Sheriff's Department took the bedding. Those linens are fresh."

Downstairs, the bell over the door jingled. Bailey barked outside.

"I'd better check that." I shuffled from the room and trotted down the stairs.

A curly-haired, middle-aged blonde in jeans and an NRA t-shirt stood beside the desk in my foyer and scowled. Bailey snuffled at her boots.

I started and nearly missed a step for the second time that morning. "Sheriff McCourt!" I hadn't recognized her out of uniform. "Is something wrong? Are you here to see Agent Manaj?"

She cursed beneath her breath. "She's here already?"

The FBI agent appeared at the top of the stairs. "I'm afraid so," she said dryly. "Sheriff, my condolences on your loss."

"Thanks," the sheriff mumbled.

Like a villain in an old western, Agent Manaj stared down at us. All that was missing was a black hat to match her suit. "Were you here to see me?" One of the agent's dark brows arched. "Because I'm sure you weren't here to take a second look at the crime scene, since you're on leave."

Bailey looked a question between the two women. No doubt he was trying to suss out who was more likely to have treats in her pocket.

A pulse beat in the sheriff's jaw. "Right. I figured you'd want to interview me. When do you want to do this?"

Agent Manaj glanced at her watch (which was also black). "I'm in the middle of something at the moment. What about later this afternoon? Say, two o'clock at your station?"

"Perfect," the sheriff ground out.

"Oh, and Ms. Witsend, since I'll be staying in Doyle awhile, I'll need a room. Is seven vacant?"

"The murder r—?" My gaze flicked to the sheriff, and I cleared my throat. "Um, yes." The rest of the rooms were booked from Friday through Sunday by UFO hunters, but seven would be free.

"Excellent." She walked down the stairs. "I'll get my things from the car and sign in." She strode across the foyer and out the front door.

I hurried to the reception desk.

The sheriff gripped my arm, halting me. "We need to talk," she said in a low voice.

"We do?" I squeaked.

"About Tanner."

"But... Aren't you off the case?"

"Meet me in the backyard," she hissed as Agent Manaj pushed open the screen door. She nodded to the FBI agent and brushed past. The screen door clattered shut behind her.

"Problem?" Manaj asked, setting her black suitcase on the faux-Persian carpet.

"No." I hustled behind the desk and pulled the guest book from the drawer.

"You don't use your computer for reservations?" Manaj asked.

"Only for printing invoices. My grandmother was old fashioned."

"Ah, yes. You inherited this place, didn't you?"

"How did you...?" Of course, she was the FBI. She'd have checked. "Yes. Six months ago."

"Has it been difficult?" she asked. "Switching from accountant to B&B manager?"

My insides quivered. She really *had* done her homework. *In control, I am in control...* "I worked here every summer growing up, so I know how Wits' End runs." My ribs squeezed, and I blew out my breath. The only difficulty – the sledgehammer-through-the-heart difficulty – had been losing Gran. I penciled her name into the ledger. "Have you got a credit card and ID?"

She pulled a man's wallet from the back pocket of her slim, black slacks and handed me a credit card.

I signed her in, swiped her card.

"How did Tanner McCourt pay?" she asked.

"Cash, up-front for three days."

"But he was here over two weeks."

"Yes," I said, feeling stupid. "He asked to extend his stay, and since I happened to have a room vacant, I let him." What an idiot I'd been. "I asked for his credit card at check-in, but he'd told me he'd misplaced it and would bring it down to me as soon as he could. He never did. Sign here... and here." I slid the room contract across the desk, and she signed.

"I'd like to take a look at that guest book," she said.

"Sure." I pushed it towards her. I probably should have asked for a warrant or something, but I wanted this investigation over and the killer caught and life back to normal. Fast. Besides, having an FBI agent in the room might exorcise Tanner's ghost. Metaphorically speaking. It seemed weirdly right that a federal agent was in room seven after a criminal had died there. Like a balancing of scales.

She tucked the book under her arm. "I'll return this in an hour." Grabbing her black suitcase off the floor, she marched up the stairs.

I waited until I heard her door shut. "Come on, Bailey. Let's go outside."

Tail wagging, the beagle followed me into the front yard. I found a faded, octopus squeaky toy beneath a rose bush and chucked it into the side yard. The furry octopus landed beneath the spirit house my grandmother had brought back from Thailand. The morning's incense had already burned down — a tradition of my grandmother's I still followed.

Bailey chased after the toy, and we made our way to the backyard.

The sheriff sat in the white-painted gazebo. White Lady Banks' climbing roses twined up its sides, their scent thick in the morning heat.

I walked up the two gazebo steps and sat on the bench across from her. "You wanted to talk to me?" I asked.

"I want you to tell me everything that woman does."

I stared. "You want me to spy?" *What? No, no way.* "I can't spy on an FBI agent."

"Call it whatever you want," she said.

"But—"

"Listen up, Witsend, you and I are in this together, and you're going to do what I tell you."

I bridled. "What do you mean *we're in this together*?" And also, *you're not the boss of me.*

"A man died in your boarding house—"

"B&B."

"And there were only three people in it at the time — you and your two guests. Of the three, you've got the best motive."

"The police think *I* did it?" I bleated. "That's ridiculous!"

"And then there's your jailbird cousin."

I plucked a dried leaf from the roses twining up the gazebo and crushed it between my fingers. Yes, Dix had a record, but it had all been stupid juvie stuff. Nothing violent. "Dixie wasn't even here when your husb— the victim was killed."

"How do you know when he was killed?"

I slowed my breathing. Nothing good ever came from hyperventilating. "I don't, exactly. Sometime on Tuesday. Do you?"

"Not. On. The case. But your cousin knows where the room keys are kept, doesn't she? She could have found Tanner's and killed him."

My heartbeat sped. "Why? She doesn't even know him. She's got no motive."

"You think the FBI isn't going to be looking hard at an ex-con in the house?"

"But—"

"But nothing. You two are suspects." She stretched her arms along the railing. "Smile. They probably won't arrest you as an accessory."

"I'm smiling on the inside." I scowled. "And what about you? You're the wife, and everyone knows that ninety-percent of the time, the spouse is the killer."

"Yeah, but I'm not, and I don't think you are either."

"Well, it's obvious *I* didn't," I said, mollified. "I called the police to ask for help bouncing Tanner out."

"Which would be nice cover if you'd just killed him."

"But you said—"

She waved off my objection. "Don't worry. I don't think you're clever or cold enough to pull that off."

What? I was clever. And cold. "Is that a compliment?"

"No."

Bailey trotted to me, the furry octopus in his mouth.

I wrestled the slimy thing away from him and chucked it into the garden.

"So, if we didn't kill him," she said, "that leaves someone sneaking in through the upstairs door or—"

"The Greens? But they seem so ordinary. And why would you bring your son along to a murder? Unless Ethan did it, but I can't imagine him getting up the energy to kill someone. I'm sure he's killed thousands of characters in computer games, but in real life? No way."

"That's what you think."

"What do you mean? Do you know something about him?"

"No, I'm off the case. I'm just saying, human nature can surprise you."

"What surprises me is an FBI agent showing up for a local

homicide." I glanced at the Victorian. "Don't they only get involved in federal cases?"

She rose and stretched. "Yeah. Well, Manaj and this town have history. Personally, I think she's off the rails, which is another reason why you need to watch her."

"What kind of history?"

"She was the lead agent on that big missing person's case last year."

My mouth parted. "You mean *The Disappeared*?" Rumors connecting Doyle to UFOs had circulated for years. There were two reasons for this. First saucer-shaped lenticular clouds often appeared over the mountains. Second, hikers occasionally went missing in the nearby forest. Both phenomena had rational, scientific explanations. Lenticular clouds aren't exactly unique. Hikers go missing in the California woods with sickening frequency.

But then an entire pub full of people disappeared. When the missing reappeared months later alongside a handful of vanished hikers, UFO speculation hit the stratosphere. We'd even started capitalizing the incident: *The Disappeared*. I had to ask Manaj what happened. Her perspective would be a fantastic addition to my UFO lectures.

The sheriff winced. "Don't call it that. They all came back."

"But none of them remembered what happened. And they were gone for months. Is the FBI still investigating?"

"Manaj is. Everyone else knows mass hysteria drove those missing people into the woods, and they got lost."

"Yes, but the entire building—"

"Don't tell me you believe this garbage?" She motioned to the B&B's intersecting gabled roofs. The edge of the flying saucer glinted behind a brick chimney.

"I'm agnostic on the subject," I lied. Because there's more in heaven and earth than is dreamt of in most people's philosophy, etc., etc. UFOs could be real. But under the circumstances, it didn't seem in my best interest to admit that.

She shot me a skeptical look.

"Okay," I said. "What's our plan?"

"Just watch her."

"But when should I call you to report in?"

"Don't call me. I'll call you."

"This doesn't seem like much of a plan," I said.

"Fine. You want a plan? Next time you clean her room, make note of what you can observe. Keep a log of her comings and goings."

"But what are you going to do?"

"None of your business." She stomped down the gazebo steps.

Bailey shook his head, collar jingling, the legs of the octopus wriggling in his jaws.

"I don't think this is a very equal partnership," I shouted at her departing back. To Bailey, I said, "But it is sort of a vote of confidence. If the sheriff really thought I was guilty, she wouldn't ask me to do this, would she?" I jammed my fists into the pockets of my khaki slacks.

The dog whined, skeptical.

I shuddered. "Yeah. She was kind of bossy. I *really* hate being told what to do." But it didn't look like I had a lot of choice, and the sheriff wasn't my controlling parents. "This is different," I said in a low voice. "I don't have to do this. I'm choosing to."

A figure shifted on the exterior stairs, and I glanced up.

The FBI agent quietly shut the rear door.

Chapter 4

Glancing up and down the green-carpeted hallway, I rapped softly on the door to room seven.

After a long moment, Agent Manaj wrenched it open. Her brown eyes narrowed. "Yes?"

"Hi, I never finished making up the room."

"Hold on." She closed the door. A minute later it opened, and she thrust my bucket of cleaning supplies into my arms.

I staggered from the force of the blow.

"It's fine," she said. "I don't need it cleaned." She slammed the door in my face.

My jaw tightened. Some guests liked their privacy, but I'd been burned once by Tanner keeping me out.

Did Manaj have something in the room she didn't want me to see? Something connected to the murder? Maybe the sheriff had been on to something when she'd asked — well, ordered — me to snoop. Not that I was keeping an eye out just for her sake. This was my B&B, after all.

I went about my cleaning.

Running a B&B sounds wildly romantic, until you realize that it consists mostly of playing maid. But I had a system. The bedrooms and dining area got a daily clean in the morning. All the other rooms — including my own — I rotated cleaning throughout the week. But I always gave the front room a good polish on Fridays, because that's when most guests arrived. Ah, the glamorous life of a B&B owner.

I backed from Professor Green's room (she was surprisingly messy) and locked the door.

"Isn't that my job?" a feminine voice drawled.

After I recovered from my heart attack, I turned.

Dixie stood in the hallway, her weight shifted to one side, her arms akimbo. The violet tips of my young cousin's hair matched her eyeshadow.

"Hi," I said. "I thought I'd get a start on the cleaning for you."

She shrugged. "Fine by me. But I still get paid, right?"

"Right."

Whistling for Bailey, she turned and jogged down the stairs. A screen door slammed below.

"I said start, not finish," I called after her.

Her voice drifted up the stairs. "I'll clean the gazebo."

"Sure you will," I muttered, not believing it.

Before Gran had died, she'd hired Dixie of the haphazard-work-ethic to help with the cleaning. Approximately five times a day I fantasized about firing her. But I didn't have the heart. I couldn't. If it hadn't been for Dixie, I wouldn't have Wits' End.

Dixie stayed outside as I finished cleaning Ethan's bedroom (unsurprisingly messy). I moved on to the breakfast room. And then, though it was only Wednesday, I vacuumed the near-Persian carpet in the foyer. When I'd finished, the FBI agent still hadn't emerged.

Once the vacuum cleaner was put away, the beagle nosed open the screen door and sat to watch. He hated the vacuum cleaner even more than the squirrels he waged daily and futile battles against defending the yard.

I broke out the lemon-scented furniture polish and went to work on the bannister, the desk, the window frames overlooking the front porch. I even climbed on a ladder and washed the stained-glass window.

Finally, around one o'clock, the FBI agent left. Her attaché case wasn't under her arm.

Opportunity!

I waited for her blue sedan to drive down the road, then hurried upstairs, Bailey at my heels. Heart pounding, I inserted my key into the lock to room seven.

The door opened three inches and caught on the chain.

I rubbed the back of my neck and stared at the chain, barricading my entry. What FBI trickery was this? She'd somehow chained the door *after* leaving, so presumably she had a method for unchaining it on her return. But how was a humble hotelier supposed to get inside?

True, I was trying to get inside for nefarious reasons, but still, it was my door and my room. I had every right to go inside. It was in the room contract everyone signed without reading.

I shut the door and locked it. There was probably an online video demonstrating how to defeat a chain lock, but I had an easier solution.

I strode down the hallway to the exterior stairs and stepped onto the landing. It overlooked the backyard and the A-frame cabin next door.

In the yard below, my cousin braced on her elbows and lounged on the gazebo steps. So much for cleaning.

"Dixie," I hissed, then shrugged. Today, her carelessness worked in my favor.

Bailey stared mournfully down the rough wooden stairs.

I slung one leg over the banister and slithered onto the wide, shingled overhang above the wraparound porch.

The beagle barked once.

I swallowed, grabbing a windowsill for balance. Funny, when Arsen and I had done this as kids, the overhang hadn't seemed so steep, the drop so far. I took a step, and my foot skidded six inches sideways.

The beagle yapped excitedly, and I shushed him. "Stay." Not that there was a snowball's chance of him waddling onto the roof. Bailey had a strong sense of self preservation.

Figuring four legs were better than two, I got onto my hands and knees. I crawled forward, shingles digging through the thin cloth of my khaki slacks.

My breathing grew shallow. Honestly, it wasn't such a big drop. Just one floor, plus a few feet for the porch, and some nice, soft rose beds beneath me. It might have been twenty years since I'd pulled this stunt, but I'd be fine.

I rounded the corner, the sun beating down on my neck and back. Three more windows, and I'd be there.

A bead of sweat trickled down my jawline and along my chest.

A shingle skidded from beneath my hand, and I yelped, lurching forward. The shingle flew into the garden, landing somewhere with a soft thud.

Cursing, I rubbed my burning palm and examined the scrape. Gran had just had the whole house re-shingled. There'd better be a warranty.

I crawled onward and reached the window to room seven.

I jiggled the window frame. Locked. But Arsen and I had learned how to defeat that particular window long ago. In a trice, I was clambering inside.

Manaj had made the brass bed, the UFO photos from the wall lined up atop its brightly-colored patchwork quilt. I turned them over and pried off their backs. No hidden messages lurked inside.

I returned the photos to their frames and put them back atop the bed. Was this just part and parcel of the agent's interest in The Disappeared, or did she think the framed pictures were connected to the murder?

The agent's attaché case lay, inviting, on the desk. Hurriedly, I unzipped and opened it. On top was a mug shot of an evil-looking man with a lowered brow and a jagged scar down his right cheek. Beneath the photo was a rap sheet for some guy named Guido Valducci, currently in jail for racketeering. "Sheesh."

Hand trembling, I dug into my pocket for my cell phone to take a photo and realized I hadn't brought it.

"Dammit."

I flipped through the papers, but they all seemed to be about this Guido guy. Doyle's a small town, and I'm pretty sure I'd have remembered seeing Guido. Granted, I'd never lived full-time in Doyle until now, and I couldn't claim to know everyone. But Guido was the kind of man you wouldn't want to meet in a well-lit, wide boulevard thronged with riot police. I'd remember Guido.

The floor creaked outside the bedroom door.

Heart hammering, I returned the papers to the attaché case and zipped it up.

A key rattled in the lock.

In two steps, I was at the window. I eeled through it, turned, and pulled it down as quietly as I could.

The door opened, and I ducked.

My feet skidded beneath me. I tumbled backward, too startled to shriek. The roof vanished. I was airborne. My fall was quick, broken first by an Eden rose bush, and next by the ground.

"Ooof." Pain rocketed through my back, arms, skull.

I gasped and lay still, the wind knocked from my lungs.

This is what happens when you don't have a good plan.

Above me, the window scraped open.

I froze, my arms hung up in the rose bush like a marionette's. I imagined Agent Manaj sticking her head outside and peering into the garden. For one, witless moment, I considered calling out to her for help. But then I did a mental inventory and discovered my fingers and toes could move, so the rest of me was probably mobile.

The window closed, and I breathed through the pain.

A shadow fell across my face.

Dixie stared down at me. The sun lit her like a black halo, casting her into forbidding darkness.

Then I blinked, and it was just Dixie with her black and violet hair.

"You didn't stick the landing," she said.

"Ugh." A wave of pain washed from my lower back to my neck.

"Why were you on the roof?"

Smothering a groan, I untangled myself from the thorns and sat up, my muscles protesting. I surveyed the damage. Khakis: covered in dirt. T-shirt: same. Arms: crisscrossed with red scratches. Bones: unbroken. But my neck...

I rubbed the back of it and groaned again. What had I done to myself?

"Well?" she asked.

"I noticed one of the shingles was loose," I said, "so I decided to check the others."

"Really?" She extended a hand. "'Cause it looked like you were breaking into room seven." She hauled me upright, and I bit back a howl of pain.

My laugh was shrill even to my ears. "Break in? Why would I break in when I have a key?"

"Good question."

"Did you finish cleaning the gazebo?" I asked brightly.

Dixie muttered something inaudible and wandered into the backyard.

Mournful, I gazed at the broken limbs of the rose bush. "Sorry," I whispered. My grandmother had planted these, pouring her love and attention and care into them the same way she'd done Wits' End, and my heart twisted. I'd fix the rose bush, just like I'd fix whatever fallout the murder inflicted on her B&B. I just wish I knew how. *She'd* know. "I really wish you were here." Guilt swamped me. Why would I wish this mess on my poor grandmother?

Aching, I limped up the porch steps and into the high-ceilinged foyer.

Bailey yipped from the top of the carpeted stairs.

"Shh!" I clambered up the steps and gathered him into my arms. "You really need to get over your phobia of walking down stairs," I whispered.

He licked my face.

Augh! Dog breath!

I brought him downstairs and into my private rooms. Gran had made sure she had her own personal space — a chic black-and-white Victorian sitting room, bathroom, and master bedroom.

I showered, hoping the hot water would relieve some of the pain, which had migrated into my shoulders and upper back. It didn't.

I changed into fresh jeans and a loose, blue-and-white top, and picked up my cell phone and called my chiropractor. It's easy to get out of whack when every morning is spring cleaning. My grandmother had sworn by monthly chiropractor visits. Also, the chiropractor was hot in a Prince Harry sort of way, and I had a serious crush on him. I think my grandmother had had one too. When I called, and the chiropractor himself answered, he offered me a spot that afternoon.

"Three o'clock?" he asked.

I consulted my thick day planner. "Thanks, Doctor Harwell," I said, my blood fizzing more than it should have. I'm too old to giggle over tall, red haired, and handsome men. Plus, he was my doctor.

Crushing on him was just wrong. "I'll be there."

He chuckled. "I keep telling you, just call me Zack."

"Zack. See you soon. Bye."

We hung up, and I checked my watch. It was five after two.

My stomach rumbled.

I jammed my planner into my purse, attached Bailey to his leash, and we walked into town.

Doyle had been a mining town during California's gold rush days. Today, it was all about the tourists. Main Street's old-timey, western buildings hosted wine tasting rooms instead of mining supply shops, boutiques instead of general stores. Bowls of water sat outside the doors of dog-friendly shops.

A quintet of teens in shorts and slouchy tees bounced a hacky sack between them. We dodged the hacky sack gang – taking up the entire sidewalk – and swerved toward Ground's red door. Something pinged off my head, and I turned, startled.

A sandy-haired teen grinned. "Careful." He grabbed the fallen leather ball from the flowerbed.

I scowled. "Let's go, Bailey." I tugged him past Ground's chalkboard stand. A water bowl sat beneath its red-paned windows. We paused for Bailey to get a drink and walked inside.

When the coffeeshop had burned down last year, we'd all thought the owner, Jayce, would change up the interior. But she'd returned it pretty much to its original style, with wooden floors and cloth hangings on the rough, brick walls. She had, however, indulged in a new, black quartz counter that glittered with flecks of blue, and matching tables.

Bailey's leash burning my scuffed palm, I got in line. I stared hungrily at the pastries in the window.

Behind the counter, Jayce smoothed her green apron and smiled. She was a cheerful brunette about my age, with green eyes and a penchant for jewel-toned clothes that hugged her every curve. "Hi, what'll it be?"

"Hi, Jayce. I'll take a regular coffee, black, no sugar, and a chocolate croissant, to go."

She grinned. "Comfort food." The cafe owner sobered. "I heard what happened at Wits' End. How are you holding up?"

"I'm fine." I glanced behind me, but no one else stood in line, so I was free to gossip. "I honestly didn't know Tanner well," I said quietly. "But... it happened in my house."

She winced in sympathy. Jayce reached into her apron pocket and pulled out a small, blue spray bottle and handed it to me. "It's a clearing spray, to get rid of any bad mojo. Spray it around the B&B."

Doubtful, I put it in my purse. "Thanks. How much do I owe you?"

She waved her hand, dismissive. "It's on the house. You might want to spray yourself too. I'm not one for seeing auras, but even I can feel there's some darkness clinging to you."

"That would be stress." I glanced down the counter, but didn't see Cherie, the barista who'd come to visit McCourt. "Is Cherie working today?"

"No, but she's coming in tomorrow." She turned and poured me a cup of coffee. "Do you want me to give her a message?"

The sheriff hadn't asked me to investigate - only to keep an eye on the FBI agent. But asking after Cherie wasn't investigating. It was just being polite. "No, thanks. It's no big deal."

Her emerald eyes hardened, and she slid open the glass case, retrieving my croissant. "Murder's always a big deal."

"It's not about..." But that was a lie, and I stumbled to a halt, my hunger evaporating. "You're right. It's the biggest deal there is. There's an FBI agent investigating the murder. She's staying at my B&B."

Her expression turned wary. "Not Agent Manaj?"

"Yeah. Do you know her?"

"She investigated the..." She glanced about the café. "You know."

"The Disappeared?"

"Yeah," she said. "She's obsessed. Manaj seemed to think Doyle was somehow involved in it."

"Involved?"

Her slim hands fluttered. "Like a conspiracy or something. Crazy, huh?" She passed a paper cup of coffee and a small bag across the counter. "Here you are." She handed me a doggy biscuit. "And something for Bailey. Let me know if there's anything I can do to help."

I knew she meant it, and I smiled back. "Thanks. Take care."

Bailey and I strolled onto the wide sidewalk. The two-story buildings all had balconies, providing shade on the warm day. Vines climbed the balcony supports.

We walked behind a wine tasting room and to its public picnic area filled with shade trees and metal sculptures by local artists. I found an empty bench beside a still, copper whirligig and tossed Bailey his dog treat.

Slowly, I picked apart the croissant. "So," I said to Bailey. "The question is, who is this Guido person Manaj is so interested in, and does he have anything to do with Tanner's murder?"

Bailey dropped half his treat on the brick patio and snuffled at it. Having no respect for the five-second rule, he picked it up with his teeth and resumed munching.

I opened my day planner on the rough, wooden picnic table. One of my favorite features was the quarterly sections for planning out the tasks for each project. The planner even came with color-coded stickers to organize projects. Of course, I never used them. That would be ridiculous. I used color-coded highlighter pens.

I made a note for a new project in my day planner: *Watch Manaj.*

Maybe I should use a code? I scratched out her name and replaced it with *M.*

"And what's with the UFO pictures?" I asked Bailey. "It's not like Tanner was killed by aliens."

The whirligig spun, rattling, and I gave a start. My blond hair whipped my cheek in the sudden breeze.

Bailey's mouth peeled back in a snarl, and he barked at a falling leaf. It skittered across the bricks.

Unsettled, I patted him. "Goofy dog, it's only the wind." But I finished my coffee quickly, and we trotted up the steep slope to Main Street.

Professor Green stepped from the yarn shop across the street, and I raised my hand to wave. A muscular blond woman emerged behind her, and I paused, hand in the air. It was Cherie Cavalier, the woman who'd come to visit Tanner. The two women spoke, and Professor Green nodded. She strode down Main. Cherie shook her head and walked in the opposite direction.

Did they know each other?

I checked my cell phone. It was almost three. I needed to get to the chiropractor's. But I dug out my planner and made a note of the time, date and location. Their meeting likely didn't mean anything, but the sheriff might want to know.

I tugged Bailey away from an interesting bush, and we hurried to the chiropractor's office. It was just off Main, in a low, cinderblock building with a small parking lot.

Chiropractor Zack sat behind the reception window. His long fingers zipped across a computer keyboard. He was older than me – I guessed mid-forties – definitely not too old.

Giving me a Prince Harry smile, he tossed what looked like an old pizza delivery hat from the desk to a nearby shelf. "Just give me a sec to finish entering this."

"Sure. I'm early anyway." I pointed. "What's with the hat?"

"My past life. In high school, I flipped dough at Mountain Pizza."

"I worked summers in high school too." I winced, hoping it didn't sound like I was straining for a connection. But I had fond memories of my youthful employment, working for Gran at the B&B. Those had been magical times. Once the cleaning was done, I'd had free afternoons at the lake and long nights gazing at the stars with Arsen and, sometimes, Dixie.

His fingers tapped the keyboard, and he stood. The red-headed chiropractor was even taller than Arsen, but lankier. He ambled through the door into the simple, green-painted reception area. "Is that Bailey?"

The dog woofed and tugged at his leash.

Chuckling, he bent to pet the dog, then straightened. "Come on back."

I followed him into his office, tied Bailey's leash to a table, and pressed myself against an upright and angled table.

He lowered it so I was parallel to the gray carpeted floor.

"So, what's going on?" He ran his hands lightly over my upper shoulders, and I tried not to tense.

"My neck and upper back are sore," I mumbled into the paper.

He wiggled my feet, then made adjustments to my knees with a small metal, spring-loaded device. It was much less stressful than the bone cracking manipulation I'd seen on TV. "I heard about your murder," he said. "Your muscles are really tight."

I breathed slowly. "Can you blame me? But my neck pain has nothing to do with the murder."

"What happened?" He made another adjustment, his hand skimming along the side of my thigh.

"I tripped and fell on the stairs," I said, my voice half an octave higher than normal.

He paused, his hand resting on my lower back. "I'm sorry." He laughed self-consciously. "I should have been asking about your injury, but I was really asking about the murder. I've turned into a small-town gossip. Forget I asked."

"Everyone's curious," I said, too aware of the warmth of his hand. "But I was downstairs when it happened. I'm just glad I didn't find the body."

"Me too. You don't want something like that in your head."

"Neither does the sheriff." To find her ex-husband dead like that... I grimaced, the paper crinkling. "She's the one who found him. I'd called the Sheriff's Department because..." My face heated. "It's stupid, but Tanner wasn't paying his bills."

"Ah, yes. I heard Sheriff McCourt had gone on leave. I supposed she'd have to step away from the case." He rubbed a spot beneath my shoulder blade. "Now relax."

I willed my muscles to loosen. "Where did you hear that?" My jaw crinkled the tissue paper on the head rest.

"It was in the newspaper."

A source of information I hadn't bothered to check.

"Still," he said, probing my skull, "having a murder in your B&B must have been a shock." He thunked my skull with the metal device.

"I wish I knew what really happened. The police asked a lot of questions, but they didn't tell me much."

"So, was it like you see on TV? They didn't take you down to the station, did they?" His voice warmed with concern.

"No, it was weirdly casual. They asked who I saw coming and going, how well I knew Tanner, that sort of thing."

"I still can't believe we've got the FBI here in Doyle," he said. "Again."

"I know, after last year..." I trailed off, uncomfortable. How did one talk about The Disappeared?

"My parents keep telling me to move to the big city, where it's safe." He laughed. "So, did you see anyone?"

"I heard..." He didn't need to know about the weird phone call. "No. No one."

"Coming up."

The table whirred and lifted to standing. I backed off the table, and Bailey thumped his tail on the gray carpet.

"I suggest cold packs on your neck and shoulders," he said. "They'll reduce the swelling." He walked me to the reception window, and I handed him my credit card.

"You should return next week," he said, walking through the door into the office.

"Sure," I said, trying to sound reluctant and failing. I consulted my planner. "What about Tuesday?" I braced my elbows on the open reception window.

He bent over the desk on the other side of the window and checked his computer.

We made the appointment, and I penciled it into my planner.

A bearlike man in loose jeans and a t-shirt splattered with paint strode into the office and banged the door against the wall. His nose was massive, his black hair graying about the edges. My breath caught. He'd been Tanner's mystery visitor. I should have known it wouldn't take long to run into him in a town this size, though I was surprised to find him in my chiropractor's office. But now I could give his name to the sheriff.

Bailey yipped.

The man gave the dog a cold look and stopped short at the sight of me.

"Hi," I said. "Don't I know you?"

"Don't think so," he rumbled, looking away.

"You probably saw him at your rival's." The chiropractor grinned.

My brow furrowed. "My rival?"

Bailey's tail thumped the thin carpet. He strained at his leash toward the newcomer.

"The Historic Doyle Hotel," Zack explained. "Davin works there."

I schooled my expression. Davin? The Davin Markarian who'd gone to jail with Tanner? He *had* to be the same man — how many Davins were there in a town this size?

The big man grunted. "Yeah. Doc, you got some time?"

"Sure," Zack said, motioning to the chairs in the reception area. "Have a seat, and I'll be right with you."

"No, I don't think that's where I saw you." I snapped my fingers. "You stopped by my B&B last week. I called up to Tanner McCourt's room for you."

The two men stared at me.

"The police were asking about visitors," I said, "but I didn't know your name at the time. They want to speak with everyone who met with Tanner."

Wincing, Davin rubbed his hand across the rounded belly of his paint-stained tee. "I had nothing to do with Tanner's murder. I don't know anything."

"Of course not," I said quickly and took an involuntary step back. My hip bumped an end table and the spider plant on top of it rocked. I reached to steady it. "You were there days before he died. But you worked with Tanner at the county government," I said. "The police may be wondering if his death had something to do with his old job. You could be able to help them, maybe know people from his job who might have wanted him dead." Inwardly, I winced. *Smooth.*

A vein pulsed in his jaw. "You gonna go to the cops?"

Bailey growled.

Zack cleared his throat. "There was a murder in her guest house. Of course she's concerned, and I'm sure the police have had lots of questions for her."

"Right," I said hastily. "Since Tanner only returned to Doyle two weeks ago, whoever killed him must have been someone from his past. Maybe someone the police don't know about?" *Not subtle! Not subtle!*

Davin's face darkened.

"Davin, why don't you wait in the examination room? I'll be there in a minute." Zack shoved a credit card slip through the window. "Sign here."

Davin slouched into the exam room, shutting the door hard

enough to rattle the watercolors on the wall.

"He's just a little rough around the edges," Zack said in a low voice. "He's a good guy."

I signed the receipt, and was glad to see my hand didn't shake. "Do you know him well?"

He grinned. "Just his muscles and bones, and they're a little rough around the edges."

In spite of everything, I smiled. I moved toward the door. Bailey's leash tangled in my legs, and I stumbled into the end table. The spider plant tumbled to the floor, dirt scattering across the green carpet. "Sorry!"

"It's all right." He hurried through the door into the reception room and righted the plant. "Susan, you're not... playing amateur detective, are you?"

My face heated. "No! That would be totally stupid. But the police asked, and..."

"You wanted to help. I get it. But be careful. Not everyone will understand your motives."

"Right. Thanks." I untangled myself and dragged Bailey from the chiropractor's office.

At least I'd learned Davin's name. Maybe I'd been a little obvious about it, but I'd gotten the job done. This detecting business wasn't that hard after all. In a town the size of Doyle, I'd have the suspects rounded up in no time.

Right?

Chapter 5

I hurried home and called the sheriff from my kitchen.

"Davin Markarian," I said, sliding open the window over the sink. It scraped against the frame. "The guy who came to see Tanner was Davin Markarian."

"About time you remembered."

"I didn't remember." I leaned against the butcher-block counter. "I ran into him at my chiropractor's and asked his name."

"You did what?"

"Oh! And I saw Professor Green talking to Cherie from Ground." I fumbled the snap on my day planner. "Let's see, I wrote down the time..."

"You wrote...? Stop playing detective! You don't know what you're doing."

I stiffened. "I think I'm capable of writing down the correct time and date."

The sheriff growled. "Do what you're told and let the *real* detectives solve the crime." She hung up.

My jaw unclenched. Have I mentioned I don't like being told what not to do? I dug Jayce's "clearing" spray out of my purse and spritzed it around the kitchen. It smelled of ginger and orange and something spicy I couldn't identify. But I liked it.

On a whim, I raced up stairs, spritzing as I went. I stopped in front of room seven and dosed the door. Ginger-orange scented mist drifted lazily in the air.

The door popped open.

Manaj winced, sneezed. "What are you doing?"

"Sorry." I clutched the blue bottle to my chest. "I didn't know you were here."

"What is that?"

"Just a clearing spray. For auras. If you believe in that."

"Is there anything you don't believe in?"

"Love as a healer of all wounds?"

She stared at me.

"Well," I said, "I just don't. It's naïve. People need to heal their own wounds."

"So, what you're telling me, is you assaulted my door with a magic spray."

"Well, I wouldn't say magic. Or assaulted. A friend gave it to me. I mean, it can't hurt, can it? And it smells nice, and—"

She snatched the bottle from my hand and slammed the door.

I shifted my weight, unsure what to do next. Was I getting my bottle back? Had she confiscated it for good?

The door jerked open, and she handed me the bottle. "Aura cleansed. Go away." She shut the door.

"Okay. Thanks." Irritated and embarrassed, I trotted down the stairs and returned to the kitchen. I dropped into a chair at the round, wooden table and paged through my day planner. Why were women in law enforcement so bossy? Not that I knew very many. Surely Manaj and the sheriff couldn't be representative samples.

I scratched out my *Agent Manaj* project and replaced it with: *Solve Murder.*

Uncertainly, I gnawed the end of my pencil. I wasn't actually going to try and solve a murder, was I? Just because the sheriff had told me I couldn't, didn't mean I had to try.

We had police for that sort of thing.

And even if the sheriff was off the case, I had a perfectly good FBI agent upstairs.

Beneath the table, Bailey snorted.

"*Stay out of this*, she said."

The dog laid his head on my foot.

"I'm not going to investigate, but only because I'm too busy. Not because she told me not to."

But if I *were* going to investigate, the first task would be to identify the suspects. Idly, I listed that in the left "task" column. The objective column marched down the page beside it. What was the objective for identifying suspects? I left it blank. Second task - *Interview suspects.* Objective - *Determine motive and opportunity.* Third task - *Watch Manaj.*

I closed the planner. "Don't worry," I told Bailey. "This is all a mental exercise. Mostly."

*****

Thursday passed, and the crime remained unsolved.

In fairness, it takes time to solve a murder, but this Friday afternoon wasn't looking good for it either.

I sat at the B&B's reception desk and perused the local paper. The murder had been downgraded to a paragraph on page five. Absently, I rubbed the newspaper ink from my thumbs. The story ended with a plea from the Sheriff's Department asking the community for information.

I snorted. "Ha. Like they'd listen."

Beneath the desk, Bailey yawned.

Footsteps clunked up the porch stairs.

I checked the collar of my blouse, tugged up the waistband of my navy skinny slacks.

The newest batch of guests pushed open the screen door and tramped into the foyer. Their faces glowed pink from the summer heat. They ranged from middle-aged to senior citizens, and all had a sleek, well-fed look.

Their leader, an elderly man with wispy white hair, set his duffel bag on the carpet. He approached the reception desk. "Ms. Witsend?"

I stood and smiled. "That's me. Welcome to Wit's End. How was your drive?"

"Our journey through the Sierras was glorious." He rubbed his wrinkled hands together. "We're a bit earlier than we'd expected. Do you, perchance, have our rooms ready?"

"I do. Let me sign you all in, and I'll take you upstairs."

One of the women sidled to a wooden rack filled with brochures. She examined a copy of my grandmother's slim, self-published book: *The UFOs of Doyle*. (A deal at $3.99).

A hard lump formed in my chest. My grandmother had died right after The Disappeareds had returned, so she hadn't been able to include the story. I should update the booklet myself, but I hadn't the heart to tackle it yet.

The five signed and gave me their credit cards to swipe.

"Breakfast is from six-thirty until ten o'clock," I said. "Check out is at eleven in the morning. The front door is locked at eleven at night." I handed the leader, Mr. Sorenson, his keys. "The key with the number on it is your room. The second key will unlock the front door should you stay out late." And if I knew UFO hunters, they would. "If I'm not around, my cousin, Dixie, usually will be."

He chuckled. "Understood. We should be able to fend for ourselves if we can't locate you." He leaned closer and lowered his voice. "I understand this B&B was recently the site of a tragedy?"

My stomach roiled. *Please don't go. Please don't go.* "Yes, but don't worry. None of your group has been put in the room where... it happened."

His face fell. "Oh, but I wouldn't mind."

He wouldn't? "I'm sorry, but someone's already in there."

"Oh, well." He blew out his breath. "It's disappointing, but I'm not surprised someone snatched it up. Is it true the victim was a UFO hunter?"

I blinked, startled. "I... I don't know. He never mentioned it."

The rest of the group crowded closer.

"But he must have been," Sorenson said. "Why else would he come here? Everyone knows this is the place for UFO enthusiasts. Maybe that's what killed him. Was there any evidence of alien encounter? Perhaps an abduction gone wrong?"

"I didn't notice any signs when I cleaned the room." I hadn't gotten close enough to the body to check for implants. Not that I'd ever want to.

"No blood?"

"No."

"But don't you see?" His eyes glowed. "Absence of evidence could be evidence in and of itself!"

Since I didn't know what to say to that, I pasted on a smile.

"We'd arranged for a guide?" Sorenson asked.

"Yes, that will be—"

"Arsen Holiday, at your service." Resplendent in an olive-green microfiber tee and hiking slacks, he bounded into the foyer. He smiled at the ladies and gripped their leader's hand. "Are you Mr. Sorenson?"

"That I am, young fellow. I understand you'll be able to take us to some spotting areas?"

"Yes, and Sue's got maps if you'd like to do some scouting during the day." Arsen winked. "She's labeled the wine tasting rooms too."

"Which will guarantee we see lights in the sky." The older man chuckled.

I handed his group photocopies of hand drawn maps.

Mr. Sorenson scanned his. "I see you've included the most famous UFO site, where all those people reappeared."

"I could hardly leave that off." I'd added it to the map myself.

"Should I pick you up at eight?" Arsen asked. "I can meet you here or in town, if you're having dinner."

"I'm not sure what our plans are. Do you have a cell phone?"

"I do, but reception can get spotty in the mountains."

Arsen and Sorenson exchanged numbers.

I passed out more keys, and, assuring me they could find their own rooms, the UFO hunters trooped upstairs.

Arsen jammed his hands in the pockets of his khaki slacks. "They seem easygoing."

"I'm surprised you didn't offer to take them around today to pre-scout the area." I lowered my head to study him. "I'm sure they would have paid for it."

A pained look crossed Arsen's face. "Prior engagement."

"Oh?"

Bailey crept from beneath my desk and sniffed Arsen's boots.

He bent to scratch the dog. "Professor Green is leaving the whine-oceros with me while she goes into the mountains alone."

"Whine—? You mean Ethan?"

"Who else?"

"Oh." It was one thing for Arsen to haul the occasional moaner into the mountains for a day hike. Another to be stuck with babysitting duty. "Wait, isn't she going to be up there for a week?"

He nodded.

"But you've got clients!" My clients, to be specific. "You're not going to take him with you tonight, are you?" Ethan would drive the UFO folks crazy.

"Don't worry. I just need to get Ethan settled into my place this afternoon. He's a big boy, he can take care of himself." But Arsen's bronzed forehead wrinkled.

On the other hand, this might work in my favor. Ethan had been upstairs when the murderer had been in Tanner's room. Now I'd have the chance to ask him about it. "How did you get roped into this?"

"Professor Green is a friend of my aunts."

"Which one?"

He groaned. "All of them."

Ouch. No wonder Arsen couldn't say, *no*. "It won't be that bad. Like you said, he's of age." Wait a minute. Is that why she'd chosen Wits' End? Had Arsen recommended us?

Before I could ask, Professor Green glided down the stairs. Her son trailed behind her. Backpacks were slung over both their shoulders.

Guiltily, I clamped my mouth shut, hoping they hadn't overheard.

"We're checking out," the professor said.

"How was your stay?" I sat behind the computer and pulled up their invoice.

"Adequate," she said.

I stiffened. "Only adequate? Is there something we could have done better?"

"Not had a murder."

"He had it coming," Ethan said.

I eyed him. I would definitely ask him later about *that* comment. "I'm sorry you had to go through that," I said lamely, and pressed "print." The printer rattled and hummed.

"Sorry? My son and I were interrogated. Twice."

"Twice?" I asked.

"Once by the local police," she said, "and the second by that FBI agent. She came to our rooms. How could you have given her our room numbers?"

"Did she?" My shoulders curled inward. "What did the FBI agent ask?"

"The same things the police did. Where was I that day? Did I know the victim? If we hadn't been out hiking with Arsen that day, I think they might have taken us both to the station."

My eyes narrowed. But there had been a window, after they'd returned to Wits' End and before Tanner's body had been discovered. The mother and son had separate rooms. She'd said she was going to take a shower, but had she? Or did she slip over to Tanner's room and kill him? And why would Ethan think Tanner had it coming? And why had she been talking to Cherie? "So, they think Mr. McCourt was killed while you were out hiking?" I handed her the warm invoice.

"Who knows what they think?" The professor turned to Arsen and pulled out a folded sheet of paper from her pocket. "Here's the list of what Ethan can and can't eat. Bedtime at eleven o'clock and no later. You have my number if there are any problems, though I doubt there'll be much reception in the mountains."

I stiffened and glanced at Ethan. Professor Green was as bad as my parents. At least the kid would get some freedom while she was in the mountains.

Arsen took the paper and scanned it. He blinked, his face reddening.

"Now while Ethan is in your care," she continued, "I want you to make sure that he gets plenty of healthy exercise. No sitting around playing computer games all day. Perhaps he can accompany you on your night hikes?"

Behind her back, her son and I shook our heads frantically. I sympathized with the kid, but I couldn't imagine Ethan on a UFO hunt.

Bailey woofed. The dog and I were on the same page about Ethan.

"I act as a private guide," Arsen said. "My clients pay for—"

"Nonsense. Just tell them Ethan is your trainee or assistant or something. He needs some work experience for his resume."

Arsen raised his hands in a warding gesture and stepped backward. "That might work for the day hikes, but the night hikes can be treacherous. It would be safer—"

"You intend to leave Ethan alone? At night?"

Her son's face reddened. "Mom..."

"Your aunts assured me Ethan would be in good hands. Abandoning him while you tramp around the mountains? No, it's out of the question."

No. No, no, no. I could picture the future reviews from my UFO hunters. Was it possible to get less than one star? "Ethan can stay here, with me," I said. And once I got him alone, I'd soften him up with carrot cake, and we could have a nice, peaceful interrogation. After all, we seemed to have a lot in common, the poor bastard. "Arsen has to return the UF— night hikers here anyway, and he can collect Ethan then." And then I could ask why Ethan thought Tanner had had *it* coming. I was an evil genius.

"What would Ethan do at Wits' End?" the professor asked.

"I've got a private sitting room," I said, walking around the desk to her. "What does he usually do in the evenings?"

"Normally," she said, "we have a quiet dinner, followed by exactly one hour of video game playing, and then we listen to NPR. I believe in a balanced mind."

I cleared my throat. Forget the UFO seekers. I had to save Ethan like Gran and Dixie had saved me. "Well, I'm not sure if we get NPR here in the mountains—"

"You do."

"Then, he could relax here until Arsen gets back."

She turned to her son. "Ethan? What do you think?"

He shrugged. "It beats stumbling around in the dark."

"Great!" Arsen jammed her list into one of his pockets. "It's a plan. Ethan, let's get you settled into my place. Mrs. Green—"

"Doctor Green." She lowered her chin, bullish.

"Doctor Green," he corrected, "can I drive you somewhere in town?"

"Yes. Come Ethan." She marched outside, and her son slouched after her.

Arsen squeezed my hand and kissed me lightly on the cheek. "You are a lifesaver." He hurried after them.

I touched my cheek, then cleared my throat. Maybe there was hope for Ethan after all.

Agent Manaj wandered downstairs and perused an open file folder in her hands. Not looking up from her manila file, she stopped in front of my desk. It looked like the same manila file I'd snooped through.

I hoped I hadn't left fingerprints.

"There's an unfamiliar SUV out front," she said in her monotone voice. "New guests?"

"Yep, it's a summer weekend, and the B&B has got a full house."

"Who are they?"

"Some UFO enthusiasts."

Her nostrils flared. She closed the file folder and tucked it beneath the arm of her black business suit. "Who exactly?"

"Does it matter?" It was one thing helping the FBI when a murder had been committed. But these UFO hunters weren't involved in Tanner's death, and they deserved their privacy. "They arrived after the murder. They can't have anything to do with Tanner McCourt."

Her brown eyes lasered into mine. "Who are they?"

I straightened. "Guest information is private. Unless you have a warrant, you'll have to ask them yourself."

She gave me another, long look. "Are you sure you want me to do that?"

I imagined Manaj interrogating Mr. Sorenson. "No." I handed her the guest book.

She tucked it and the folder beneath one arm. "By the way, someone broke into my room. I'll let you know when I find out who." She strode up the stairs.

"Great," I said to no one. I was starting to see the downside of having an FBI agent on the premises. But who knows? Sorenson and his gang might find it thrilling.

Grabbing my cell phone off the desk, I walked out to the back garden, sat in the gazebo, and called Sheriff McCourt.

"McCourt here."

"Hi," I whispered. "It's Susan."

"Why are you whispering?"

"I don't see Agent Manaj, but she's at the B&B. I'm in the garden."

"So?"

"I may have some information for you."

"And you're drawing out the dramatic suspense? If you've got something to say, say it."

My jaw tightened. That seemed a little rude, but the sheriff had to be super stressed. After all, she'd found her ex-husband's corpse. "First, when I went into Manaj's room, she had all the UFO photos from the walls on the bed. I checked their backing, but there wasn't anything hidden inside."

"No kidding. We already checked."

"I thought you were off the case."

"I may be off the case, but my deputies wouldn't ignore proper procedure just because I wasn't watching over their shoulders. If they'd found something, they would have taken it in as evidence."

"Oh. Right. Then why would Manaj be examining the photos? She has access to whatever your guys found, doesn't she?"

"She does," she said slowly.

"So, it's kind of weird."

"Maybe, maybe not. I told you, Manaj is a UFO freak. She's a real-life Fox Mulder, or at least she was until it blew up her career. She's more circumspect now, but just as batty. Did you find anything else?"

"No," I said. "Have your deputies questioned Davin Markarian—"

"That's police business, not yours."

"But—"

"Listen to me very carefully, Witless—"

"Okay, that's really unoriginal."

"We are not partners," she said. "*Not* partners. And you are not a detective."

"But—"

"Do you have a private detective's license?"

"No, but—"

"You're not qualified, and you'll just get in the way."

"I don't—"

"Stop questioning suspects! Stay at Wits' End and watch Manaj." She hung up on me.

Nostrils flaring, I stared at the phone.

Here's the thing. Organization might be my superpower, but being told I can't do something is my.... It just makes me mad.

I wasn't a total incompetent. Earning a CPA license wasn't exactly child's play. Neither is running a B&B, which, by the way, my parents had insisted I couldn't handle. What was the big deal about asking a few, subtle questions?

I was done being the sheriff's flunky. And I didn't have to stay at the B&B if I didn't want to.

I bustled upstairs and checked on my guests. They agreed they didn't need anything, so I told them I was leaving to run an errand.

I put a "*Back in 1 Hour*" sign on the reception desk and returned outside to my Crosstrek. I opened the door. A blast of heat sent me reeling backwards.

Steeling myself, I slid inside, closed the door, and froze, seatbelt unbuckled, heart thumping.

A cassette tape lay on the dashboard.

A cassette tape I hadn't put there.

The seatbelt zipped from my lifeless fingers and clattered against the window.

Someone had been in my car.

Chapter 6

My gaze darted around the B&B's front yard. Rose bushes swayed in the warm breeze, scraped against the picket fence.

A curtain moved in an upstairs window.

Grabbing the steering wheel, I yelped with pain. Hot! I rubbed my palm on my navy skinny pants and winced, staring at the tape cassette on my dash.

Cautiously, I picked it up with my fingertips. It was unlabeled. Black as Agent Manaj's hair. And it wouldn't fit in my CD player. How the devil was I supposed to listen to a tape? The thing was ancient.

I took deep breaths, trying to calm myself. If someone was watching me, I had to play it cool. They'd expect me to run into the house like a schmuck. But I wasn't going to let my schedule be manipulated. I'd been on my way into town, and right now, the idea of being somewhere public appealed. And then I'd figure out where I'd last seen Gran's old tape player.

Roughly, I jammed my keys into the ignition and pulled from the gravel drive. I drove the looping, tree-lined roads into Doyle and parked in the alley behind Ground.

The coffee shop was a cheap and easy place to get a grip on myself. And if Cherie Cavalier happened to be working her shift at Ground, so much the better. The sheriff couldn't blame me for coming here. Ground was the only real coffee shop in town.

During the drive, the cassette had slid into the far corner of the dash. I didn't want to leave it in the hot car, so I jammed it into my slouchy leather purse.

The café was cool, the rough bricks retaining last night's chill. I sidled to Ground's black quartz counter. Ferns and spider plants dangled above it. Shaggy-haired millennials filled the coffeeshop. They tapped on computer keyboards and made their single cups of coffee last.

Cherie glanced at me. She was a muscular blond in her mid-forties with cropped and tousled hair. She reminded me of those smiling blond lifeguards you see on TV shows. Except Cherie's smile didn't sit naturally on her tanned face.

"Good afternoon," she said. "What can I get you?"

"Coffee. Ethiopian. Regular size."

She adjusted the green apron around her waist. "For here or to go?"

"Here." *Ask her about Davin and Tanner.* I ran my fingers along my leather purse strap and imagined I could feel the tape burning a hole through my purse and heating my thigh.

Cherie turned her back on me and poured a cup from a pot behind her. She handed me the ceramic mug, and I paid.

I dug out my wallet and swallowed. *Ask her now!* "Have you got a minute?"

She looked around the coffee shop, at its wall hangings, the faded brick, the heads bent over keyboards. No one else stood in line. "I guess. What do you want?"

I handed her my cash. "I run Wits' End, the B&B at the bottom of Grizzly Court?"

"With the UFO in the roof and the corpse in the attic?" She made change and handed it to me.

"That's... Tanner wasn't in the attic," I blundered on. "He was in his room. Room seven."

She stared at me, her expression a careful blank.

I dropped the change in the tip jar and added a dollar. *Develop rapport.* Hadn't I seen that on a crime show? "There's an FBI agent in there now." I lowered my voice, though the other patrons seemed oblivious to our conversation. "Investigating. I mean, she's staying there, but she's investigating too."

"And?"

"And it's a little weird, having an FBI agent in the house after someone was killed there."

"Weirder than someone getting killed in your B&B?"

I rubbed my free hand down the thigh of my slacks. "No. That was awful. But the FBI here implies that his death is somehow a federal case."

She made a noise somewhere between a "hmph" and a grunt. "And? If you want advice, go to Antoine's Bar."

I took a deep breath. "You used to know Tanner. Do you have any idea who would have wanted him dead?"

Her face reddened. "Aside from me, you mean?"

"Oh, no. I'm sure you didn't—"

"Save it. The Fed already questioned me." Her blue eyes narrowed. "Some narc told the cops I visited Tanner at your B&B."

"Did they?" My voice cracked.

"I'll tell you what I told her. I don't know what happened to Tanner. I was a minor cog in the operation, and I wish I'd never gotten involved. Tanner betrayed everyone." She deflated. "But I have no one to blame but myself for what I did. No one put a gun to my head and forced me to get involved. I was greedy." The barista looked toward the mod-print curtains blocking the kitchen. "You want someone who wanted Tanner's head, talk to Davin. I'm sure you know who he is."

"I will. Thanks." I wavered at the counter.

"What?" she asked.

"Where were you—?"

She rolled her eyes. "I was here, working, when Tanner was killed."

"Did the FBI agent tell you when he died?"

"Some time on Tuesday, when I was pulling a double shift. I was here all Tuesday afternoon."

"That's great." Now I could cross her off the suspect list.

Her blond brows pulled inward. "You think having to work in a coffee shop is *great*? I have an MBA."

Ground's owner, Jayce, brushed through the curtains that blocked the kitchen from view. "Hey, Cherie. Your shift's done. I'll take over."

Wordlessly, Cherie turned on her heel and strode through the curtains.

Jayce, her brown hair pulled into a ponytail, smiled. "Anything I can get for you?"

I raised my coffee mug. "I'm okay. Thanks." Now all I wanted to do was run home and listen to the cassette.

But I wasn't going to.

Exercising every ounce of self-control I could muster, I sat at an empty table and opened my day planner. It should be easy enough to confirm whether Cherie had been working here all day Tuesday. The cops had no doubt already figured that out. I made a note and jotted down a rough transcript of our conversation.

How tight was Cherie's alibi? Jayce was no slave driver — she would have given Cherie breaks. It only took five minutes to walk from Ground to Wits' End if you knew the shortcuts. I hadn't seen Cherie around the B&B on Tuesday. But the point of having a B&B is once breakfast and check-outs are done, I'm not chained to a desk waiting to help guests. They came and went as they wished, and so did I. Cherie could have walked in, killed Tanner, and left without me seeing. I added a question mark beside her name in my journal.

I sipped my coffee. But that didn't make sense. Someone had picked up the phone in Tanner's room minutes before Sheriff McCourt had arrived. Either Tanner had been alive to answer the phone, or his killer had picked up. Or could it have been someone else, snooping in his room after Tanner was already dead?

At any rate, the killer couldn't have been the sheriff. She hadn't the time, and I would have heard his body fall if she'd been the one to kill him.

But who had left the mysterious cassette in my car? The only way I'd find out was by listening to it. And I was dying to listen to it. But was I being watched?

Finishing my coffee, I jammed my planner into my purse and ambled down Main Street. I paused in front of a boutique in an old-west building and scanned the reflection in the window. A middle-aged tourist couple with a German shepherd strolled past. I didn't notice anyone loitering, watching me, but as the sheriff was so fond of pointing out, I was no detective.

Casual. Find Davin like you'd planned and act casual. I strolled to the Historic Doyle Hotel. Independence Day had come and gone, but red, white and blue bunting still hung from the hotel's iron balconies.

Inside the reception area, the air conditioner ran at full blast, and I sighed with delight. The reception was painted deep blue with white wainscoting. A velvet rope blocked off a dining area to the left.

I approached the reception window.

The receptionist, in the hotel uniform blue polo shirt and khaki shorts, smiled.

I knew Erica from Chamber of Commerce events. She'd always been friendly, even if we were competitors.

"Hi, Susan." Her tanned face crinkled in sympathy. Freckles dusted her nose and cheeks. "A murder at your B&B," she said loudly. "How are you holding up?"

Two guests perusing the brochure rack turned to stare.

My shoulders tightened. "Fine, thanks for asking."

She shivered dramatically. "I don't know if I could stay in a place with a *murder*."

That was rich. There had been a murder in this hotel not that long ago.

I must have given her a look, because she laughed.

"Sorry," she said, "I couldn't help myself. And I suppose UFO hunters aren't put off by a little thing like murder."

"No, they're a different breed. Hey, I was looking for Davin. Is he around?"

An expression I couldn't read crossed her face. "He's out back, repairing the bear-proof garbage bins."

"Weren't they bear-proof enough?"

"They worked on the bears just fine. Last night, a guest crashed into one with a Buick."

"Ouch." At least I wasn't the only hotelier with problems. "Thanks.

I'll check outside." I headed through the rear door and into the parking lot. A wave of heat rippled off the macadam, and I stifled a gasp.

Davin's head and broad shoulders were visible above the top of one of the bins. He stood inside, banging out a dent – with a sledgehammer, judging from the clangs.

"Hi, Davin," I shouted over the din.

The banging stopped. The bearlike man straightened and rested the massive hammer against his shoulder.

I eyed it warily. "We met at the chiropractor's office. Zack's great, isn't he?" I said a touch too enthusiastically.

He grunted and banged out another dent.

"I guess with the sort of work you do, you must have lots of aches and pains," I babbled, unsure how to lead into the Tanner question.

"My biggest pain is dead." He hammered more loudly on the bin.

Well, that made it easy. Honestly, being a detective wasn't so hard. I didn't understand why cops got so shirty about amateur involvement. "You mean, Tanner?"

He didn't look up.

I cleared my throat. "I'm sorry to bother you, but weird things have been going on at Wits' End. There's an FBI agent snooping around and—"

His round face screwed up with anger. "We've met. *Someone* told her I'd visited McCourt after I suggested snitching would be unappreciated."

My face warmed. "Really? And then someone was in my car—"

"Why is any of this my problem?"

"It isn't, but you knew Tanner before he went to jail."

He clambered out of the bin and rested the sledgehammer on the macadam. "I didn't kill him. And I didn't break into your car." His fist clenched and unclenched on the wooden handle.

I tried not to stare.

"I believe you." Sort of. "I wouldn't be here otherwise." *Or would I?* "You weren't anywhere near the B&B on Tuesday, were you?"

His thick brows lowered.

I gulped. "Um, where were you Tuesday afternoon?"

"Home. Sleeping."

"In the afternoon?" I asked, disbelieving.

"I had an unscheduled night shift Monday, and Tuesday was my day off." He shut the lid on the bin and shot the bolt. "So yeah, I was sleeping, like I told the cops. What of it?"

"Nothing. Never mind."

Shoulders hunched, he stormed toward the hotel's open, rear door.

So that was that. The two best suspects in Tanner's murder didn't have strong alibis, which the police must have already figured out. Why was I doing this again? Oh, right. Because the sheriff had knocked my ego out of joint. It wasn't a very good reason.

He turned. "I wasn't the only one with a beef with Tanner. Ask your chiropractor."

"What do you mean?"

"I mean Tanner owed him money." He stomped inside the hotel.

Tanner owed *Zack* money? The jerk! He'd probably taken advantage of the chiropractor like he'd done with me. There was no way Zack had killed Tanner over it. But I couldn't ignore this lead just because Zack was a sexy ginger.

Thoughtful, I returned inside the air-conditioned hotel. I sat in one of the blue lobby chairs and recorded my conversation with Davin in my planner.

"Oh, hey, Susan." Erica emerged from behind her counter. "Are you going to the next Chamber meeting?"

I looked up from my notes. "I guess so. Why?"

"I'm supposed to go, but I can't, and I heard a rumor they might be raising the hotel tax. Can you let me know what you hear?"

"Sure." I added Zack to my list of people to question and shut the day planner, opened my purse.

"Thanks! And let me know if there's anything I can do for you." She rolled a pencil between her fingers. "So... Arsen. Are you two like a thing?"

The day planner fell to the blue carpet, and I snatched it up. "Arsen? Ew! Cooties. He's like my brother." Or at least like my cousin.

She brightened. "So, you wouldn't mind if I asked him to the next concert?"

My stomach twisted oddly. "No, why would I?" I stood.

She smiled. "Great. Thanks!"

I nodded to her and strode out the front door. A red pickup drifted down Main Street, and I waited on the sidewalk for it to pass.

So far, my so-called investigations had been a bust. But at least I could finish my shopping for the weekend's breakfasts. "Shopping it is," I muttered.

I started down the wide sidewalk.

"Susan! Look out!"

I turned toward Zack. The chiropractor raced across the street.

Above, a metallic groan.

Behind, an explosive crash. I jumped, shrieked, whirled.

Where I'd been standing, an air conditioning unit lay on the sidewalk, its metal crumpled. Screws pinged along the concrete walk.

Heart rabbiting, I looked up.
From the hotel window overhead, a curtain fluttered.

Chapter 7

"Zack told me he didn't see anyone," I said to the sheriff, who was planted irritatingly at my kitchen table. "Just the wobble of the air conditioner."

My nerves jumped as I rolled the coffee cake dough into a double spiral on the butcher-block counter. The kitchen was normally my happy place. Last year, Gran had redecorated it with white subway tile walls, a new black stove, and plain wooden shelves.

Out my kitchen window, twilight turned the mountains purple and blue. A waning crescent moon hung like a scimitar above their jagged peaks. I wasn't one for omens, but the signs couldn't be clearer — a sword dangled over my head.

My stomach tightened. Someone had unscrewed that A/C unit this afternoon and pushed it out the window.

The sheriff shifted at the kitchen table. "Good for Zack. Anyone else tell you anything?"

"No." Erica had been properly horrified by the "accident." I suspected she would have been more bothered if I'd been a guest rather than a fellow hotel owner.

Davin had been suspiciously impassive, not that I'd seen much emotion from him in the past. But he was the obvious suspect. Tanner's old partner had had time to go into the empty hotel room, loosen the bolts on the window unit, and shove it onto the sidewalk below.

And to make matters worse, the sheriff had been waiting at the B&B when I'd returned late that afternoon. She showed no signs of leaving. I itched to find Gran's old tape recorder and listen to the mystery tape. But if I told her about the tape, she'd confiscate it before I could hear what was on it.

Frustrated, I brushed the flour from my hands and turned to the sheriff. She sipped coffee, her legs extended, a plate dotted with carrot cake crumbs at her elbow.

"Davin *must* have shoved that air conditioner out the window." I picked flour from my pink nail polish. "I'm on to something, and he didn't like me nosing about."

She arched a brow. Without her usual sheriff's uniform, she looked more relaxed. Her short blond hair was tousled, her t-shirt loose about her slim waist. "And why were you nosing about?"

Bailey, still hopeful scraps might be on their way, sat near her booted feet.

"Only someone with a key could have gotten into that hotel room." Hastily, I turned a burner to low and set the tray of spiral dough near it to rise.

"You said its door was wide open," she said. "That the guest had checked out, and the maid had gone downstairs for more cleaning supplies."

"It would have taken time to loosen the bolts holding the air conditioner in place," I said.

"For all we know, they could have already been loose, ready to drop."

"Well, who else could have done it?" I soaped my hands in the sink.

"I dunno, maybe a jealous rival?"

I snorted. "Jealous rival? Rival for what?"

Her mouth turned down. "Come on. Are you really pretending you don't know Arsen is the hottest bachelor in town? The Holidays are loaded. Hell, I'd take a crack at him if I didn't know better." She sipped her coffee. "Fortunately for you, I do know better."

"Arsen and I are just friends," I said loftily. "And if you're implying Erica dropped that A/C out the window, she couldn't have. She wouldn't have had time to run upstairs and..." Unless those A/C screws really had been pre-loosened. I bit the inside of my cheek. "Well, she wouldn't have," I said, uncertain.

"I told you to stop playing detective. Keep it up, and one of my deputies might notice. They'll toss your butt in jail for interfering in an investigation."

"Pot. Kettle. Black." I pointed a soapy finger at her. "You're not hanging out in my kitchen for the coffee. You're waiting for that FBI agent to return, so you can grill her."

"*I* am a seasoned and credentialed investigator."

"Who was chucked off the case for conflict of interest."

Her face tightened. "You screwed up. You screwed up when you ignored my warning. You screwed up and tipped off a killer that you're in the mix."

The distinctive rumble of an ancient VW Bug sputtered to a halt outside.

I swallowed. "So, you don't think it was an accident."

The sheriff lurched to her feet, and the chair she'd been sitting in skidded backwards.

Bailey jumped up and howled.

"Are you even listening to me? Stop blundering around this case!" She stormed from the kitchen.

A door banged in the foyer.

Finally!

I dried my hands and put the chair back where it belonged. Whatever insanity had led me to believe I could help catch a killer had evaporated. What had I been thinking? My so-called interviews had all been busts. Someone had tried to kill me with an air conditioner. And I was no closer to figuring out whodunnit.

Though Davin Markarian was high on my list.

I hadn't said anything which could have made him consider me a threat, but you never could tell. Maybe prison had made him more suspicious?

Maybe the mysterious tape cassette would hold some answers.

My cousin Dixie wandered into the kitchen. She opened the refrigerator door and peered inside. "Don't you have anything good in here?"

I tossed the dishtowel on the table. "Don't you have your own kitchen?" Dixie lived in an old Airstream trailer on a lot not far from here. Both lot and trailer had been willed to Dixie by my Gran. She and Gran had been close, even if they weren't directly related. Dixie and I were cousins, but not through Gran's side of the family.

I guess I was a little jealous of their relationship. And I didn't like that Dix had banned me from the Airstream. But a part of me was glad she was here. We might not be best buds, but we were family, and I couldn't get the falling A/C out of my head. Or that stupid cassette.

She leaned further inside the open refrigerator. "My kitchen's a disaster."

I sighed. "There's a carrot cake in the microwave." I'd baked it after my near miss. The sheriff and I had eaten nearly half in one go.

Straightening, she sauntered to the microwave and withdrew the cake. "Why'd you put it in the microwave?"

"To keep the ants away from it."

"Ew, you have ants?" She set the box on the metal counter and got a plate from the cupboard, a knife from the drawer.

"No, I'm ant free, because I keep food sealed tight." I sat at the table, hoping she'd join me. "What are you doing here?"

Bailey laid his head on my bare feet.

Her face tightened. "Is there a crime against it?"

"No, but I didn't expect to see you until tomorrow morning."

"I heard you were almost smashed by an air conditioner."

She'd come to check on me? That was kind of... nice. "It was an accident. I'm fine."

"So, if you die, do I get the B&B?"

I folded my arms. "Seriously?"

"I'm only curious," she said. "You're always telling me I should plan better."

"Not for my death." Offended, I grabbed the sheriff's discarded plate and put it in the sink.

She sliced a thick wedge of carrot cake. "Hey, it's not like I dropped the air-con on you."

"You..." I snapped my mouth shut. "Anyway, no one was hurt. What did you—?"

Arsen and Ethan strolled into the kitchen. The younger man wore a tank top and red and orange board shorts. His eyes were glued to his phone, his thumbs zipping across the keypad. He stumbled against a kitchen chair and glanced up.

"Hi, Dixie," Arsen said, ready for night hiking in cargo pants, boots, and a lightweight jacket. A backpack dangled from his fingers. "Thanks for coming."

"You invited her here?" I asked, confused.

He turned to me. "I ran into Sorenson in the foyer. It looks like the group is ready to leave." He clapped Ethan on the shoulder. "Sure you don't want to come with us?" he asked insincerely.

Ethan raised his head and glared.

"Who were you thanking for coming?" I asked. "Because I live here."

Arsen jerked his head toward the sitting room. "Mind if I have a word? Business," he said to the other two, who ignored us.

I followed him into the sitting room. My grandmother had decorated it in a modern Victorian style. White-and-black toile wallpaper. A black velvet, high-backed sofa. A shiny black coffee table and cabinets. White rugs.

UFO in the roof aside, Gran had style.

Arsen shut the door behind us.

"What gives?" I asked, looking at him more closely. First Erica had asked about dating him, and then the sheriff had said he was the best catch in town. I couldn't deny he was good looking, with his tan and muscles. He filled out his hiking slacks nicely. But... he was Arsen.

"Dixie and Ethan are roughly the same age," he said. "They can entertain each other."

I goggled at him. "Are you nuts? Dix will eat him alive." How was I supposed to question/rescue Ethan if Dixie was hanging around?

"Ethan's not that lucky." He shifted the backpack to one shoulder. "I'm sure they'll find something to do."

"That's what I'm afraid of."

He laughed. "Don't be such an old person."

"How well do you actually know my cousin?"

"If you're talking about her little run-in with the cops, that was just adolescent hijinks."

"Hijinks? Now who's the old person?"

"I might have heard your grandmother use the word," he admitted. "It's a small town. It's Doyle. How much trouble can they get into?"

Shaking my head, I stalked into the kitchen and drew in a sharp breath. Bailey sat alone. He stared at the closed door to the side porch.

"Where'd they go?" Blocking Bailey with one leg, I opened the door and peered out. The porch and side yard were empty.

"Who cares?" Arsen asked, exasperated. "They found something to do."

"But where?" I walked into the foyer. Mr. Sorenson's UFO group chattered excitedly at the base of the stairs. They were dressed for their night hike in lightweight jackets. The group gripped hiking sticks and wore backpacks slung over their shoulders.

"Ah, Mr. Holiday." Sorensen brandished his hiking stick. "As you can see, we're all here."

"Great," Arsen said.

"Did you see a young man and woman go past?" I asked.

"Yes," Sorensen said. "They stepped outside. Will they be joining us?"

"They'd better not." I hurried onto the screened porch. Dixie's purple VW bug was gone from the driveway.

Arsen and Bailey joined me at the railing.

"They've gone." And my mission was up in smoke. I hated it when a plan didn't come together.

"Perfect," he said. "They'll entertain themselves, and you don't have to play babysitter. I've done us both a favor."

My stomach knotted. A man had been killed and someone had nearly killed me. What if I was being watched? What if Dix became a target? What if I didn't get another chance to quiz Ethan? "Weren't you supposed to watch him?"

"Professor Green's a helicopter parent, and Ethan's old enough to drink and go to war. I'm sure he can handle Doyle."

"It's not Doyle I'm worried about." But maybe I was making mountains out of molehills. Maybe Arsen was right. Dixie had nothing to do with Tanner McCourt. She wasn't stupid enough to drive drunk, and they both were of age. For all the trouble she'd gotten herself into over the years, she had a keen sense of survival.

He clapped me on the shoulder. "Stop worrying. Everything will be fine."

"Right," I said, not believing it.

I watched the UFO hunters pile into Arsen's steel-gray Jeep Commander and waved as his lights backed down the driveway.

Returning to the kitchen, I gulped down another thin slice of carrot cake.

Bailey's gaze tracked my fork.

"I have officially turned into my parents," I told the dog. They'd been all about rules, control, structure. If it hadn't been for my summers in Doyle, I'd never have known what it meant to be free. My breathing slowed, the memories taking over. I missed those trips to the lake, running through the hills at night with Arsen and one of Gran's dogs, the ghost stories by the fireplace. Gran had never cared if Arsen brought back a frog from a nearby pond, or if my clothes were covered in muck from falling in said pond.

I shook myself. "I don't need to worry about Dixie. She's an adult. Ethan's an adult. And maybe Arsen's right, and this is just what Ethan needs."

Bailey gave a skeptical woof.

"At least Ethan took some initiative," I said with less certainty. I ran my hand across my day planner on the kitchen table.

I stood and lifted the damp towel off the coffee cake. It was rising nicely. So, I walked into the sitting room and stared at the black cupboard doors. I hadn't cleaned out the cupboards after Gran's passing — I hadn't wanted to get rid of the last traces of Gran. And I was pretty sure the tape player was inside one of them.

Bailey thumped his tail on the floor, turned around three times, and curled into a ball on his dog pillow.

Unable to remember which cupboard held the tape recorder, I worked my way from left to right. I found the dusty machine in the last, far right cupboard, atop a faded pile of *National Geographic* magazines.

My cell phone rang on the end table, startling me. I reached for it too quickly, and it skidded onto the fluffy white throw rug beside Bailey's head.

The beagle's eyes opened, and he shot me a reproachful look. Red-eyed, he returned to his doggy dreams.

I snatched the cell phone off the floor. "Hi, this is Sue."

"Sue? It's Jayce."

"Oh, hi," I said, surprised and pleased. I didn't know the café owner well — I didn't know many people well in Doyle aside from Arsen — but I liked her.

"Hey, I'm at Antoine's, and I think maybe you should get over here."

"Why? What's going on?"

"The thing is, Antoine's sick tonight, and his replacement, well, it's me. Antoine and I go way back, and no one knows this bar better than I do, so I was happy to do him a favor."

Shifting with impatience, I plugged in the tape player.

"But I'm not really the best person at enforcing rules," Jayce continued. "And far be it for me to get in the way of a little innocent fun, but—"

"What innocent fun?" I froze, finger poised above the eject button.

"Your cousin Dixie. She bet some guy that he could swing his way across the bar from the chandeliers—"

"Oh, no." Dread puddled in my stomach. All Dixie needed was an arrest on her adult record.

"And then her friend tried to start a fight with some cowboys—"

"*Ethan* did?"

"I managed to calm everyone down with a round of drinks. Look, I don't want to call the police - I caused my share of trouble when I was that age, but—"

"I'll be right there." I hung up and slid my tennis shoes on, then jammed the cassette into the recorder so I wouldn't lose it.

I sprinted to my Subaru and drove into town as fast as I dared. Parking off Main Street, I jogged to the bar.

Music and light poured from the bar's windows. A pink, neon cocktail shaker blinked above the balcony over its door. I pushed through the old-timey swinging doors.

The bar was dimly lit and cowboy themed. I peered through the crowd of cowboys, bikers, and middle-aged tourists. Framed photos of old Doyle lined the dark-wood walls. Three brass chandeliers hung above the curved wooden bar. Behind it, Jayce, her hair long and loose, poured drinks. I breathed a sigh of relief. At least the chandeliers were still in place.

Dixie perched on a barstool and toyed with a swizzle stick. At her arm sat a cola drink loaded with cherries. She swiveled toward the lit juke box in the corner.

Ethan clung to the bar beside her. In a just universe, he'd have a black eye.

I strode to them, determined to get Ethan out of here.

"What are you doing here?" Dixie asked me.

"What do you think?" I turned to Ethan. "I know how it feels, not having any control over your life. And I can understand why you'd take the chance to cut loose. But this isn't healthy. Why don't you come back to Wits' End, and we can talk?"

He loosed a window-rattling belch.

"Seriously?" Dixie said. "Talk therapy? Forget it. He's plastered."

She was right. I wouldn't get through to him in his lubricated state. But I might be able to take advantage of it and get some answers. "Ethan, you said Tanner McCourt deserved to die. Why?"

Ethan's legs folded. He slithered down the bar and sat hard on the sawdust-covered floor. With a sigh, he closed his eyes and leaned against Dixie's bare legs.

So much for that.

"You were here thirty minutes, tops," I said to my cousin. "How did he get so drunk?"

"He's got a flask. He's been drinking since his mother left."

"What?" How had Arsen missed that? "Did you really dare him to swing from the chandeliers?"

She smiled dreamily. "I read it in a Wodehouse story."

"Great. At least you were inspired by literature."

"I didn't think he'd do it. I didn't know how drunk he was."

Ethan nuzzled her calf.

A movement near the batwing doors drew my eye.

Agent Manaj strode into the bar. She met my gaze, and her expression turned hard and hostile.

I shrank on the barstool. She couldn't have figured I'd broken into her room. Could she?

Chapter 8

"The intruder came in through my window. You need better security." Agent Manaj stared into her beer mug and sighed. "They must have been wearing gloves. The only prints in my room were yours and mine. Nice cleaning job by the way."

I clung to the bar. "Thanks." I hadn't even thought to wear gloves.

Tourists and cowboys two-stepped around the tiny dance floor.

"No wonder the FBI stuck me out here," the agent said. "I'm hopeless."

Perched on her barstool, Dixie leaned across me. Her jade eyes widened. "Through the window? Are you sure?"

"They walked across the porch overhang and landed in one of your rose bushes on the way down."

My shoulders hunched. Why hadn't I gotten around to pruning those branches?

"I'm surprised no one saw the intruder," Dixie said.

Ethan snored at her feet.

"Maybe someone did," Manaj said. "I'll talk to the neighbors tomorrow."

Beads of sweat dampened my forehead. "The neighbors?" Gulp.

Dixie prodded Ethan with her toe.

He snored more loudly.

"Best let sleeping drunks lie," the FBI agent said, voice even.

"I guess." I wasn't sure how I'd get him back to Wits' End, and we were coming up on closing time.

"Colonel Fitzgerald, in the A-frame next door, would have had the best view," Dixie said.

Dix *knew* I was the culprit. What was she doing? I nudged her foot.

"Ow! Why are you kicking me?"

I glared at my cousin. Oh, right, she was being a thorn in my side. I was already starting to suspect the universe was out to get me, but did my flesh and blood have to pile on?

"I should have expected the intrusion." The agent reached across the bar and hooked a maraschino cherry from the metal bin. "This town. That case. UFOs. Fairies. It's like there's some weird cabal in Doyle, hiding the truth."

"Cabal?" *Fairies?* I'd never seen Manaj this chatty before.

"The Disappeared. The last time I was in Doyle..." She shook herself. "Never mind. I met your grandmother back then, did you know?"

"You did?" I asked. "Were you staying at Wits' End?"

"I interviewed her about UFOs, figured she might have some insight. Into what the locals believed, I mean," she added quickly. "Whoever pulled off those people's disappearance knew the lore."

Beside me, Dixie shifted.

"She told me that I had about as much chance of catching a UFO as her beagle did of catching the cars he chased," the agent said. "And even if he did catch one, he wouldn't know what to do with it. She was right, but not the way she thought. The thing is, there are no UFOs."

"Huh?" I asked, unable to follow her leaps of logic. She must have had a drink or two before she got to Antoine's.

Manaj tied the cherry stem into a careful knot. "Something's going on, but no one will talk. It's a small-town conspiracy. And that scares me a helluva lot more than little green men."

"I should go," my cousin slid from her barstool.

Thank you and goodbye. "My grandmother?" I prompted the FBI agent.

Dixie exited through the old-west batwing doors.

"This town." Manaj ground her thumb into the damp bar. "It's happening all over again, but this time, a man is dead. Tanner McCourt."

"Right," I said, watching the doors in case Dixie returned to needle me some more. I didn't trust the universe. Or my cousin.

"Someone knows something." She snapped the stem and popped the cherry into her mouth.

"I wish I did."

She shook her head. "You weren't here last year when those people returned. You're in the clear."

"Are you saying you think Tanner's death has something to do with The Disappeared?" Because that was just... incredible. Incredible, as in hard to credit. Tanner hadn't been around last year either. He'd been in jail. Maybe the sheriff was right about Manaj's obsession.

Jayce sidled down the bar. "Last call. Can I get you anything else?"

"I think we're all right here," I said. "Agent, could you help me with Ethan?"

"Why not?" She slid off her stool, and it tumbled to the sawdust-covered floor.

Shooting Jayce an apologetic look, I righted the barstool.

Together, Agent Manaj and I woke Ethan and hauled him upright.

Bits of sawdust clung to his cheek and bare arms.

We maneuvered his slender form out the door and around the corner to my waiting Crosstrek. I unlocked the doors, and Manaj shoved him into the back seat.

Ethan collapsed in a heap, mouth open, breathing heavily.

She slammed the door and trotted to the passenger side. "Good thing you're driving. I think I'm over the blood alcohol limit."

"Really?" *Hashtag: sarcasm.*

In the light from the nearby streetlamp, Agent Manaj flushed. "What?"

"I was just surprised. You don't seem like you've been drinking at all." I rubbed my arms, covered in goosebumps. The night had grown chill.

She slid inside my Crosstrek and struggled with the seat belt. "What's up with this guy anyway?" She jerked her thumb over her shoulder and toward the back seat. "I thought he and his mother had checked out."

"They did." Grim, I started the SUV and pulled from the curb. "Ethan's staying with my friend Arsen for a few days while his mother does her bear tracking thing in the mountains."

"So why is Ethan snoring in *your* back seat?"

"Arsen's busy with some of my guests tonight. They're on a night hike looking for UFOs."

We drove past an iron streetlight. It flooded the car with beery light, and then we were in darkness.

The FBI agent frowned. "Arsen leads UFO tours?"

"He knows the best places to stargaze," I said, "and of course we have the old reports of sightings to go by. But I'm sure you know more about that than me."

"I doubt that."

I cleared my throat. "I'd love to get your take on The Disappeared. For my UFO lecture."

"Gas leak. Mass hysteria."

"But... that doesn't make sense. They were missing for months."

"Lost in the woods." She folded her arms.

"But you mentioned a conspiracy—"

"Did I?" The FBI agent settled back in her seat.

Damn. The alcohol must be wearing off. "Can I ask you about something else?"

"As long as it's not about the McCourt case."

Rats. "When did you first become interested in UFOs?"

Her lips pursed. "Who says I'm interested?"

"Believing in UFOs is nothing to be embarrassed about."

"I'm not embarrassed, because I don't believe in UFOs."

"But why couldn't life exist on other planets?" I asked.

"The question is, how could aliens get here? It's impossible to travel the huge distances required. Haven't you heard of faster-than-light travel?"

"No."

"Because it's impossible, and that's what you'd need to cross galaxies."

"Just because it's impossible for us now—"

"Physics," she said. "Those laws don't change. It can't be done."

I turned down Grizzly Court to Wits' End. The crescent moon had vanished behind the jagged mountain peaks. Arsen and the UFO hunters would have a spectacular night for stargazing.

"It was an impossible situation," she said beneath her breath. "It wasn't fair."

"What?"

"Nothing."

"Any good leads on the McCourt case?" I asked cheerfully.

"Just da—" She snapped her mouth shut and glared. "I can't talk about the case."

"Sorry, I forgot." *Da* for Davin? After the falling air conditioner incident, he was my number one pick too. I turned into the driveway, tires crunching on the gravel. "Here we are," I sang out.

I twisted in my seat and regarded Ethan unenthusiastically.

He snored, lips flapping.

"I don't suppose we could just leave him here?" I asked, hopeful.

"When's your hot friend getting back?"

"My hot—You mean Arsen?" I asked, disbelieving. Sure, he had killer abs and thighs and other muscles, and a great smile, and twinkly hazel eyes and...

Fine. He was hot. "In an hour or two."

She stepped from the SUV, staggered. "The kid will keep."

I glanced again at Ethan, shrugged, and followed her up the steps and into the homey foyer. After all, I couldn't do anything for him while he was sleeping or while the FBI agent was around. "Can I get you anything?"

Manaj trudged up the stairs. "Find me the killer, will you, so I can get the hell out of this town?"

"Ha, ha. Right." Riiight. It would serve her and the sheriff right if I did.

In the kitchen, the coffee cake was fully risen. The carrot cake was gone, by which I deduced Dixie had returned, departed, and was still mad at me. Leaving the dirty cake plate for me to clean was a low blow, but I'd rise above it.

I wrapped the unbaked coffee cake in foil and put it in the fridge. Grabbing an ivory throw blanket off the sofa in the sitting room, I walked into the front yard.

Overhead, the stars blazed, and for a moment I just stopped and stared. The Milky Way was a brilliant, wavering trail. I never got tired of those stars. Never.

I shivered and opened the rear door of the SUV.

Its back seat was empty.

"For Pete's sake!" I tossed the blanket into the back seat and slammed the door. "Ethan?" I grabbed a flashlight from the glove compartment and flicked it on, scanning the front yard.

No Ethan beneath the rose bushes. No Ethan sprawled on the lawn. No Ethan draped over the white picket fence, and anxiety bubbled in my chest. Cursing, I walked out to the road and aimed the beam up the court.

Nada.

He couldn't have gone far. I stomped around the side of the house, past the rose bush I'd broken, and to the back garden.

A dark form sat slumped in the gazebo, and I breathed a sigh of relief. "Ethan?"

He didn't respond.

Uneasy, I slowed on the darkened path. He'd probably fallen asleep again. But I couldn't help thinking of another still form, lying on my grandmother's rag rug. I swallowed, shook myself. Balderdash. He was just sleeping it off.

I climbed the three gazebo steps. Muscles heavy, I raised the flashlight, revealing Ethan's dirty sneakers, his board shorts, his white tank. His head canted downward, his face obscured.

"Hey, buddy, it's a little cold out here. Why don't we go inside?" I reached a shaking hand toward his shoulder. He wasn't dead. Not dead, not dead, not dead. I touched his bare shoulder.

He rocketed from the bench. "Gagh!"

"Augh!" I jumped backward and clutched my chest.

He glowered. "You shouldn't wake someone like that."

"You shouldn't fall asleep outdoors at night without a sleeping bag. You could freeze or get eaten by a bear."

"My mother's a specialist in bears. I won't get eaten. Mauled, maybe, but not eaten."

"Whatever." I reminded myself that he was a lost and trampled soul. He needed me. I forced a smile. "You can't sleep here," I said more gently. "Come inside, where I've got a nice, soft couch."

"There's no empty room I can crash in?"

"Sorry," I said. "We're fully booked."

"I don't feel so good." He bent double.

"Not on the—"

He vomited.

"Gazebo," I finished, resigned. Why couldn't he at least have fertilized the roses? Now I was stuck with the cleanup. "Come on. You need water."

I steered him into the house, through the kitchen and into the sitting room.

He collapsed on the black velvet sofa and rubbed his face. "I'm thirsty. Why does this room look like a chess board?"

"Don't move." *Or throw up.* I proceeded to play nurse — fetching water, getting him a blanket, and making sure there'd be no accidents on Gran's new couch.

Fuming, I returned outside and hosed off the gazebo. I couldn't see what I was doing, but I'd check my work in the morning. It wouldn't do for my paying guests to find Ethan's dinner splattered across the gazebo bench.

I only had myself to blame. But the night wasn't over yet. The drinking, the acting out, clearly Ethan needed some guidance and structure. And I was the perfect one to give it to him. After all, I'd been through this. True, I'd never gone off the rails and tried to swing from a chandelier, but I *got* him. My pulse seemed to slow, sympathy welling inside me.

I returned inside. "Ethan, can I get you some more water?" I pushed open the door to the sitting room.

Ethan snored on the couch.

I forced a smile. I'd just help him later.

I grabbed the tape recorder and took it into the kitchen. Glancing at the closed door to the sitting room, I plugged in the cassette player, set it on the counter, and pressed PLAY.

There was a faint crackling sound. "Leave this case alone," a woman whispered.

Cold fingers trailed up my spine. Was there a conspiracy in Doyle?

I leaned closer, ears straining. But that seemed to be the end of it. I hit rewind and listened more closely. The message didn't change, and I didn't pick up any noises in the background that might have given me a clue to where the tape had been made. Though it was a pretty good bet it had been made in Doyle.

I gave a tiny head shake. I couldn't identify the woman's voice, much less any background noise that might identify her.

I ejected the tape and turned it over. Where did people even buy cassette tapes anymore?

An hour later, the front door opened, and the sound of muted chatter drifted into the kitchen. I pocketed the cassette tape and went to greet my guests.

Mr. Sorenson awkwardly palmed a bill into Arsen's hand. The rest of his group tromped up the stairs.

"How did it go?" I asked in a low voice.

"We saw some shooting stars," Sorenson said, "but no UFOs."

"I'm sorry," I said to the older man. "How disappointing."

"You can't expect a spaceship every time you look at the sky," Mr. Sorenson said. "It was still a fascinating excursion. Mr. Holiday knows his UFO lore and these mountains well."

"Thanks," Arsen said.

"Good night to you both." Mr. Sorenson ambled up the stairs.

Arsen turned to me. "How did it go?"

"Not so good. Ethan and Dixie snuck out of the house and went to Antoine's. Ethan got drunk, challenged some cowboys to a duel, and made a general pest of himself. Then he vomited all over my gazebo."

Arsen winced. "Ouch."

"It's not his fault he doesn't know how to handle himself without parental supervision. He's never had a chance."

He grimaced. "Maybe not, but it's time he learned."

"I'll talk to him."

"It doesn't look like talking's done him much good so far."

I smothered my annoyance. But how was Arsen to understand? He'd only known me during those halcyon summers in Doyle and now, when I was free and easy at Wits' End. He didn't know what my other life had been like, and I wasn't about to tell him. It was too embarrassing. "How was I to know what he'd get up to? I got a call from Antoine's asking me to come and remove him. I had to go. I don't go to that bar often, but I'd like to be able to go back."

"Was it that bad?" he asked, leaning against the scuffed wooden desk.

I blew out my breath. "I'm not sure. He passed out not long after I got there. Jayce didn't seem too mad—"

"Jayce?"

Footsteps creaked above us – Mr. Sorenson in his room – and I glanced at the ceiling. The chandelier swayed.

"She was taking over for Antoine tonight," I said more quietly. "He's got a summer cold or something."

"Well, that's okay then. Jayce is cool."

"That's not the point," I whispered. "How are we going to help him?"

He quirked a brow. "Why would we want to? And what's this we business anyway?"

"You're right," I said, crestfallen. "You're taking the UFO hunters out again tomorrow night."

He patted my shoulder. "You'll figure something out to rescue poor, misunderstood Ethan."

My muscles tightened. "What's that supposed to mean?"

"It means you shouldn't waste your sympathy on him. He's got enough mothering in his life."

"I don't think it's a waste," I said stiffly.

He angled his head. "I get the feeling you're annoyed about more than one drunk kid."

"Did I mention he threw up in the gazebo?"

"You weren't able to turn up anything on the murder, were you?"

"How d— I don't know what you're talking about."

He grinned. "Don't worry. Just because I've been turning up all sorts of leads, doesn't mean you're a bad investigator."

"You've— What have you learned?" It was one thing for me to investigate. After all, I was a CPA. I understood the finer points of analysis and the darker points of human nature. But Arsen? I gnawed my bottom lip. He could get hurt.

His expression turned serious. "If I tell you, I might have to kill you."

"Arsen..."

"Sue, a man's dead." He braced his roughened hands on my shoulders. "Someone's not playing around. Who knows what else they might try? I don't want you to get hurt. There's no shame in staying out of it."

"What about you?"

He kissed the top of my head. "Don't worry. I've got this."

That was exactly what I was afraid of.

Chapter 9

Ethan was snoring loudly when Arsen and I returned to my sitting room. After some negotiating, we agreed to let him stay on my couch.

He had to wake up eventually.

But Ethan was still dead to the world when I got up at six the next morning to start breakfast and let the dog out. I needed to find out what he knew so I could tell the sheriff. She needed to solve this case before Arsen did something stupid. But my third degree would once again have to wait until Ethan was on his feet.

Sigh.

I heated the oven and set the breakfast room table, clanking down the silverware harder than necessary.

Determined to shake my mood, I returned to the kitchen and pulled the coffee cake from the freezer. When the oven was hot enough, I slid the cake inside. Then I started on the bacon and scrambled eggs.

By the time Mr. Sorenson drifted down to the breakfast room, I was setting the eggs in the warmer and not feeling like such a grouch.

"Good morning." I'd guessed Sorenson would be an early bird.

He rubbed his wrinkled hands together. "And good morning to you, Ms. Witsend. Did you sleep well?"

Once I'd found a set of earplugs to dampen Ethan's snoring. "Yes, but I should be asking you that."

He filled a plate at the sideboard. "So far, everything has been delightful. We're all looking forward to your lecture this evening."

My stomach tightened. Rats. My lecture. A couple years back, Gran and I had created a presentation on the Doyle UFO legends and UFO photography techniques. I needed to update it. By tonight. "Is seven o'clock still okay?"

"Perfect. We can't go hunting until well after sundown anyway. This will give us something to do until then."

My shoulders relaxed. "Great!" I hurried to my bedroom, booted up my computer, and got to work on the show, taking breaks to check the food levels in the breakfast room.

At eight, the sounds of Ethan stirring emerged from the sitting room.

Striding past him and into the kitchen, I poured him a tall glass of water and grabbed the aspirin bottle. I returned with both to the sitting room.

Bleary-eyed, Ethan slumped on the ebony couch. He reached beneath his stained, white tank and scratched his belly. My gran's quilt pooled around his waist.

"I feel terrible." He ran his fingers through his lank, raisin-colored hair.

"Good. Drink this, and here are some aspirin." I set them on the shiny black coffee table.

He gulped down two aspirin with the water and set the glass down, missing the coaster. He sniffed. "Is that bacon?"

"Yes." I shifted the glass onto the coaster.

"Can I have some?"

At least he'd asked rather than assumed. "Sure, but first I have some questions."

He groaned and rolled sideways, burying his face in a velvet throw pillow. "Not you too," he said, his voice muffled.

"About Tanner McCourt."

He stilled. "Tanner?"

"The guy who died."

He sat up and stared at me.

"You said he had it coming," I said. "Why?"

His gaze shifted to the garden window. A stellar jay landed on the sill and stared back at him. "Everyone knows he was a crook."

I hadn't known Tanner's reputation when I'd checked him in, and Ethan wasn't a Doyle resident. "Where did you hear about that?"

He curled his toes in the fluffy white rug. "People talk. *You're staying at the UFO B&B? I heard that embezzler's staying there.*" He shrugged again. "That sort of thing."

I didn't believe it. Until last night, I'd never seen Ethan socializing — he'd been too engrossed in his tech — and last night had been a disaster. I had a hard time believing he'd been exchanging gossip with strangers. "People were saying this to you?"

"To my mother."

That made more sense. "Why did you think he deserved to be murdered?"

"Okay, maybe he didn't deserve it. I don't know." He rose, and the blanket fell to the ground. "Where are my shoes?"

I pointed beneath the end table.

He sat heavily on the couch and grabbed the expensive hiking shoes.

"Now about last night and the drinking—"

Arsen ambled into the room. "Good," he said unenthusiastically. "You're up." He wore cargo pants and one of those fancy hiking shirts — SUV protection, sweat wicking, the works — long sleeved and khaki colored.

Ethan grunted a response and jammed his foot into a shoe.

Arsen motioned to me.

Frustrated – *again* – I followed him through the sitting room door to the wraparound porch. The morning air was cool and crisp, smelling of pine and damp grass.

Bailey trotted up the steps, and Arsen scratched him behind the ears.

Arsen jerked his thumb toward the sitting room window. "Did you get anything out of that hurtbag about the murder?"

"Ethan?" Wary, I pursed my lips. I'd hoped Arsen had been teasing about running his own investigation. "No. Why? Do you think he would know anything?"

"He was here when McCourt was killed, wasn't he?"

"Yeah." And I didn't quite believe Ethan's responses this morning. He'd seemed genuinely angry when he'd said that Tanner had "deserved" it.

I walked to the railing and stared out at the side yard. The rose blossoms glistened with dew.

"Hey, what's wrong?" Arsen massaged my shoulders.

Unthinking, I leaned back against his broad chest. "I think Ethan knows something, but either he's not talking, or I haven't had the chance to get it out of him."

"Frustrating," he rumbled, his mouth close to my ear.

I shivered. "If he knows something, it might put him in danger."

"It might put you in danger."

A door banged shut behind us, and I jumped.

Crunching a piece of bacon, Dixie ambled onto the porch. "What do you want me to do today?"

"The same thing you do every morning. Clean empty rooms." I eyed her. She wore skintight jeans, a painted-on tank top, and more eyeshadow than usual. But she didn't look any worse for wear after last night, unless her makeup covered dark circles. "You're early. Why are you early?"

"I was hungry. You get Ethan home okay?" she asked Arsen.

"He's inside." Arsen pointed.

Silently, she turned and strode into the kitchen. The screen door banged shut behind her.

"Maybe she can wheedle information from him," Arsen mused.

"Why would she want to?" I shifted, uneasy. Dixie wasn't interested in Ethan, not after last night. She'd never respect someone who couldn't hold their liquor. Plus, Ethan was a suspect, and I didn't want my cousin anywhere near him.

"They're about the same age."

"And?"

"And a little summer romance never hurt anyone."

My chest burned. "You would know." I'd heard all about the guys who worked at those resorts and their new romances every weekend.

He pressed a broad hand to his chest. "What's that supposed to mean?"

I gave him a look.

"What?" he asked.

"I'm doing my UFO lecture at seven. What time are you picking up the group for their night hike?"

"Nine. I'll drop Ethan by then."

"And this time, I'll make sure Ethan stays here." He wasn't leaving until we had a serious talk about self-sufficiency and murder. "What are your plans for him today?"

"Do I need plans?" he asked. "He's an adult male. He doesn't need coddling."

"No," I said, "*you're* an adult male who doesn't need coddling." I blinked, realizing the truth of it. Why had I been thinking of Arsen as irresponsible? I trusted him with my hikers at night in dangerous mountains.

"He just needs a bit of freedom so he can find his way," he said.

"Freedom in small doses. The shock of this freedom has clearly gone to his head. He nearly got into a bar fight last night."

He kissed the top of my head. "Trust me. I've got this."

"That's what you always say. And you don't have it." And what was with all the top-of-the-head kissing?

Two sheriff's SUVs pulled into the front driveway. The deputies from Tuesday stepped from the vehicles.

Frowning, I walked around the corner of the enclosed porch to the front and met them at the top of the steps.

"What's going on?" Arsen asked Deputy Denton.

"We're looking for Dixie Witsend," the taller dark-haired one said. "Is she here?"

I nodded, my stomach twisting with anxiety. Why Dixie? She had nothing to do with Tanner. "She's inside. But—"

"Thanks." The dark-haired deputy climbed the steps and walked past us, into the B&B.

"What do you want with Dixie?" Arsen asked Denton.

"It's just routine," he said. "A few questions." He nodded to me and walked inside.

Arsen and I looked at each other, then hurried into the foyer.

Arms crossed, Dixie glared up at the two officers.

"...down to the station for some questions," Denton was saying. Her lips pressed together in a white slash.

"Why to the station?" I asked, my voice rising. "Why not here?"

"It'll be more private at the station." Denton's hands dropped to his sides.

"Does she need a lawyer?" My gaze darted from the two cops to Arsen.

"It's only questions," the dark-haired one said blandly.

"But—"

"Please, ma'am," Denton said. "We've got a job to do."

Gently, Arsen pulled me from the doorway.

I watched, unable to do anything, while the officers led Dixie outside and put her into the back of a police car.

I grasped Arsen's arm. "They didn't handcuff her. Maybe this really is just routine?"

He shook his head. "Your idea of getting a lawyer isn't a bad one."

"But I don't know any lawyers." An icy weight hardened my stomach. I wasn't sure I could pay for a lawyer. I was certain that Dixie could not.

"It's okay," Arsen said. "I know a guy."

A faint moan escaped my lips. "Thanks. Do you have his number?" I'd figure out how to pay for the lawyer somehow. Gran wouldn't have let Dixie get dragged to the sheriff's station without doing something. I could do no less. Not after what she'd done for me.

I closed my eyes and images flashed into my head. That awful, rainy night in San Francisco after Gran had died. My parents bringing in a lawyer so I could sell the B&B. They'd had it all arranged, and I'd been too numbed by grief and habit to fight.

And then Dixie, rain and tears streaming down her accusing face. *She wanted you to carry on. You! You can't sell Wits' End.*

Because of Dixie, I hadn't.

Because of Dixie, I'd found the strength to tell my parents no.

Because of Dixie, I had Wits' End. A life. Independence. Control.

The sheriff's SUVs backed down the driveway.

Arsen laid a hand on my shoulder. "Dixie barely knew Tanner McCourt. They're just nosing around because she's got a record. It'll be okay."

I swallowed. I didn't believe him.

Chapter 10

I clung to the porch banister while Arsen called the lawyer. The roses in the front garden swayed in the breeze flowing from the mountain peaks.

"Heathcoat," he said jovially. "How's it going...? Yeah, I've got a little problem. A friend of mine's being questioned by the police about a local murder..."

"Let me talk to him," I said.

He shook his head. "Right, that one... No, they're just going after her because she's got a record... Petty stuff, when she was a kid... She works at the B&B where he died."

I grabbed for the phone, and he turned away, blocking me. "Arsen, I'm hiring him. I should talk to him."

"Yeah," he said, "she's at the station now... Thanks." He hung up. "I got this. Nick's headed to the station."

I folded my arms. "Why didn't you let me talk to him? I'm not even sure I can afford his fees." Not that that would have stopped me. Gran would have figured out a way to pay, and so would I. But it would be nice to know what I was getting into.

"He's my friend. I'll take care of it."

"Arsen, you can't just *do* that." I glanced at the screen door to the foyer. Had any of the guests heard me?

"Do what?"

I lowered my voice. "Throw money at problems. This is my responsibility." Which I'd taken on without consulting Dixie. Was I as high-handed as Arsen? But what else was I supposed to do?

"I don't know how else to hire a lawyer without throwing them money. Nick's a good guy, but he just had a kid. He's got bills to pay. Diapers. Doctor's bills. College savings funds."

My breath came in quick gasps – a sure sign of my plans getting derailed. I'd just have to be flexible. I could be flexible. "I know lawyers need to get paid. I just..."

"Just what?"

"This wasn't what I'd planned," I said feebly.

"You can't plan on your cousin getting arrested for murder."

"She wasn't arrested," I said, shrill.

"Sorry, you're right. Taken in for questioning." He checked his dive watch. "Look, I'm guessing you can't get away from the B&B right now. Why don't I head down to the sheriff's station?"

"What about Ethan? I can't watch him while I'm cleaning rooms."

His jaw clenched. "He's twenty-three. He'll survive on his own for a few hours."

Arsen had an optimistic view of human nature. Ethan wouldn't be able to break decades of conditioning overnight.

"He's not your problem," Arsen said. "He's mine. And he's on his own for the morning."

"Fine," I said, the roller-coastery feeling in my stomach subsiding. "And thanks."

Arsen squeezed my hand and jogged down the porch steps to his Jeep Commander.

Dazed, I returned inside and checked the blue-curtained breakfast room. A few yellow scrambled eggs crumbs lay scattered across the bottom of the warming tray.

On auto-pilot, I walked to the kitchen and cooked more, then ladled them into the lidded metal tray.

That done, I sat behind the reception desk and opened my day planner. Arsen was right. You couldn't plan for everything, but my planner was a beacon of orderly comfort in the morning's chaos. It even had a section to write the top three things I was grateful for that day. I'd been leaving that blank the last few days, but I filled it out today: *Arsen and Dixie and..."* The ceiling fan stirred my hair. Sweat dampened my lower back. *"...air conditioning."*

I rubbed a curled knuckle over my bottom lip and crossed off the last item. Air conditioning was marvelous until units came raining down from the sky.

I ran down my top three goals for the week — *update website, call electrician to fix bathroom heater in room 4,* and *blog the latest UFO news.* I'd finished them all. Life wasn't as out of control as it felt.

After breakfast, I washed up, my phone on the butcher-block counter in case Arsen or Dixie called. Cleaning the rooms took more time without Dixie. Fortunately, this batch of UFO hunters was neat, and Agent Manaj had hung a DO NOT DISTURB sign on her doorknob. By one o'clock, I was sweaty and finished.

I returned to the Victorian-chic sitting room.

Ethan wasn't in it. He wasn't in the yard either.

I checked the phone. "I have faith in Ethan," I said to Bailey. But my insides quivered.

He thumped his tail on the rag rug.

I showered and changed into a fresh, white tank top and green shorts. Jamming phone and planner into my oversized leather purse, I headed into town for the weekend shopping.

Why hadn't Dixie or Arsen called yet? An unpleasant knot squeezed my midsection. The police should have been done asking Dixie questions by now, shouldn't they?

I parked behind the bookstore on Main Street. A flyer for Arsen's hero, Xavier Ultra, was taped in its front window between a display of hiking books and romance novels.

Sweating, I walked past, down wide sidewalks shaded by balconies and elm trees. A young tourist couple paused in front of a shop window filled with biker tees. Their German shepherd lapped water from the bowl outside the door.

I unpeeled the tank top from my spine and wove through the green, metal tables in front of the cupcake shop. I needed a bundt cake for tonight's UFO lecture. Normally, I'd bake it myself. But Arsen or Dixie might call, and I didn't want to be stuck in the kitchen when they needed me.

The cashier boxed the cake, tying it with a thick string. Pink box dangling from my fingers, I stepped outside and hiked to the local grocery store. Like most of the other shops on Main Street, the grocery was small, and in an old, western-style building with a false front.

Loaded down with eggs, bacon, flour, milk, coffee, I shuffled outside, pausing at a green wooden bench to adjust my bags.

A prickling feeling heated the spot between my shoulder blades, and I stiffened. Casually, I looked over my shoulder. An F-150 rolled past on Main Street. Tourists strolled beneath vine-covered balconies. A golden retriever sat, its leash tied to a hitching post, and panted outside a shop.

I shifted the bags in my arms and hurried to my Crosstrek. Was I being paranoid? Or was someone watching me? At the corner, I glanced over my shoulder. No one seemed to be following.

Definitely paranoid.

In the parking lot behind the bookstore, I loaded the bags into my SUV and checked my phone. No missed calls.

And I'd forgotten something.

I checked my planner and thunked my forehead with my palm. It was pickup day at my wine club. I locked the doors and hurried to the Country Rose Winery's tasting room.

Pink climbing roses twined up the sides of the 19th century wooden building and filled the front garden. Music and laughter flowed through the closed door, the pick-up party in full swing.

I hurried up the front steps and inside the air-conditioned tasting room. The door swung shut behind me, and the muscles between my shoulders relaxed, as if I'd reached a safe haven.

Ridiculous.

I'd only imagined being watched. But a man *had* been murdered in my B&B. An air conditioning unit had nearly squashed me. And I still hadn't heard from Arsen or Dixie. Who wouldn't be tense?

Wine t-shirts and crackers and dipping sauce sat on neat displays scattered throughout. Adjusting my purse over my shoulder, I strode to the crowd at the tasting bar. I squeezed between a bachelorette party and a retired couple and braced my elbows on the polished quartz.

One of the women behind the counter looked up and smiled. "Hey, Susan! Can I get you a drink?" Fidelity touched her auburn hair, knotted in a bun at the nape of her neck.

"No, thanks. I'm only here to pick up my wine." I glanced toward the closed front door.

She frowned. "Is something wrong?"

"What? No. It's been a crazy day." A crazy, paranoia-filled day.

"Okay..." She checked her clipboard. "You're on the four-bottle plan." She ducked behind the counter and handed me a tall, black wine carrier with a cardboard handle. "You're all set."

"Thanks." I ticked off the "pick up wine" note in my planner. Gripping it to my chest, I turned from the bar and crashed into my chiropractor's broad chest.

I took a quick step back, bumping my hip against the cool marble. Why was I always such a klutz around him? "Sorry, I didn't see you, Dr. Harwell."

He grinned down at me and jammed the sleeves of his lightweight, plaid shirt to his muscular biceps, and my pulse quickened.

"How many times have I told you to call me Zack?" His red hair was mussed in a sexy, windblown sort of way, and I gulped.

"It's habit. Are you a wine club member?"

"The only club worth being a member of is a wine club. Because... wine."

I laughed, an odd falsetto, and rubbed my thumb across my planner's pages. Its pen slipped from the holder and rattled to the floor. I set down the box of wine on the red tiles and something slammed into my head.

"Ow."

I gasped, reeling backward, clutching my skull.

Wincing, Zack rubbed his head. "You okay?" He handed me the pen. "Sorry, that one was on me."

"I'm fine," I said, embarrassed.

"Here, turn around." Firmly, he braced his hands on my shoulders and turned me. He ran his hand up the back of my head, and I shivered. "I don't think our collision knocked you out of alignment," he said. "But it's a good thing you're coming in for another adjustment next week."

I swallowed and turned, casually bracing my elbow on the counter. *Curse you for your red-headed sexiness, Chiropractor Zack!*

"Hi, Doc Harwell," Fidelity said. "Two-bottle plan?"

"That's right," he said to her. "What are you up to today?" he asked me. "Aside from collecting wine."

"Running errands." Hastily, I jammed the pen into its leather holder. This was ridiculous. Crushes were one hundred percent chemical. No basis in reality. None. At. All. Though someone had once told me if you're attracted to someone, odds are they're attracted to you back.

"It sounds like things are getting back to normal." he asked. His voice was low and husky, and I stepped closer to hear him over the noise of the pickup party.

"Hardly," I said, tapping the planner with one finger. "You've probably heard that FBI agent's taken over the investigation."

"Mm. I think it was in the paper." His brown eyes crinkled with concern. We were close enough I could see the gold flecks in his irises.

"But how are you doing?" he asked. "You look tense."

I shrugged one shoulder, shifting my purse. "Oh, you know how it is when you find a dead body in a bedroom."

He smiled crookedly and crossed his arms, his muscles flexing. "Fortunately, I don't."

"It's a good lesson in how to deal when you're not completely in control." I laughed, false sounding, and jammed my planner into my slouchy purse. "To make things worse, the police have taken my cousin in for questioning, which is totally ridiculous—"

"Dixie?" His reddish brows rocketed upward. "Why? She can't have anything to do with this."

"I know, right?" I raked my hand through my loose hair. "It's crazy. I think they're grasping at straws. After what he did, Tanner must have had tons of enemies." Including Zack? I eyed him. "Tanner was behind on his room bill, and I doubt I'll ever get paid now. I heard he owed you money too. Do you think you'll ever collect?" A woman edged to the counter and nudged me, bumping me close enough to smell Zack's swoon-worthy cologne, a light, spicy blend.

He grimaced. "It was all so long ago — from before he went to prison — that I've written it off. Best to just let it go. You should too, or it will make you crazy."

Disappointed, I fiddled with the clasp on my planner. "Was he a client?"

"No, it was a personal matter." His ears reddened. "A bet we'd placed on a football game. So, I'm not really out money, but the whole thing left a bad taste in my mouth. I didn't realize he was such a weasel until then. But I guess none of us did — not even his wife. And if he could fool his wife..." He shrugged.

The poor sheriff. I couldn't even imagine what that betrayal must have felt like. "Out of curiosity, how much was the bet?"

"Five hundred dollars." He colored, his freckles darkening. "We'd been drinking beer. Never drink and gamble."

Or shop. The gift shops in wine tasting rooms were my special bête noire.

He put his hand on mine, warmth flowing from his touch. "Don't worry about Dixie. I'm sure it's all just routine questioning. The police must be getting close to figuring out what happened."

"They're not," I said sharply.

"That would surprise me," he said, his gaze searching. "There aren't many secrets in a town this size."

"I'm not so sure."

"What do you mean?"

"I mean the *police* have no idea what happened." Because Dixie was *not* involved, and if they really thought she'd killed Tanner, then they were barking up the wrong pine. I reached into my purse for my planner, realized what I was doing and jerked my hand away. Was I turning it into some sort of security blanket? "Tanner McCourt spent the last days of his life in Wits' End. I may not know the whole story, but I know Dixie didn't kill him."

"Have you spoken with the police yet?"

Like they'd listen. "I'm starting to think the Sheriff's Department isn't much use."

His tawny eyes flickered. "If you know something, you should be careful."

"I'm not the only one," I muttered, thinking of Ethan.

One of the retirees stepped sideways and bumped into my wine box, standing on the floor. He stumbled against Zack.

"Careful," Zack said, steadying him.

"Whoops," the older man said. "I didn't see that box."

"It's my fault." Face warm, I picked up the box. "I shouldn't have left it there. I'll see you later, Zack. And thanks for letting me vent."

"Any time." His mouth curved in a thoughtful smile.

I strode out the door and into the sunshine. Had I been imagining Zack's interest? Not that it mattered. With Dixie in trouble with the police, I had more important things to worry about than my love life.

In the bookstore parking lot, I checked my phone.

Dixie hadn't called.

Neither had Arsen.

And no news was not good news.

I called them both. Neither responded.

No, not good news at all.

Chapter 11

Worried, I set the lemon bundt cake in the microwave and shut its door. Sunlight streamed through the open kitchen windows, glinted off the white subway tile walls.

Bailey looked up at me with a mournful expression.

"No cake for you." But I got him a dog treat off the top of the refrigerator. His tail thumped the linoleum floor. "Do you want a treat?"

More enthusiastic tail thumping.

"Here you go." I tossed it to him.

Bailey lurched upward on his hind legs, snatching it from the air. The beagle crunched the treat into pieces, scattering them across the floor.

I gripped the butcher-block counter and stared, unseeing, out the window to the side yard. Why hadn't Dixie or the lawyer or *someone* called?

I nodded, decision made. My need to investigate wasn't about the sheriff ordering me not to. I'd been in the B&B when Tanner had died. If anyone could help Dixie prove her innocence, it would have to be me.

Opening my thick day planner on the kitchen table, I sat and studied the projects section. First task: *make list of suspects*. I flipped to a blank note page and wrote *Suspects* across the top and divided it into three columns: *name, motive, opportunity*.

Cherie Cavalier and Davin Markarian were two obvious suspects. Tanner had helped send both to jail, and I wasn't convinced by either of their alibis. Plus, they'd both visited Tanner. That was suspicious.

Markarian had been at the hotel when its air conditioner had fallen. He was the most obvious suspect, but I didn't have a list of everyone who was on the scene at the hotel. Someone could have seen me go in, followed me inside, and then decided to lie in wait for me to walk out.

But why? I drummed my fingers on the kitchen table.

And what about the sheriff? She had motive - divorce and the humiliation of being a sheriff married to a felon. Her finding the body reeked of convenience.

But had she had time to kill him? I just didn't know. I hadn't heard a struggle. And despite myself, I *liked* the sheriff. Anyone who could get reelected after what she'd gone through with her husband had to be worth something. With a sigh, I added her name.

Bailey sat on my foot.

I shifted, nudging him off.

The dog huffed and trotted through the open door to my sitting room.

"Sorry," I called after him.

Ethan Green and his mother had both been on the scene when Tanner had been killed. I gnawed the end of my pen. But I wasn't sure when Tanner had been killed. All I knew was that someone had picked up the phone in his room. That had happened after the Greens had returned from their hike.

They'd both had opportunity to kill Tanner. For the life of me, I couldn't figure out why they would, though Ethan had seemed hostile after Tanner's death.

I wracked my memory. Had he or Professor Green encountered Tanner while he was alive? I didn't remember seeing them together, not even at breakfast. But I added their names to the list and left the *motive* column blank.

There was a lot of blank. I didn't have many suspects, which was probably a good thing. But Zack knew Davin, one of the suspects, and he'd known Tanner. Should I add him to my list? I gnawed on the pen. No, an old debt of a few hundred dollars wasn't much a motive for murder.

I studied my list and a weight lifted from my chest. I was making forward progress. Now I just hoped the lawyer could free Dixie from the Doyle Sheriff's Department.

Bailey trotted into the kitchen, a filthy tennis ball in his mouth.

I checked my phone. The display was blank. No missed texts or messages from Arsen or Dixie. Frustrated, I banged it on the wooden table. Where *were* they?

I called the sheriff.

"Yeah?" she asked.

"Hi, this is Susan."

"I know."

"Did you know my cousin's been taken in for questioning?"

"Has she?" she asked, a note of caution in her voice.

Bailey dropped the tennis ball on the linoleum floor. It rolled to a stop against my tennis shoe. I picked it up with my finger tips and tossed it in the air.

He barked once and chased after it.

"Sheriff, you must know she's got nothing to do with Tanner's death. Dixie's got no motive. They're just picking on her because of her record."

"She stole a sheriff's car and dumped it in the lake."

"That was ages ago and a far cry from murder. Plus, she didn't dump it. She crashed it." I still couldn't quite believe she'd done it. What fifteen-year-old steals a police car?

"And it wasn't her first offense."

"But there was nothing violent. This isn't right. Someone else killed Tanner, and the police are wasting their time on Dixie. She's got no connection to him."

The sheriff blew out her breath. "Yes, she does."

My stomach lurched. "You mean the B&B? Tanner rarely left his room. He didn't let any of us in to clean."

"Dixie worked in Tanner's department at the county a couple years back. She only lasted two weeks, but it's a connection."

Bailey dropped the ball at my feet.

"What?" I croaked.

"You heard me."

"What happened? Why did she leave after two weeks?"

"Tanner fired her."

I pressed my hand over my face and closed my eyes. "Dixie wouldn't kill someone just because he'd fired her, especially if it happened years ago." But my cousin *had* turned up right after Tanner's body had been discovered, and that, now that I thought about it, was weird. Dixie wasn't the sort for afternoon strolls around Doyle. I bit the inside of my lip. Why had she really stopped by that day?

"She accused him of sexual harassment."

I stared at the kitchen table. "She accused your hus—"

"Her accusation came after she was fired," she said, voice tight. "There was no evidence to support it, so Tanner got a warning, and the whole thing was dismissed as retribution."

The *sheriff* had dismissed it as retribution. How did she feel about Dixie now? I swallowed. "Why did Tanner say he'd fired her?"

"Petty theft. She was taking home office supplies. Your cousin denied it. The loss wasn't enough to call the cops in, but it was enough to let her go."

"Now I know this is bogus," I said, on firmer ground. "My cousin would never steal office supplies."

"She stole a sheriff's car."

"Yes, a car with flashing lights and serious horsepower. That, she would consider exciting. But office supplies? What was she going to do with them? Work on her novel? Resell paperclips on the black market? Office supplies aren't Dixie's style."

She made a doubtful noise. "Doesn't matter. If he lied about the theft to get rid of her, it's an even stronger motive. You'd be amazed what people will justify when they think they've been treated unfairly."

"There's something else going on," I said. "Someone put a cassette tape in my car the other day. A voice on it warned me off the case."

"What? Have you given it to the police?"

"Not yet."

There was a long silence. Then, "I suppose your finger prints are all over it. Put it in a plastic bag anyway. I'll get it later."

"So, you think there *is* something more?" I asked.

"I don't think anything. We don't have enough information. Do you have any idea whose voice was on the tape?"

"No," I said, "but it was a woman's."

"Dixie's?"

"I think I'd have recognized my own cousin. There's got to be something we can do to get Dixie out of the station."

"We?" she said. "There's no *we*. You're an informant, not a detective."

An informant? That was just insulting. "But—"

"Have you got anything for me on Manaj?"

"No, but—"

"Don't call me again unless you do." She hung up.

"Dammit!" I slammed shut my planner. I was severely tempted to move the sheriff to the top of my suspect list. But a good detective doesn't pick suspects based on how irritating and unhelpful they are.

And speaking of irritating and unhelpful...

I called Arsen.

"Hey," he said.

"What's going on?" I asked. "Where are you?"

"Outside, with Dixie."

"What?" I raced to the front porch and shoved open the screen door.

Dixie stepped out of Arsen's massive Jeep. Her violet-tipped hair fell limp against her drooping shoulders. She trudged up the steps. "I'll get started cleaning."

I sagged with relief. "No, it's okay. I did it all."

Her emerald eyes flashed. "So, I suppose I'm not getting paid?"

"I didn't know when you'd return," I sputtered. "But I didn't get a chance to clean the foyer and hallways. You can do that."

"Never mind." She turned on her heel and strode down the gravel driveway.

"Dixie?" I called anxiously.

Arsen walked up the steps and laid a broad hand on my arm. "Let her go. She's had a rough day."

"What happened?"

"I wasn't in the interrogation room with them, but Nick said she was uncooperative — a good thing where the cops are concerned, not so good for her lawyer."

"Do the police have a case?"

He nodded. "I'm afraid they might. She's got motive and opportunity. The one saving grace is Tanner's neck was broken, and they can't figure out how Dixie might have pulled that off."

"Broken?" I was definitely adding that detail to my murder book/day planner.

My cousin's wiry form turned at the fence and strode up the court.

"She's strong," I said slowly, "but I don't think she's strong enough to break a man's neck."

"Neither do I. But she needs to stop fighting her lawyer and let him help her."

"Dixie can be kind of stubborn."

He grinned. "I wonder where she gets that from?"

"Did she say anything to you about... anything?"

"She thanked me for the ride. You need to talk to her. Nick's on her side. She needs to trust him, tell him what she knows."

I gripped the porch railing. "What she knows? Why would she know anything about a murder?"

"Just talk to her."

I rubbed the back of my neck, which had grown increasingly sore as the day went on. I'd talk, but would Dixie listen? Or was she hiding something too?

Chapter 12

Straight-backed, I stood at the end of the breakfast room's oval table. I'd changed into blue skinny capris and a loose, white blouse for my UFO talk.

The curtains in the octagonal room were drawn, the lights on the brass, hanging lamp off. In the gloom, the wallpaper's blue flowers looked deep gray.

Mr. Sorenson's UFO group sat around the table and stared fixedly at the screen. Eerie music played in the background, a touch I was especially proud of.

"Nineteen-eighty-six, of course, was the famous mass sighting," I said. "Twenty-eight Doyle residents reported seeing saucer-shaped UFOs hanging over the mountains. These were long-term residents. They'd seen plenty of lenticular clouds in their lifetimes and knew the difference."

Agent Manaj, black suited and impassive, slid into the room and stood against the wall, beside the sideboard.

My confidence evaporated. I fiddled with my silver bolero-style necklace.

Swallowing hard, I clicked the remote. A slide of an empty lot backed by unyielding pines replaced the Bell and Thistle. "But our most famous UFO case was more recent. Last year, an entire pub and the twenty-two people inside vanished."

"The Swiss psychologist Carl Jung posited that UFOs were projections of our unconscious," Agent Manaj said. "He believed they represented synchronicity, when external events mirror internal psychic states."

The people around the table started, noticing her for the first time.

I tensed. "Sorry, I haven't introduced you. Agent Manaj is another guest at Wits' End." I cleared my throat. "The twenty-two reappeared months later with no memory of what had occurred, but the pub itself never returned. Even stranger, their numbers had increased. Hikers who'd been missing for years returned with the twenty-two. And *the hikers hadn't appeared to have aged.*"

I paused for effect, and murmurs erupted around the table. It was the weirdest aspect of the entire story, and never failed to raise the hair on my head.

"People are still struggling for an explanation," I continued. "Most of the world believes it to be some sort of hoax." I carefully did not look at Manaj, ramrod straight in her midnight pantsuit. "The official explanation for the disappearing people is a gas leak. It caused an explosion that destroyed the pub."

"But there were no remains of the pub found," Mr. Sorenson said. "Correct?"

"Correct," I said. "This is one of those instances where UFOs really do seem to be the most plausible theory. Though there is a story going around that fairies took the people and the pub." I winked.

A chuckle rippled around the oval table, and I joined in.

"Carl Jung equated visions of UFOs with fairy sightings," Manaj said. "And the literature of fairy kidnappings bears striking similarity to those of UFO abductions. They appear to be the same psychic phenomenon."

"Whatever happened," I said, ignoring her, "if Doyle was known as a UFO hotspot before, it's even more so now." And hoorah for that. Not a weekend went by that the B&B wasn't fully booked. "But we're just happy everyone's back, safe and sound."

"I have a hard time believing that." A middle-aged woman clasped her hands on the tablecloth.

Manaj shifted, a whisper of cheap fabric.

"Sorry?" I rubbed my thumb over the plastic remote. Why wouldn't we be happy about the Return? This was a small town. Losing twenty-two people had been traumatic, even for a summer resident like me.

Sorenson cleared his throat. "I believe my colleague was alluding to the emotional state of the Returned."

The woman nodded.

"Abductees are typically traumatized by their experience," Sorenson said. "And you said they have no memory of what happened. It must be terribly confusing."

The woman who'd spoken earlier leaned across the table. "Do you know any of the abductees personally?"

"No," I said. "I'm afraid I was only a summer resident here until recently."

She leaned back in the antique, wooden chair with a disappointed sigh. "Too bad. I would have loved to interview someone aside from that Frank Haslett. We only talked to him for thirty minutes, and I can already tell he'd tell anyone anything."

And Frank charged a steep fee for those thirty minutes.

"You talked to Haslett?" Agent Manaj asked sharply. "He's a

charlatan."

And I didn't need her hassling my guests. What did she care if they talked to crazy Frank Haslett?

"He was kind enough to grant us an interview," Sorenson said.

Manaj folded her arms, the fabric of her suit rustling. "He'll grant anyone an interview for the right price."

"You're probably right," Sorenson said. "I suspect he has no memory of the event and was inventing elements to justify his fee. Still, it was a useful interview."

"How so?" the FBI agent asked.

"One must talk to fabulists to be able to identify them in future," he said.

I clicked the remote, showing a stunted and barren pine silhouetted against the Milky Way. "And here's where Arsen will be taking you tonight."

The group around the table made appreciative noises.

I checked my watch. Arsen hadn't arrived with Ethan yet, but it was still early. "You're lucky. There's no moon tonight, so you'll see even more stars, and hopefully, other celestial objects."

The UFO hunters applauded.

I turned on the lights and clicked off the music. "I'll leave you so you can prep for your hike."

Agent Manaj approached me. "I wouldn't mind getting a copy of that slide show."

I fiddled with my notes. "Um, sure, but why? None of my UFO materials are connected to the murder."

"Personal interest." Bland, she turned and filed from the room with the UFO hunters.

I returned the projector to its cubby beneath the sideboard and parted the floral-print drapes. A figure shifted in the window's black reflection, and my grip tightened. The curtain rings rattled.

I released the drape and turned. "Mr. Sorenson, what can I do for you?"

The elderly man glanced around the room. "What sort of agent is Ms. Manaj?"

"FBI."

"How well do you know her?" he asked in a low voice.

"I don't. Why? Is something wrong?"

"It's probably my imagination."

"What is?"

"Isn't it a little strange that the FBI would take over this investigation? There are other investigators who can step in for the sheriff."

"I suspect there's more to it than that."

He nodded. "As do I. Don't you find her interest in UFOs... odd?"

"She says she's not interested. And during my lecture, she provided alternate theories."

"She managed the case of The Disappeared." He glanced around again and stepped closer. "She's famous in UFO circles. And she always wears black," he whispered.

I tugged my hand through my loose hair. "Does she?" I hadn't noticed.

His snowy brows rose, and he gave me a significant look. Unfortunately, I had no idea what the significance was.

"Mm," I said, nodding wisely.

"Exactly! I knew you'd understand."

"Of course." Understand what?

"She's a man in black."

I bit back a laugh. In UFO mythology, men in black are mysterious figures in black suits who warn people who've sighted UFOs to keep quiet. The first mentions of them date from the late nineteen-forties. Men in Black feature in one of my favorite *X-Files* episodes of all time – *Jose Chung's From Outer Space.*

"But she's a woman," I pointed out.

"I'm sure whatever secret government agency she really belongs to has opened up to the fairer sex by now. This *is* the twenty-first century."

My phone rang in the pocket of my capris, and I winced. It should have been turned off for my lecture. I checked the number. *Arsen.* "Thanks for the warning," I said. "I need to take this."

"Certainly." Mr. Sorenson walked from the breakfast room.

I answered the phone. "Hey, what's going on?"

"Help," Arsen whispered, strain thick in his voice.

The hair rose on the back of my neck. "What's wrong?"

"It's Ethan. You've got to come to my place." Alt-rock music played in the background.

"Why? What happened?"

"Just get over here," he hissed and hung up.

I hurried to the kitchen and grabbed my purse and keys off the butcher-block counter.

Hopeful, Bailey lumbered to his feet on the rag rug in front of the sink.

"Sorry," I said. "No time for a walk." I raced outside and to my Crosstrek. Arsen was never stressed. When I thought of cool, calm and collected, I thought of Arsen. What had Ethan done?

I buckled up and called Dixie.

"Yeah?"

"I have to run an errand for Arsen. Can you stop by the B&B and hang out here until I get back?"

"Am I getting paid?"

"Yes! Fine!" I flattened my lips, regretting losing my temper. I opened my mouth to apologize.

"I'll be there." She hung up.

Spitting gravel, I roared from the driveway and drove as fast I dared in the waning twilight. I zoomed around a curve, my headlights glinting off the pond that backed against Arsen's yard.

Arsen lived in a stone cottage, ramshackle on the exterior, with ivy plucking at the window sills. Music and shrieks of laughter blared from the cottage, and light flowed from its windows. A black stretch limo sat parked in front of Arsen's humongous Jeep. Beside a slender driver in a black jacket and hat, Arsen leaned against the limo, his muscular arms crossed.

I blew out my breath and parked on the street. Arsen was okay. I crunched across the dirt verge to the driveway.

Arsen straightened off the limo. "Thank God. It took you long enough."

The limo driver eyed me and rolled a toothpick between his teeth.

"What's happened?" I asked.

"Ethan is what's happened," Arsen said. "I left him alone for a few hours, and when I got back, he was throwing a party. I can't leave for the UFO hike with that going on."

He'd dragged me here for this? "So, throw them out."

He quirked a brow. "I'd like to see you try."

"Arsen, you're six-foot-whatever—"

"Two. And seriously, I'd like to see you try. Please try."

"—and I'm sure you can look menacing if you want. Just tell them the party's over."

"It's a *bachelorette* party."

"And?" This was so Arsen. He hated confrontation.

"Ethan told them I was the stripper."

I blinked, laughter and outrage vying for prominence. "You didn't— They didn't— I mean—"

He scowled. "Of course, I didn't." His blue eyes widened, pleading. "You can see why I can't go in there. And even if I could, I can't strong-arm women."

And Arsen didn't deserve to be mauled by drunken bachelorettes. "You're making it really hard to stay angry at you. But you did say all Ethan needed was..."

A woman in a skintight, pink mini-dress staggered out the front door. Gripping the window sill, she leaned over a juniper bush and made retching sounds.

"At least she stepped outside," I said weakly.

The woman tottered into the stone cottage and slammed the door.

Arsen flinched. "You have to help me. Ethan's inside, and I've got to get to the B&B to collect the UFO hunters."

I rolled my eyes. "Fine. I'll tell the girls they have to go."

His shoulders slumped. "Thanks. I owe you." He hopped into his Jeep and drove off.

The limo driver removed the toothpick and studied it. "Good luck."

"They're bachelorettes, not a motorcycle gang." I nodded to him and started to the front door.

His voice floated after me. "A gang would be easier."

Ignoring the sour odor by the juniper bush, I stepped onto the flagstone path and opened the front door.

A wave of alt-rock music hit me, and I took an involuntary step back. Swallowing, I stepped inside. Honestly, I wasn't a big fan of confrontation either.

When Arsen had returned to Doyle, he'd bought the cottage and gutted it completely. Now, its stone walls were covered in wood paneling. A concrete fireplace stood angled in one corner. The floors were of an indefinable, glossy gray stone. Floor-to-ceiling windows vibrated from the music and opened onto a concrete deck. Lights from homes across the pond reflected on its surface.

A half-dozen young women in various states of dishevelment whooped on the porch. Empty bottles and plastic cups littered the mid-century modern furniture.

Ethan, in a tank top and blue board shorts, stood atop the metal porch railing and faced the pond.

"Jump! Jump! Jump!" the women chanted.

I strode to the complicated-looking sound system and stepped in something sticky and yellow. *Please let that be margarita mix.*

Cursing, I searched for the power button. When I couldn't find it, I yanked the plug from the wall.

Blessed silence fell.

I strolled onto the concrete balcony, and Ethan crawled down from the steel and cable railing.

The ladies stared.

"Hi," I said. "I'm Susan. I'm sorry, but the homeowner had to leave and asked me to shut down the party."

"It's okay," Ethan slurred. "I'm here. Ladies, let the festivities continue!"

They cheered.

My jaw clenched. "Ethan, don't you remember? You've got an appointment tonight."

A blonde tittered. "What, is she like your butler or something?"

"Or something," Ethan said, and they laughed.

A bachelorette chose that moment to tumble into the pond. She shrieked, flailing her arms.

Another woman peeled off her top, exposing a lacy bra, and jumped in after her.

"You shouldn't be in there," I said futilely. "You have to leave."

Ethan hopped on one foot and tugged at his hiking boot. "What's your problem?"

"I'm supposed to be back at Wits' End and so are you," I snapped, and a wave of heat flushed my chest. I'd sounded just like my mother.

"So, go," he said.

Giggling, three more women tumbled into the pond.

"This isn't your house, and I promised Arsen I'd shut down the party."

Ethan extracted his foot from the boot and tossed the latter over one shoulder. It hit a window and thunked to the concrete. "This party's going nowhere."

The thought of these women demanding Arsen take off his clothes burned. I raised my voice. "It's just that there are leeches in the pond—"

Shrieks drowned the rest of my words. Bachelorettes stampeded from the pond. They shivered in the tall grass and checked each other for leeches.

I'm not proud of it, but it had required a certain degree of cunning to survive my parents' martial reign. There were no leeches in the pond. But in that moment, I wished there were. I tossed discarded clothing over the railing to them. "Sorry, no towels!"

I herded them, grumbling, to the limo.

Wearing one shoe, Ethan tried to worm inside the limo after them.

"He's underage," I whispered to a tall brunette at the door.

"I am not," Ethan said.

With one stiletto-clad foot, the brunette shoved him away from the car. She slammed the door.

The limo pulled away.

In the driveway, Ethan jammed his hands into the pockets of his board shorts and glowered. "Are you happy now?"

"Not really." How was Ethan going to trust me when I'd just acted like... his mother? I was certain that deep within him there remained a nobility of spirit, even if it was buried very deep indeed.

His eyes glittered oddly, his face flushed with alcohol. "Then why'd you break up the party? We were having a good time!"

"Because if something went wrong," I said calmly, "Arsen would be liable. He can't be here to manage the situation."

"Nothing ever goes wrong!" He stepped backward and stumbled, waving his arms. "I *want* something to go wrong. Do you have any idea what my life's been like? My mother manages everything — what I eat, what I wear, how I spend my free time — not that I've got much of that. And now I've got a few days of freedom, and you're ruining it."

My heart squeezed in sympathy. He could have been ticking the boxes from my own youth. And college years. And after college years. When I'd been a kid, I'd been jealous of Dixie and her freedom. My aunt didn't care what Dixie did.

At all.

Now, as an adult, I understood that came with its own set of complications.

But tonight was about Ethan. I stuffed my hands in the pockets of my navy capris. "Look, I get it. You want to control your own life. You deserve to control your own life. But the operative word is *control*, and you've been way out of it with this drinking. There are other things you can do that don't include starting bar fights and wrecking Arsen's house."

He stuck out his bottom lip. "I didn't wreck it."

Dixie had been right. Talk therapy wasn't the answer. I was moving on to tough love. "Then you won't mind cleaning up the mess your friends left."

Grumbling, he limped inside.

Beneath a kitchen sink the envy of a Michelin-star restaurant, I found a bucket of cleaning supplies. I handed him a clean rag and a bottle of cleaner. "Wipe up the spills with this."

Ethan aimlessly wandered the living area, bottle and rag in hand.

I collected the cups and empty bottles in a garbage bag and deposited them in the bear-proof container outside.

When I returned, Ethan stood in the center of the gray stone floor. His head lolled, the cloth and bottle dangling, limp, from his fingertips.

I stopped short. Was he asleep? Standing up? I shook my head. It didn't matter. I wasn't Arsen's maid, and Ethan wasn't my problem. So why did I feel... guilty?

I walked onto the balcony and tidied up more party debris. Full dark had fallen. Stars littered the sky, reflecting in the pond. I inhaled deeply, enjoying the cool scent of the pines. The night was still aside from the faint lap of water against the shore.

Something shifted in the forested hill to the left, and I whipped my head toward the movement. Palms damp, I grasped the metal rail and stared, the pines black prison bars against a darker night.

The figure vanished in the trees, and I shivered.

Chapter 13

My Crosstrek glided to a halt in the B&B's driveway. The Victorian's lit windows painted trapezoids of light across the gravel drive, the rose bushes, the lawn.

I breathed a sigh of relief. The person in the woods had probably been one of Arsen's neighbors, out for a night walk along the shore. *Paranoia! It's not just for breakfast anymore.*

But I was glad to be home, glad for the light, glad even for Ethan, sullen in the passenger seat.

He crossed his arms over his seatbelt, his jaw jutting mulishly forward in a pose reminiscent of Dixie. "I'm not going in."

It had taken me thirty minutes of arguing and finally, locking him out of Arsen's house, to get him into my Subaru. "Fine, then let's talk."

He pulled his phone from the pocket of his lightweight jacket. The screen lit his face, making the soft angles of his chin and cheekbones ghoulish. "I'm not talking about my mother."

"Then let's talk about the afternoon Tanner McCourt died. Did you see or hear anything after you and your mother returned to the B&B?"

He stared vacantly at the phone.

"There's bundt cake in the kitchen," I wheedled, opening the door and stepping out.

His thumbs tapped the phone's keyboard.

"It's lemon poppy seed," I said hopefully.

No response.

With nothing left to bribe him with, I grabbed my purse off the seat. Maybe he'd be more reasonable when the booze wore off. I reminded myself we were fellow soldiers in the battle against helicopter parenting and softened my tone. "I'm not going to try to tell you what to do any more. But the door's open, so you can come inside when you start to get cold." I strode up the front steps. Helping Ethan had left me with a certain dissatisfaction pooling in my gut. It had also taken longer than I'd expected. I hoped Dixie wasn't too annoyed by the delay.

Bailey barked, steady and irritating from somewhere deep inside the house. Why wasn't Dixie keeping him quiet?

I beelined for the kitchen to shush him before the FBI agent complained.

The microwave door hung open. On the table lay a plate scattered with crumbs and an empty pink cake box. I sighed. *Dixie!* I really could have gone for a slice of bundt after my night.

Gran's leather-bound book of recipes was open to her chocolate bundt cake recipe. I guessed that was either a hint or a rebuke from Dixie. I straightened the loose pages and closed the book on the table, snapping the clasp shut.

Bailey's barking continued.

"I'm coming," I sang out, pushing through the swinging door to my private sitting room. "I'm—"

The door slammed back on me, cracking my elbow and knocking me to my butt on the linoleum floor. My head rocked backward. It struck something unyielding. Pain blazed through my skull. I gasped, stunned, unable to speak, shout, scream.

Bailey's barks grew more frenzied.

A figure clothed in a black ski mask, pants and top raced past.

Anger flared inside my chest. I rolled and grabbed at him, catching the hem of his (her?) trouser.

His momentum dragged me across the linoleum.

"Help!"

He pivoted, swinging a clumsy kick at me.

I let go, covered my head with my arm.

The blow struck my shoulder. I shouted in pain and fear and outrage. Swiveling on the floor, I kicked out. My leg tangled between the intruder's.

He stumbled, crashed against the kitchen table. The plate smashed on the floor.

Where was Dixie? Where was Manaj? Horrified, I realized I was on my own. What on earth was I doing fighting?

Scrambling to my feet, I ran, plunging through the swinging door. I skidded to a halt in the sitting room.

Dixie lay sprawled on the fuzzy white rug. One strap of her olive-colored tank top had slipped from her shoulder. Books and the contents of Gran's cabinets lay on the floor.

My heart thundered in my ears. I panted, fists clenched, and turned to face the kitchen door.

Bailey howled from behind my closed bedroom door. His claws scrabbled on the wood.

A screen door banged shut, and then a second.

I fell to my knees beside Dixie. "Dix? Dixie!" I grasped her shoulder.

Her green eyes opened, and I started breathing again.

"Sue? What—?" She jolted upright, her tanned legs extended, and clasped one hand to her head, groaned. "Someone was in here."

"I know. They're gone now." I hoped. Fumbling in my pocket, I pulled out my phone and called the sheriff. This was awful. But I was in control. Taking back control. My breath rasped.

The sheriff picked up on the first ring. "This had better be good," she snapped.

"Someone broke into the B&B." I hurried to the bedroom door and opened it.

Bailey bolted from my bedroom and raced in circles around my feet.

"Isn't that place always unlocked?" the sheriff asked. "And what the hell's that racket?"

"It's Bailey. The intruder attacked Dixie."

"Is she all right?"

"She's talking, but she was unconscious when I got here."

"All right. I'll call it in. Stay put."

I hung up. "What happened?" I asked Dixie.

"I'm not sure." She levered herself onto the black velvet couch. "I came in here to watch TV. The window was open." She pointed over her shoulder with her thumb. Curtains fluttered at the open window above the sofa. "I remember thinking it was odd because you have A/C in here, and then I heard someone behind me. I started to turn, and then I was on the floor, and then you were here." She rubbed the back of her head. "Ow. He must have hit me."

Bailey sat beside her and licked her hand.

She pulled him close and ruffled his fur.

"Where's Agent Manaj?" I asked.

"She left with the UFO hunters."

"Great." Could this night get worse? My guests thought she was a Man in Black. She was going to cause a panic.

"What was your errand?" Dixie asked.

"I had to help Arsen with..." Ethan! "I'll be right back." I raced to the kitchen, shutting the door so Bailey wouldn't follow and hurt his paws on the broken plate. I strode out the front door. Ethan's still figure sat upright in the SUV, his face lit by the screen of his phone.

Blowing out a breath, I walked to the passenger window and knocked.

He jerked, swearing, and rolled down the window. "What?"

"Did you see anybody come out of the B&B within the last five minutes?"

"No."

Was the intruder still in the house? With Dixie? "Would you have noticed if anyone did?"

"I was texting a friend."

In other words, *no*. "Okay, someone just broke into the house. The police are on their way. It might be a good idea if you came inside so they don't accidentally arrest you for lurking." I wasn't sure if they would, but I'd rather have Ethan where I could keep an eye on him.

He heaved a sigh. At a sloth's pace, he made his way from the car.

Resisting the urge to shoo him up the porch steps, I followed his achingly slow progress inside.

Dixie wandered into the high-ceilinged foyer, and his face lit. "Hey, Dixie. What's up?"

She scowled. "Someone broke in, hit me on the head, and knocked me out."

He goggled. "Seriously? Are you okay?"

"I guess."

"You could have a concussion," he said. "You should sit down. But don't go to sleep. That could be bad."

I left them to it and walked into the kitchen. Pieces of cake plate lay scattered across the linoleum floor beside a fork and the pink box. The table rocked gently on its side, the blue tablecloth puddling on the floor.

I moved to turn it upright, then stopped myself. The police would want to see this. At least the break-in should get Dixie off the hook. She hadn't knocked herself out — someone else had been in here. Maybe they'd left fingerprints? I scrunched my face, trying to picture the man. Had he been wearing gloves? But all I could remember was the black ski mask and black slacks.

The front screen doors banged shut, and murmurs drifted into the kitchen.

I hurried into the foyer.

Dixie sat propped against the reception desk. Sheriff McCourt, in civilian jeans and an olive-green windbreaker, spoke to her in a low voice. The sheriff's expression was hard and tight.

"Sheriff." I hurried across the foyer. "Thanks for coming." I glanced, uneasy, between her and Dixie. How had I not known the two had more than a history of stolen police cars between them?

McCourt grunted. "I called the paramedics for your cousin. You said she'd been knocked out?" Blue eyes narrowed, she gave Dixie a hard stare.

"She was unconscious in the sitting room when I found her," I said.

"Show me." She pointed at Dixie and Ethan. "You two stay here."

The sheriff followed me into the kitchen and whistled. "What happened here?"

"I was going into the sitting room when the intruder was coming out. We struggled."

"Was he wearing gloves?"

"I don't remember," I said.

"Of course you don't," she muttered.

"There was a lot happening."

She brushed past me. Using the back of her hand to push open the swinging door, she walked into the sitting room. The sheriff stopped short beside the coffee table. Books lay tumbled on the floor beneath their shelves. The drawers to my Gran's cabinet hung open.

"Could have been a simple robbery," she said.

"You can't really believe that."

"Or," she said, "you and Dixie could have created the scene to make her look like an innocent victim."

"What? No! And besides, I couldn't have. I was with Ethan."

"Who? Oh, the professor's kid. When she's getting back?"

"In three days." Three days that couldn't come too soon. "What if it wasn't a burglary at all? What if someone was trying to hurt Dixie?"

"Then they didn't do a very good job. Where's Manaj?"

"She went on a night hike with the UFO hunters."

The sheriff's nose wrinkled. "Figures. I can't believe they gave my job to that lunatic, even if it is only temporary. Anything missing?"

"Not that I can tell. I'd have to go through everything to be sure."

"All right. We'll wait for the fingerprint techs to get here. Where's that cassette tape?"

"In the kitchen."

"Let's go."

She escorted me into the kitchen, and I stopped short, my brow furrowing.

"What's wrong?" she asked.

I walked around the overturned table and scanned the floor.

"What?" she asked, her voice threaded with impatience.

"My Gran's recipe book was on the table when I walked in. I don't see it anywhere."

She canted her head. "A cookbook?"

"No, a collection of her recipes that she'd put into a small leather binder. You know, like a day... planner."

My mouth pursed in a silent whistle. And it looked a lot like the day planner that I carried with me everywhere. Had the intruder been after... me?

Chapter 14

The deputies examined the kitchen, fingerprinted the doors. I watched, giving them a blow-by-blow account of the fight.

"This might take a while," Deputy Denton finally said, his blue eyes glinting with annoyance. "Why don't you wait for us somewhere else?"

I stiffened. I *was* a witness, after all. "Oh. Sure." I wandered through the swinging door into my sitting room.

In Gran's black velvet wingchair, Sheriff McCourt thumbed through a local tourist magazine. Ethan watched Dixie intently. A paramedic examined my cousin on the velvet couch. Behind her, curtains fluttered at the open window, and I moved to shut it.

"Don't," the sheriff said, without looking up from the magazine.

"You might have a mild concussion," the paramedic said. She was a thick-set woman in her mid-forties with short, salt-and-pepper hair. "Someone should wake you up every two hours tonight to make sure you're not getting worse."

Ethan opened his mouth to speak.

"I can do it," I said. "Dixie, you can spend the night here."

"No way." She crossed her arms. "I sleep in my own bed."

The paramedic frowned. "Irritability is one sign of a concussion. Maybe she—"

"She's always like this," I said.

Dixie stuck her tongue out at me behind the paramedic's back.

"But she was unconscious when I got here," I continued. "Are you sure she shouldn't get a CAT scan or something?"

"I don't think we need to take that step yet." The paramedic snapped shut her black case and rose. "If anything changes, bring her in."

"Will do," I said.

We watched her leave the room.

"Where's that cassette you told me about?" the sheriff asked.

"In the junk drawer."

"Which is?"

"In the kitchen," I said. "With the deputies."

She snapped open the magazine and slouched deeper into the wingchair.

"What cassette?" Dixie asked.

"Yeah," Ethan said. "What cassette?"

"Nothing you need to worry about," the sheriff said.

Denton emerged from the kitchen. "Er, Sheriff? Mind if I have a word?"

Sighing, she rose. "Do I have a choice?"

He shuffled his feet, his face reddening.

"The question was rhetorical." She joined the deputy in the kitchen.

"What cassette?" Dixie asked me.

The kitchen door swung back and forth, swishing across the top of the rug. "I'll tell you later," I whispered.

"Me too?" Ethan asked.

"No."

A door slammed, and subdued voices drifted to us.

"That must be Arsen." I hurried through the kitchen, past the whispering cops, and into the foyer.

The UFO hunters peeled off their jackets.

"Sue, are you okay?" Arsen's brow furrowed with concern. "We saw the sheriffs' cars."

"We're fine." I glanced at the UFO hunters. "Just a break-in."

Mr. Sorenson gasped. "Our rooms?" He and a fellow hunter, a middle-aged woman with curly brown hair, exchanged worried glances.

"I don't think so," I said, "but you should check to make sure nothing's missing while the police are here."

Agent Manaj strode across the Persian carpet. She'd traded her black suit jacket for a black windbreaker, and my scalp prickled. With her black hair and intense, brown eyes, she really did look like a man in black. "What's happened?" she asked.

Muttering, the UFO hunters trooped upstairs, sans Mr. Sorenson. He loitered beside the bookshelf of UFO paraphernalia and watched, head cocked.

"No biggie," I said, not wanting to worry Sorenson. "Just a burglar. I scared him off."

"Where are the deputies?" she asked, brusque.

"In the kitchen."

She strode past me and vanished into the kitchen.

"You scared him off?" Arsen brushed the back of his hand over my cheek, and I shivered.

His eyes darkened. "Is that a bruise?"

"No, it's just bad lighting." Though my shoulder and upper arm ached from the kick. I turned to Mr. Sorenson. "How was your hunt?"

He edged closer to me. "I am growing more and more convinced there's something odd about Agent Manaj." He glanced toward the closed kitchen door. "She is more than the typical FBI agent. And now this break-in..."

"Did something happen on your hike?" I asked carefully. The Men in Black mythos was vague enough to make belief possible. There was good evidence the government did have a sort of reverse Men in Black in play, ensuring sightings of military tests were chalked up to alien encounters. But even if that were true, it didn't mean that UFOs hadn't swung by Earth. This was a big universe. It seemed arrogant to believe we were alone in it.

"Every time we saw an anomaly," Sorenson said, "she would dispute it."

"Was she right?" I asked.

"Well," he said, "I can't say she was wrong. But she was very insistent. And very intense. Those eyes... You've heard the theory that the men in black are shapeshifting aliens in disguise?"

Arsen coughed and quickly turned away.

Hm. Agent Manaj *was* rather robotic. And it was kind of weird that she was here.

"More disturbing," the elderly man continued, "she seemed interested in our little group itself. Perhaps the government has finally taken notice of us. We may be close to uncovering the truth, right here in Doyle!"

That would be... Exciting. Terrifying. Unlikely.

"The truth?" Arsen asked.

"About the aliens," he whispered. "How difficult would it be for her to break into your guest files?"

I shifted guiltily. "Well..." I never should have let her see my guest register.

He shook his head. "No offense intended, but I suspect your security is no match for a determined government agent."

Ratting out UFO enthusiasts to the Feds wasn't the sort of reputation that would endear me to the UFO community. "Mr. Sorenson—"

"If a Man – Woman in Black is here, it just affirms that there is truth to the UFO sightings." He straightened. "We may not have captured any hard evidence on this trip, but I assure you, we won't let a Woman in Black frighten us from the quest."

A cheer sounded from above, and I glanced up. The UFO group peeked over the second-floor landing.

"No sign of our rooms being broken into," the curly-haired brunette said darkly. "And you know what that means."

Sorenson nodded, grim. "Professionals." He climbed the stairs.

Arsen angled his head toward the door, and I followed him onto the enclosed porch.

He leaned against the porch rail. "What really happened?"

"I collected Ethan from your house—"

"You did it? You got those women out? How?"

"I told them about the leeches in the pond."

"What leeches?"

"Exactly."

He gave me an admiring look. "You're amazing," he said.

"Thanks," I said, warming. "Anyway, Ethan wasn't happy. When we got here, he wouldn't leave the car. So, I left him and ran into the burglar as he was coming out of my sitting room. He knocked me down. I think he stole my Gran's recipe book."

"Why would he take a recipe book?"

A moth bumped futilely against the light beside the door.

"No idea, but it was there when I walked in and gone after he left. I found Dixie in the sitting room, unconscious. She's okay," I said quickly. "The paramedic said she might have a slight concussion, but that's it. I'm going to watch her tonight."

He clawed his hands through his wavy brown hair. "I should have been here."

"How could you have known what was going to happen?"

"A man was murdered here. I should have guessed this isn't over."

The two deputies strolled onto the porch.

"There you are," Denton said. "Look, we pulled some prints, but they look a lot like yours and Dixie's. I'll have to get to the station to do a better comparison. We'll send more patrols by your B&B and keep a watch on things."

I laid a hand on my chest. "Thank you." It made me feel a lot better knowing the cops were nearby.

"You watch out for her now," he said to Arsen.

Arsen looped an arm over my shoulder. "I intend to."

I leaned into his protective embrace. Arsen was another reason I was glad I'd moved to Doyle. I couldn't imagine losing his friendship.

The deputies backed their black-and-white SUV from the driveway, their headlights blinding.

Arsen and I returned inside.

In the foyer, Agent Manaj and the sheriff glared at each other, arms crossed.

"What part of *you're on leave* don't you understand?" Manaj asked through gritted teeth.

"Leave isn't house arrest," McCourt said. "If a friend calls to tell me about a break-in, I'm going to come over, especially when she's in hysterics."

Manaj's jaw set. "So, you two are *friends*."

I smiled. *Huh.* I was friends with the town sheriff. Well, it made sense. We'd gone through a traumatic experience together. We'd bonded.

The sheriff stiffened. "Acquaintances."

Acquaintances? After all I'd done for her? Then I blinked, horror dawning. Wait a minute. Did Manaj think the sheriff and I had colluded in Tanner's murder?

"You're on notice, McCourt. If I catch you nosing around my crime scene again, you'll be on more than leave."

"I wasn't aware Susan's kitchen was your crime scene."

"It is now." Manaj stormed up the stairs.

"Whatever." The sheriff turned to me. "That item you were going to get for me?"

"Oh, right." I walked into the kitchen and opened the junk drawer. Frowning, I prospected through a tangle of loose rubber bands and extracted the cassette in its plastic baggie.

I turned.

The sheriff stood six inches from me.

Startled, I lurched backward. My lower back hit the counter, and I rediscovered a bruise from my fall off the porch roof. I sucked in my breath.

"I'll take that." The sheriff snatched the cassette from my hand and tucked it into the back pocket of her jeans. "See you." Tossing a wave over her shoulder, she walked through the swinging door to the foyer.

Arsen poked his head inside the kitchen. "All clear?" He ventured inside and whistled, staring at the overturned table, the smashed plate. "He did all this?"

"Like I said, he knocked me down."

His gaze narrowed. "But the door to your sitting room is way over there." He pointed. "How'd the table get overturned?"

"It happened kind of fast," I said, vague. "Ethan's in the sitting room."

Arsen walked past me and opened the door. He stopped short in the doorway. "Where?"

I crowded behind him and peered beneath his arm.

Dixie sat alone on the couch. Head lolling, she stared at the ceiling. "Hey, Arsen. Good hike tonight?"

He stepped inside. "Where's Ethan?"

"Ethan?" she asked. "He left."

I gaped. "How? We were right outside the door the whole time." Well, not the *whole* time. Arsen and I had been on the front porch, and... Oh no.

"He said he had a party to go to."

Arsen cursed. "Where?"

"Antoine's."

Swearing beneath his breath, Arsen charged out the door.

"Couldn't you have kept him here?" I asked.

She raised her head. "Why?"

"Because Arsen's supposed to be watching him, and you know what happened last time he went to Antoine's."

"Ethan's one of those guys who needs to learn things the hard way. I did you all a favor."

"Fine," I ground out. "Then do me another favor and stay here tonight." Because I really didn't want to spend the night in her cramped trailer.

She rose, tossing her violet-tipped hair, and winced. "I'm going home."

My muscles knotted with frustration. Pain spiked along the back of my neck and shoulders. I needed to relax, or I wouldn't make it to my next chiropractor's appointment. "I'll drive."

"You don't have to babysit me. I'm not Ethan."

"You're a million times smarter than Ethan, but you heard what the paramedic said. Someone needs to make sure you don't get worse tonight."

"I'll use an alarm and wake myself up."

"It won't work. If you do get worse, you might not realize it. Someone else needs to be there."

"Whatever." She stomped past me and into the kitchen.

Following, I grabbed my purse off the butcher-block counter and strode to my Subaru Crosstrek, where Dixie waited. Her trailer was walking distance from the B&B, but in fairness, it was late, and we were both tired.

"Did you get a good look at him?" she asked.

"No. But at least I'm pretty sure it was a man."

"Pretty sure?"

"It all happened so fast. Now I'm doubting myself. I didn't get a sense of size, just... power."

I drove the looping road to the plot of land she'd inherited from my Gran. The old Airstream sat beside a stand of pines, bricks stacked beneath its trailer hitch to keep it balanced. Colored twinkle lights blinked behind the blinds shading the windows.

Shivering, Dixie dug a set of keys from the pockets of her olive-colored shorts. She unlocked the trailer and stepped inside.

I moved to join her, but she turned, blocking the door.

"My trailer is private."

"I need to come inside if I'm going to watch you tonight," I said, exasperated.

"All right." She licked her lips. "But I don't want you telling anybody about what's in here."

"What's in there?" I asked sharply.

"Nothing illegal," she said. "Mostly." She stepped away from the doorway.

"Mostly? What's mostly?" I stepped inside, and my eyes widened.

The walls of the trailer were plastered with news clippings about UFOs. Little gray men stared out from sketches. A complicated-looking radio sat on a built-in shelf. A mobile of the solar system turned slowly from the ceiling.

"Wow," I said.

"Yeah."

"You should be giving the UFO lecture, not me."

"No way. My interests are my own business."

"Now I get why you and Gran were so close." A stiletto of jealousy stabbed my heart. I'd always maintained an open-minded skepticism, but Dix was a true believer.

"Yeah," Dixie said. "She was one cool lady."

My throat thickened. Dix had been the one to find Gran that awful day. I'd been in the Bay Area, at my job, as usual. Dix had always been here for Gran.

I turned to examine an article about mass UFO abductions. "Yeah. She was." And I still missed her. "I'm glad she had you here."

"You can sleep on the floor." She lugged an air mattress from a tiny cupboard beneath a built-in bench, and a pile of martial arts equipment, including old belts, fell out.

I picked up the brown belt.

"Don't start," she said. "He jumped me from behind. It could have happened to anyone."

"I didn't say anything." I handed her the belt. According to Gran, Dixie had gotten pretty good at martial arts. She still went to the dojo on Main Street.

Together we blew up the air mattress, and Dixie bounced on it. "What was with the cassette the sheriff was talking about?"

"Someone left it in my car. It was a woman — or the voice on the tape was a woman — warning me to stop investigating."

"So that's why you broke into Manaj's room?"

"It's complicated." I sat beside her on the air mattress, and she swayed.

"I'll say. Telling the sheriff about the tape was a bonehead move."

"What was I supposed to do? It *is* a murder investigation."

"And she's off the case," Dixie said. "You don't know what she's going to do with that tape. What if she gives it to the Feds?"

"She should. It might be evidence."

My cousin rolled her eyes. "Didn't you pay any attention to your grandma? You can't trust the government."

"Dix, a man was murdered. This is their job."

The colored lights winked in the windows, disorienting.

"Well, you're not supposed to be investigating, and you seem to be doing it anyway."

That was different. I had a unique, inside perspective on the case. It was my duty to investigate, especially when Dixie had become a lead suspect. "What's with the humongous radio?" I asked, changing the subject.

"You can't tell anyone about it."

"Why not?"

"I use it to keep track of sightings."

I pursed my lips. "Are the UFOs using radio frequencies to communicate?"

"No, dummy. But people radio each other to report sightings."

"People," I said slowly. "Wait, is that a police scanner?"

"It's more than that, but yes, it picks up police frequencies."

"Is that legal?" *Please tell me it's legal.*

"No, which is why you need to keep your trap shut."

I raised my hands in a warding gesture. "Fine, I won't tell."

The twinkle lights winked more rapidly, and my stomach rolled.

"And I won't tell anyone about your amateur attempt at B&E."

"B&E?"

She snorted. "Breaking and entering, duh."

"Oh, right." My eyes widened. "Is that how you knew...?"

"What?"

"The afternoon Tanner's body was discovered. That's why you came by, wasn't it?"

"No." She scowled. "I left my wallet at Wits' End."

"Oh. That's not very helpful."

"What do you mean?"

"If you'd heard it on the radio, you'd have an excuse if the police asked why you were on the scene when Tanner was discovered."

"Hello? Weren't you listening? The police can't know about the radio."

"But they were questioning you. You're a suspect."

Her nostrils flared. "I can take care of myself."

But I had the sinking feeling she couldn't.

I settled Dixie on her narrow bed and laid down on the air mattress. The plastic was cool through the thin sheet, and it felt good against my battered body. But every twinge reminded me of the danger I – we – were really in.

Chapter 15

In the gray dawn, I stumbled up the B&B's porch steps. I yawned and unlocked the front door. Dixie hadn't gotten any worse during the night, but I was so sleep-deprived *I* felt concussed. Her air mattress couldn't be completely filled, and I'd bobbed on it like a cork in an ocean storm. It didn't help that I'd had to wake Dixie every two hours.

Bleary-eyed, I staggered to the kitchen. I stared at the wreckage – the overturned table, the pieces of broken plate, the stale bundt crumbs on the linoleum.

Bailey yipped behind the closed door to the sitting room.

"I'll be right there," I called softly.

I righted the table, swept up the broken plate, and retrieved Bailey from my sitting room.

He danced around my ankles as I refilled his food and water bowl. I opened the kitchen door to the side porch. The dog raced outside and around the corner to the backyard.

I watered the spider plants atop the kitchen's thick, wooden shelves, then started on the scrambled eggs, whisking them in a bowl.

The kitchen door creaked open, and I jumped. The bowl slipped from my hand. It shattered on the floor, eggs splattering the linoleum.

Arsen winced in the doorway. A five o'clock shadow darkened his jaw. "Sorry."

"It's fine." I took a step toward the butcher-block counter and skidded in yellow muck.

Arsen was at my side in an instant, wrapping one arm around my midsection, steadying me.

The shock of his touch quivered through my torso.

"Hey." His breath was hot against my neck. "Are you all right?"

I swallowed, nodded, and stepped away. "I'm only tired," I said, trying to convince myself. "What are you doing here so early?"

"I wanted to make sure everything was okay after last night. How's Dixie?"

"Grumpy, but no concussion."

"Why don't you let me make breakfast? Take a nap. Take a shower."

"Are you telling me I stink?" I yawned, too tired to argue.

He smiled. "Never."

"Thanks." I stumbled to the stove and opened Gran's metal recipe holder. "Here are the recipes for the eggs and country potatoes. There are three tubes of biscuit dough in the fridge. Use two. And if you could cut fruit into a bowl for the vegetarians, that would be great too."

He beamed. "No problem."

I hesitated. Good breakfasts were pretty critical in the B&B biz. "On second thought, I'll be quick. If you just cut the fruit, I can do the rest."

"It's breakfast. You don't trust me to make breakfast?"

"I do, but it doesn't feel right—"

He bustled me through the door into the sitting room. "Go. Sleep."

Leaving Arsen to it, I showered and felt less terrible. My bedroom lightened. Golden beams of sunshine streamed through the windows and danced across my Gran's tree of life quilt. This was the only room I'd redone after moving in – painting the walls pale blue and adding my own, comfy furniture.

I hurriedly changed into skinny white slacks and a blue peasant top.

Utensils clattered from the kitchen, and the scent of comfort food drifted into my bedroom. I whisked on extra blush so I looked less haggard and strode into the kitchen.

A pile of pans and bowls tottered in the sink. Arsen's size eleven boot prints left tracks in the now powdered crockery on the floor.

I frowned. Gran's ancient waffle iron sat on the counter. What was that doing here?

Suddenly hungry, I followed the egg and biscuit smells into the blue-and-white dining area.

Arsen closed the lid on a warming tray. "I thought you were going to take a nap?"

"I'm too hungry to sleep."

He motioned toward the sideboard. A pitcher of orange juice sat beside rows of glasses, stacks of dishes, neatly arrayed silverware and napkins. Tea lights were lit beneath two metal chafing dishes. A bowl of cut fruit sat on the other end of the table.

Outside the octagonal breakfast room's tall windows, Bailey raced back and forth in the front yard.

"This looks great," I said, surprised. Arsen had outdone himself. Well, he'd done what I do every day, but it looked good.

"I've eaten here often enough to know the layout." He handed me a plate.

"Thanks." I opened a chafing dish and stared at what looked like mutant waffles with cheese guts squeezing out the sides. What. The. Hell?

I slammed shut the lid and hastily opened the second. Yes, it was filled with country potatoes. I returned to the first and opened it again, eyes bulging. "What's this?"

"I just thought I'd, you know, throw some things together," he said. "Get creative."

Frantic, I searched the sideboard. "And where are the biscuits? Where are the scrambled eggs?"

"Those are the biscuits." He pointed to the first warmer. "I put the scrambled eggs inside."

"Inside the...?"

"Inside the biscuits. You had cheddar cheese in the fridge, so I threw some of that in too, added some of those bell peppers for the potatoes, a little onion—"

"You— I gave you recipes," I said weakly. Carefully, I set the plate on the oval table, covered in a crisp, white cloth.

"I didn't want to just *bake* the biscuits, like it said on the package. That would be boring."

"But that's how you make biscuits."

"I wasn't sure if the waffle iron would work," he continued blithely. "But in the end, it was all about the timing. Sorry about the eggs and cheese. Some got burnt into the waffle iron grooves. But don't worry, I'll clean it."

Horrified, I scrubbed my hands over my face. "Arsen, I don't experiment on guests." I'd tested and crafted these breakfast recipes. Or Gran had. But the point is, they all worked!

"It'll be fine. Don't worry."

"Don't—"

Footsteps clunked down the stairs.

He rested a hand on my shoulder. "You're welcome."

"You...!" This was so like him!

Sorenson and three members of his crew entered the breakfast room.

"Good morning, Ms. Witsend," Mr. Sorenson boomed. "Mr. Holiday."

It was too late to fix this. "Hi." We had to be nearly out of eggs. I'd dropped eight on the floor, and Arsen must have used at least as much on his Franken-waffles. But maybe I could whip up some pancakes, or French toast...

Sorenson ambled to the sideboard. "How is your cousin feeling?"

I edged in front of the chafing dishes. "Dixie's fine, thanks for asking."

"I'm relieved to hear it." Mr. Sorenson poured a glass of orange juice and set it on the nearby table. "Have there been any more... developments?"

"None," I said.

The UFO hunter's face fell. "Ah, well. I'm sure there's more to come."

"Um. You know, with Dixie under the weather, I'm a bit behind in the breakfast—"

"So, I did the cooking," Arsen nodded toward the warming trays. "Bon appétit."

Grinding my teeth, I edged aside.

Sorenson lifted the lid on the chafing dish and paused, cocked his head, frowned. "What are these?"

"Biscuits and scrambled eggs," Arsen said. "With cheese."

"Hm." He plucked one from the tray with a pair of tongs and dropped it onto his plate, then moved to the tray of potatoes. His friends followed and arrayed themselves around the table.

Damn, damn, damn. Maybe I could order in?

"Oh, my God!" the middle-aged, curly-haired woman bellowed. Brown eyes wide, she gazed at the waffle/egg/biscuit.

I could fix this! "If you don't like it—"

"Don't like it?" she asked. "It's delicious! Sorenson, have you tried these?"

He took a bite, and his face brightened. "I thought your coffee cake was delicious, but this is truly inspired, Mr. Holiday."

Arsen rocked on his heels and grinned. "Wits' End has the best breakfasts in the Sierras. The egg-waffle-biscuits are my own creation."

"Were you a chef in a former life?" Sorenson asked.

Arsen shrugged, modest. "I did a little cooking in one of my old jobs."

Grrr... Did Arsen *have* to be a super star at everything? Maybe I should let him take over the case. "I'll refill the orange juice," I said tightly. I strode into the foyer.

Behind me, a chair scraped back. "Oh, Ms. Witsend," Mr. Sorenson said in a low voice.

I paused in front of the kitchen door.

He glanced at the staircase. "Is there a space we can speak in private?"

"The kitchen?"

He nodded and followed me inside.

"What can I do for you?" I asked, ignoring the wreckage.

He checked that the swinging door was closed. "You understand, on most of our UFO hunts, we don't find anything."

I nodded. At heart, UFO hunts were about the tease, the mystery, the possibility.

"But I'm afraid I have bad news," he said, his expression stern.

"Oh?"

"The so-called FBI agent, the murder, and now the break-in."

I steeled myself. This was it. They were going to leave a bad review.

"I believe..." He glanced around the kitchen. "You stand at the center of a conspiracy." Mr. Sorenson raised his chin.

He was talking about a UFO conspiracy, of course. But maybe he'd noticed something odd – something related to the murder – that I hadn't. "What do you mean?"

"I know that where there's a government cover-up, it's because there's something to cover up." Dramatically, he angled his head back to gaze at the white ceiling. Room seven, Agent Manaj's room, was directly above us.

I swallowed. "You mean...?"

"Extraterrestrials," he whispered. "They're here."

I made a noise in my throat. "Here... You mean, living amongst us?" I asked, disappointed. The rumor would be good for business, but what I really wanted was to know who killed Tanner McCourt. I refilled the pitcher with orange juice.

"They may have a base in the mountains somewhere. Would you mind putting Mr. Holiday on that? He seems like a capable fellow. And do you have any free weekends next month? We'd like to book rooms again. If all the excitement didn't convince me, your breakfasts have. Wits' End is well worth a second visit."

They wanted to return! But we kept pretty busy during the summer. "I'll have to check the bookings," I said cautiously.

He took the pitcher from my hands. "We'll only need two rooms. Any weekend you can manage, please let me know."

"Sure. I'll go check now."

Sorenson returned to the breakfast room with the orange juice.

Hurriedly, I swept up the mess on the kitchen floor, then trotted to the foyer. The reservation book lay open on the desk. *Yes!* We had two rooms available in late July.

Agent Manaj, wearing a black blazer, black blouse, black slacks, glided down the steps. Without acknowledging me, she walked into the breakfast room.

Something rustled by the front door. The exterior screen door banged shut.

Frowning, I walked onto the porch and peered through the screen to the yard. Aside from my SUV and the UFO hunters' cars, the driveway was empty.

I turned and stepped on a newspaper.

Puzzled, I lifted my foot. It hadn't been delivered by an overzealous paperboy, because I didn't get delivery. I collected the paper and brought it inside.

Arsen emerged from the breakfast room, and I dropped the newspaper on the reception desk.

I could admit when I was wrong, and I straightened my spine. "Thanks for helping with breakfast," I said. "Your creation was a hit."

"You're welcome."

"I should never have doubted."

"It's all right." He backed toward the front door. "I should be going. Are you sure you're going to be okay?"

"I'll be fine."

"Good. Um." He rubbed his calloused hands together. "There's something else."

"About?"

"About Ethan."

"Hm?" Idly, I flipped open the paper, and the hair rose on the back of my neck. A plain white envelope lay inside its folds.

"So, I found him last night."

"That's good," I said, studying the envelope. "Where was he?"

"Jail."

My head jerked up. "What?!"

"Okay, gotta go." Catlike, he zipped out the door.

"Arsen!"

The screen doors banged.

I rubbed my temple. How had things gotten so out of control? Again? But one thing I'd promised myself was I'd never try to control others, only myself. If I truly believed Ethan was his own man – or could be – I had to let him walk his own path. I opened the envelope and pulled out a sheet of typing paper. One word was written on it: *bandstand.*

Bandstand? What was that supposed to mean? If this was a ransom note, it wasn't particularly informative. There wasn't even a time.

I called Arsen.

"Are you going to yell?" he asked.

"Is that why you wanted to put distance between us?" I grumped. "If I didn't scream at you after you experimented on my guests, what was I going to do to you about Ethan?"

"Well, you couldn't yell at me in front of your guests."

I clenched my teeth. "Ethan is none of my business."

"True, but you have a soft spot for the oppressed."

How could I not? I'd spent enough time as one of them under my parents' thumbs. "Why is Ethan in jail?"

"He started a fight with the hacky sack gang at Antoine's."

"Those hacky sackers are really irritating," I said, grudging.

"And then he punched a deputy."

Whoops. I massaged my temple. "Oh, no. Did he do much damage?"

"Not even a bruise. From the sound of it, punching Denton was an accident, but the police frown on that sort of thing."

"They would. I don't suppose you can bail him out on a weekend?" Thanks to Dixie's youthful misadventures, I knew more about our criminal justice system than I wanted. If you got arrested on a Friday night, you were pretty much in for the duration.

"No. I can't. And I'm thinking of leaving him there until his mom returns."

I tore my gaze from the weird note. "Arsen, you can't *do* that." Sure, the Doyle jail was safe and modern. But still.

"Why not? The kid wants to experience life. What's more visceral than life behind bars?"

"Arsen..." I rubbed my burning eyes.

He sighed. "Well, it's a nice fantasy. At least he's off my hands for today. Hey, I meant to ask—"

"While you were running from the B&B?"

"Do you want to come to the lake this afternoon?"

"Um..." I stared at the letter, Sorenson's words echoing in my mind. A conspiracy in Doyle...?

"Sue? Is something wrong?"

"N—no. I was just trying to figure out my schedule. I have to clean the rooms, and then we've got a guest coming in around four."

"That gives us time to grab lunch at the lake and get in some paddle boarding."

A weight lifted from my chest. Could I manage it? Because my insides still felt odd and shaky when I thought of last night's attack. I *did* want to see Arsen. Lately, I only really felt safe in his cheerful, muscular presence.

Sorenson's group was checking out at eleven. And I didn't have to clean all the rooms this morning — only one for the new guest who'd arrive around four. That would give me time to stop by the only bandstand in town – in the park – and then meet up with Arsen. "I'm not sure I'm up for paddle boarding."

"Let me rephrase. I'll paddle board, while you lounge on the beach."

"Lounging I can manage." I was exhausted. I deserved a break. "Let's say one o'clock?" Assuming Dixie arrived late after her near concussion, I might be able to talk her into staying a little later this afternoon.

"I'll pick you up then."

We hung up, and I flipped through the newspaper. Rectangular holes dotted pages where the letters had been cut for the bandstand note. I returned to page one. The break-in at Wits' End had made the front page, and my stomach clenched. This wasn't good publicity.

I scanned each page for any hidden messages, but all I found was a circle around an ad for dental services in nearby Angel's Camp.

"Enough," I muttered. I was fed up with mysterious messages. An FBI agent was staying in my house. It was time to make this her problem.

Note in hand, I returned to the dining area's entrance. Inside, a frail-looking UFO hunter gazed up at the FBI agent with a petulant look on her face.

"My cat disappeared twenty-five years ago," the elderly woman was saying. "You're the UFO expert. What are you going to do about it?" she demanded.

Agent Manaj's face pinched. "Cats go missing all the time."

"But they aren't taken by UFOs," the woman persisted.

"There's no such thing as UFOs."

"But it wasn't just the cat," she said. "There was missing time."

"What does that even mean?" Manaj asked wildly.

"I'd just set the tea pot on the stove," the gray-haired woman said. "Mr. Tiddles was in his favorite chair. And then Mr. Tiddles was gone, and the water was boiling. Missing time!"

Or... maybe I could puzzle out the mysterious note on my own. I backed from the room and tiptoed into the kitchen.

To my surprise, Dixie rolled in at eleven and started cleaning while I managed the check-outs. Mr. Sorenson booked the two rooms for July, and his group bought UFO tchotchkes before leaving.

At noon, I grabbed Bailey's leash off the hook on the porch. I wasn't worried about going to the bandstand alone. It was a sunny Sunday, and the park would be filled with picnickers and families.

The two of us shambled to Doyle's small park, our journey slowed by Bailey's insistence on sniffing every bush and mailbox. The fresh air and sunshine woke me up a bit, but I was yawning when we reached the park.

The bandstand stood beneath a copse of elms at the far side of the park. A stream trickled, hidden, in the gully behind it. The lawn was spotted brown, but that didn't stop an elderly couple from spreading out a blanket. A trio of children raced, shrieking, around the park.

Bailey strained at his leash toward a collie playing catch with his owner. The collie ignored my dog.

"Don't feel bad," I said. "She may be long-haired and beautiful, but you don't need to waste time on a snob."

I tugged Bailey past the empty benches bracketing the wooden steps and up the stairs. We surveyed the deck. Empty, of course. Why had I assumed otherwise when there wasn't even a time on the note?

I walked to the railing. White paint flaked from the banister, and there was a bird's nest wedged between a ceiling beam and the octagonal roof.

I checked my phone.

Five minutes had passed.

Bailey looked up at me, a question in his caramel eyes.

This was stupid. I had to meet Arsen. Who knew when the letter writer would show, if at all?

I picked up Bailey and tromped down the steps, my feet making hollow, clunking sounds.

"Hsst!"

I jerked, straightening.

Bailey yipped and squirmed in my arms.

Setting him down, I looked around the park. The collie raced after a tennis ball. A father and son tried to launch a kite into the air.

Bailey whimpered, his tail wagging. It wasn't hard to guess what was going through his doggy brain. What was the point of going to the park if I wasn't going to let him play?

"Hsst!"

Head cocked, I peered around the corner of the bandstand.

An elderly woman in movie-star glasses and a scarf over her gray hair stood at the opposite end of one of the benches. The woman motioned to me. She wore a shapeless blue dress and sensible shoes, and had a stout, stern look about her.

But she didn't appear dangerous, so I walked over. "Can I help you?"

She edged deeper into the shade of the elms and vanished around another of the bandstand's many corners.

Old lady or not, I wasn't thrilled about being lured into the trees, where no one could see me. "Hello?"

No response.

Gritting my teeth, I crept around the corner.

The old woman dug a pink e-cigarette from her handbag and stuck it in her mouth. Her lipstick had faded, deeper shades of red clotting the wrinkles of her lips. "Susan Witsend." The e-cig's tip glowed green. She coughed out a stream of smoke.

"How do you know me?" I asked. "Who are you?"

"Who I am doesn't concern you."

"Did you put a newspaper on my porch this morning?"

"I told you to leave this case alone."

"So, it was you who left the cassette in my car."

"You're jeopardizing the future of Wits' End... And your own. Your grandmother wouldn't have wanted that."

Bailey yipped an agreement.

"How do you know my grandmother?"

A breeze rustled the leaves above us.

"Never mind." She coughed. "You've seen things you shouldn't have, things that weren't meant to be seen."

"What?" I wished I hadn't seen Tanner's corpse, but what was she talking about? "Do you know something about Tanner McCourt's death?"

"Tanner's murder was only the tip of the iceberg."

A headache throbbed behind my eyeballs. Did she have to be so cryptic? "What do you mean?"

"I mean that your life may be in danger."

"No kidding. Someone tried to drop an air conditioner on me from the Doyle Hotel."

Her mouth pinched. "I know."

"Was it Davin Markarian?"

"You shouldn't have gone to speak with him. Or with Cherie Cavalier. Leave this alone."

Bailey howled, tugging me backwards.

I spun, heart pounding.

The collie dropped a mangy tennis ball at my feet. Bailey lunged for it.

I swept up the tennis ball and chucked it across the park.

The collie raced after it. Bailey shot me a dour look.

I turned to the woman.

She had vanished, leaving only the faint scent of vanilla smoke behind her.

"Seriously?" I walked to the rear of the bandstand. A narrow path wound through a clump of coffee bushes and down to the creek bank. I squeezed through the brush and looked up and down the path.

Leaves whispered, dappled light shifting on the empty, dirt path.

Wavering, I rubbed my jaw. Where had she gone? The woman was eighty if a day. She couldn't have moved that quickly. I returned to the bandstand and searched the bushes for clues. But it was as if the old lady had vanished beneath the earth.

Chapter 16

The sun beat through the pines, and a rivulet of sweat trickled down my back, dampening my blue peasant top. Thinking hard, I walked Bailey down the looping roads to Wits' End.

I tightened my grip on his leash. It would be easy to write the mystery woman off as a batty old lady. But how had she known I'd spoken with Davin and Cherie? And she'd implied — I thought — that they were somehow connected to Tanner's murder. Otherwise, why shouldn't I have talked with them?

Unless she was using reverse psychology to get me to talk to them again. They'd been partners with Tanner. What did they know? I needed to talk to them again, but next time, I'd be careful. Keep it public.

We turned down Grizzly Court. Above the pines, sunlight glinted, blinding, off the silvery UFO crashed into the gabled roof of Wits' End. Bailey strained at his leash, and we jogged the last hundred yards home.

I unhooked the beagle's leash, and he trotted around the corner of the Victorian. I never worried about Bailey running into the street. Gran had trained the dog to stay in the yard.

Inside the B&B, Dixie pushed a vacuum cleaner around the foyer rug. She yawned, face pale.

"I can do that later," I shouted over the roar.

She turned off the vacuum and planted one fist on the hip of her khaki shorts. Her white tee was oversized with a high V-neck, and looked like it might be a man's. "What?"

"I said, I can do that later."

She shrugged. "I'm almost done anyway."

"How are you feeling?" I asked.

Careful not to meet my gaze, she unplugged the vacuum and wound the cord around its hook. "Fine. In fact, I was wondering if I could pick up some extra hours."

Huzzah! Now I wouldn't have to ask her for a favor while I went to the lake with Arsen. But if I looked desperate, she'd just find a way to take advantage later. I rubbed my chin. "I don't know..."

"You must need me around for something."

"I suppose you can today," I said, feigning reluctance. "The next guests aren't supposed to arrive until four, but it would be handy to have you here in case they arrive early."

"I'll do it." She glanced toward the ceiling. "By the way, that FBI agent left."

"You mean, she checked out?" I asked, holding my breath. Had she already solved the case?

"No, I mean she left for the day. She was wearing hiking clothes."

Rats. "You don't have to report guests' comings and goings."

She gave me a look. "Right. Oh, and she's dressed in all black, like she's paramilitary or something."

"Maybe she's in mourning."

"This isn't the Victorian era."

"Mr. Sorenson thought she might be a Man in Black."

Dixie snorted. "He would."

"I thought he was nice."

"Nice but gullible. He told me their last three UFO-hunting trips were near military bases."

"And?"

She rolled her eyes. "And everyone knows the strange lights over bases are military tests. The whole Men in Black shtick is a misinformation campaign by the government. They want people to think what they're seeing are UFOs instead of top-secret test flights."

Relief unfurled inside my chest. That had been my thinking, and I was oddly glad Dixie and I were on the same page.

Her emerald eyes narrowed. "It's really muddied the waters though. With all the fake information, it's harder to tell what's real and what's not. Some people think it's a double-fake. They believe UFOs hang around military bases because they're working with the government."

"What do you think?" Managing a UFO-themed B&B, I'd heard it all. But I was curious about her take.

"Any species smart enough to figure out intergalactic travel would be smart enough not to team up with the government."

"That... makes a weird sort of sense."

She stuck her hands in the pockets of her shorts. "It's only logical."

"Pick up any interesting radio chatter?" I asked casually.

"No. And if you mean about the murder, no. Why?"

"Something weird happened. You know that tape someone left in my car?"

"The one you gave to the cops?" Her mouth twisted with disdain. "Yeah."

"Someone slipped me a note asking to meet at the bandstand."

She sneered. "And you gave it to the cops?"

"No, and the letter writer turned out to be a little old lady. She wore big glasses and a scarf, so I couldn't get a good look at her. Any idea who she might be?"

"Why would I? Do you think because I'm interested in UFOs, I'm friends with all the local crackpots?"

Arsen, in cargo shorts and a hiking tee, strode into the room. "Hey, Dix. Want to come to the lake with us?"

She tossed her violet-tinted hair and picked up the vacuum. "*I'm* working."

"Then it looks like it's just you and me." He grinned.

"Let me get changed." I hurried into my bedroom and put on a bathing suit, then slathered on sunscreen. I slipped into shorts and a loose t-shirt and rummaged for a floppy hat in my closet. Grabbing my tote bag, I stuffed two beach towels, sunscreen, my wallet and day planner inside, and walked into the foyer.

Arsen and Dixie stood in deep conversation beside the reception desk.

He straightened when he saw me. "Ready?"

Dixie shoved the vacuum into a hall closet. "I'm going to start on the other rooms."

"Thanks," I said. "I've already cleaned room four." When had Dixie grown a work ethic? Suspicious, I let Arsen lead me to his ginormous Jeep. His paddle board was strapped to the top.

I buckled in, and we cruised into town, past tourists idling on the sidewalks, past tasting rooms and restaurants in old barns. A wave of exhaustion hit me, and I closed my eyes.

"You okay?" he asked.

I yawned. "Just tired. I didn't get much sleep last night."

"I'm not surprised. Have the police told you anything? Any idea who the guy was?"

"Nope," I lied. I still was betting on Davin.

"The break-in's got to be connected to Tanner's murder." He turned left onto the highway, lined with pines.

"I think so too, but why are you so sure?"

"I've been poking around."

"Arsen..."

His hands clenched on the wheel, his biceps flexing beneath his short-sleeved tee. "I don't like that someone nearly killed you with an air conditioner."

"I don't much like it either." And I was starting to regret having told him last night. "But it *could* have been an accident."

He slowed for an RV, crawling up the hill. "Right. Because the hotel is in the habit of letting air conditioners drop from its windows. You were grilling Davin Markarian, weren't you?"

"I wouldn't say *grilling*."

"I knew it. What did you find out?"

"What did *you* find out?" I asked. "You said you've been poking around."

"I asked you first."

"And I asked you second, and it's my B&B at risk."

The road straightened, and he accelerated, passing the camper. "*You're* at risk."

"Did you notice anything odd about Agent Manaj on the hike last night?"

"Last night? No. But Manaj? Yes." He smiled, grim.

"What?"

"I thought there was something strange about her taking over the case. So, I contacted a friend."

I gnawed the inside of my lip. "What sort of friend?"

"The sort who's connected. It turns out Tanner McCourt was connected to a federal case. He was cellmates with a federal informant."

Stunned, I blinked at the unfurling road. Pine trees flashed past. That was the sort of information the FBI wouldn't want leaked. Arsen's "friend" must be high up indeed. I smoothed the front of my baggy shirt. "What sort of informant?"

"The sort who was murdered after Tanner got out."

I sucked in my breath. "Tanner's cell mate was killed? And Manaj thinks Tanner's murder is connected?"

"That was all I could get," he said.

"Who was the informant?"

"My friend wouldn't tell me. She shouldn't have told me that much, but she owed me one."

"She?" I asked before I could stop myself.

"Sorry." He grinned. "No names."

"You're enjoying this way too much."

He sobered. "Honestly, I'm not."

I needed to get back inside Manaj's room. I'd been interrupted the first time, but she'd brought the file on that villainous-looking Guido person for a reason. Did he have a connection to Tanner McCourt?

"Have you heard anything from Ethan?" I asked.

"He's in jail. What's to hear?"

I shook my head, and told myself for the eighth time that Ethan was in jail for a good reason. If he was ever going to get some freedom, he needed to learn self-control.

We drove up to the seven-thousand-foot level, and the lake flashed between the trees. Arsen parked along the side of the narrow highway.

Arsen dealt with unhooking his paddle board and oar from the roof, and I wandered down to the water. Groupings of pine trees sprouted impossibly from the white stone islands dotting the lake. It being Sunday afternoon, the tourist hordes had thinned, starting their return treks to the Bay Area.

I found a shady spot on an empty stretch of gravel beach and laid down my striped towel. Rolling the other into a pillow, I got settled, dropping my floppy hat over my face to block the sun.

Arsen's board splashed into the water, and I heard the soft dip of his paddle. But soon all I could hear was the gentle lap of waves against the shore.

I must have fallen asleep, because the next thing I knew, cold drips of water were falling on my bare midriff.

Hissing, I snapped upright, my hat falling to the ground, and shielded my eyes.

Arsen loomed over me like a bronzed Apollo. I squinted, fiddling with the hem of the towel. How had I not noticed how well built he was? Though I wasn't counting, I think he might have had an actual six-pack going. I tore my gaze from his abs.

He shook his head like Bailey, splattering me with water.

"Hey!" I wiped droplets from my face. "Did you fall in?"

"Went for a swim. Want to join me?"

I yawned and pressed a finger to my leg. It left a white mark when I lifted it away. "No thanks. I think I was out in the sun too long."

"How irresponsible," he said lightly.

Annoyance flickered through me for no good reason. I checked my phone and leapt to my feet. "My next guests will be here at four."

"It's only two-thirty."

"But it takes twenty minutes to get back, and the guests could arrive early."

"And heaven forbid you go off schedule."

I scooped up the towels and stuffed them into my beach bag. "What's that supposed to mean?"

"Dixie's at the B&B. Let her take care of them. That's what you pay her for, isn't it?"

"Yes, but—"

"But you don't trust her."

"It's not that," I said.

"And I'll bet your day planner is in that tote bag."

I clutched it to my chest. "Is not," I lied.

"It is, isn't it? You actually brought your day planner to the beach."

I might have had time to do some editing. "What's your point?" I asked.

"My point is, you might want to try a little spontaneity."

My mouth pinched. Said the trust fund baby who'd run away to join the circus and hadn't had a steady job since.

"Fine," I said. "You want spontaneity? How about a surprise visit to Davin?" I dug out my day planner and checked the time. "If we leave now, we can interview him for twenty minutes and still get me back well before my next guests arrive."

He shouldered the paddle board. Beads of water dripped, glistening, down its side. "It's not spontaneous if you're checking a calendar."

"Day planner. And are you coming with me, or do I go it alone later?"

He rolled his eyes. "Fine. Let's go."

We trudged up the low bank to the Jeep.

I waited in the shade beside the bike path while Arsen strapped the board and paddle to the top.

Twenty minutes later, Arsen maneuvered into a parking spot behind the Historic Doyle Hotel. "How do you know he's working today?"

"I don't." I unbuckled my belt and hopped from the Jeep, careful not to ding the door of the blue Miata nearby. A wave of heat rippled off the macadam. "I'm being spontaneous."

Arsen emerged holding a small plastic grocery bag. "Let me dump this trash," he said, nodding to the dumpster at the rear of the hotel. "See, I can think ahead too."

I strode to the hotel's back door and waited, tapping my foot.

Arsen ambled to the dumpster and lifted the lid. "There's spontaneous," he said, "and then there's..." He stared into the open dumpster. His face paled.

"What's wrong? Did you forget your wallet at the beach?"

He dropped the lid with a clang. Movements jerky, he pulled his cell phone from the pocket of his cargo shorts.

"Arsen?" I moved to the dumpster.

"Don't touch it," he said sharply.

My nostrils flared. He so wasn't the boss of me! Lifting the lid, I peered inside.

And reeled away, gasping.

Davin Markarian lay coiled atop brown garbage bags. His neck twisted, wrong, broken.

Chapter 17

The sheriff's deputies arrived at the hotel first, the tires of their SUVs screeching on the parking lot asphalt. Agent Manaj wasn't far behind in her blue sedan. Briefly, I wondered if Dixie was listening in on her radio. But she couldn't be, because she was at Wits' End, doing my job while I'd lounged at the lake and stuck my nose where it had no business — in a murder.

Arsen leaned, arms and legs crossed, against his steel-gray Jeep. He bent his head toward me. "We just stopped by so I could dump some garbage," he murmured.

The deputies — Denton and his dark-haired partner — emerged from their SUV.

I shook my head. "But we weren't."

"Do our motives here really matter?" he asked.

I opened my mouth to protest and snapped it shut. Arsen was right. Neither of us had anything to do with Davin Markarian's death. Explaining why we'd come to the hotel would only cause more trouble.

Denton snapped on a pair of gloves. Opening the lid of the dumpster, he peered inside, shook his head. "Call the crime scene team. This guy didn't get in here on his own."

Agent Manaj, dressed like she was in a SWAT team, looked over his shoulder. "Davin Markarian." She turned, her gaze boring into Arsen and me. "Interesting." The FBI agent pointed. "You. Come with me."

Sweating, I trailed after her to the opposite edge of the parking lot.

A crow pecked at a potato chip, broken into three pieces on the macadam.

"What were you doing poking around the hotel garbage bins?" she asked.

I sucked in my cheeks. "I wasn't. Arsen needed to throw something out."

"And he doesn't have his own garbage cans?"

I shrugged. "Maybe they were full. The hotel was on our way back from the lake."

"What were you doing at the lake?"

"I was sunbathing. Arsen was paddle boarding."

"Don't you know sunbathing is bad for you?"

I crossed my arms, wrinkling my oversized tee. "Does the FBI have an SPF division now?"

The crow made a low, clicking noise, and flew into a nearby redwood.

"How long were you at the lake?" Manaj asked.

"Arsen picked me up from Wits' End at one o'clock. I don't think you were there at the time," I said. And what had she been up to?

But Manaj didn't enlighten me. "And then?"

"And then we drove to the beach. We'd talked about getting a late lunch, but I guess I fell asleep, so we came straight back into town. Arsen called you as soon as we found the body, which was just a minute or two after we drove into the parking lot."

She rubbed her dark brow. "Why'd you come here?"

"I told you, Arsen decided he needed to use their dumpster to empty some trash."

"That he was carrying around in his Jeep?" she asked, her voice thick with disbelief.

"I guess so. He had a bag." I nodded toward Arsen, speaking earnestly to the dark-haired cop. The small plastic bag dangled from his fingertips. "We didn't have a huge discussion about it."

"Wait here." She strode across the lot to Arsen and the dark-haired cop and jabbed her finger at my friend.

Arsen pressed a hand to his chest, his eyes widening.

Apprehensive, I adjusted my t-shirt. "Here" being a vague and subjective term, I edged closer.

Denton threw back his head and laughed, a rich sound. "You don't know Arsen," he said. "Using someone else's garbage can is exactly the sort of thing he'd do."

I stopped beside a dusty blue Prius, and my cheeks warmed. Arsen had come here because of me. Now, he was letting himself look foolish to protect me. True, he had a long history of looking ridiculous — the circus incident being a case in point. But this wasn't fair.

Arsen hung his head, as if chagrined. It was a good thing he didn't mind what people thought. But he'd never minded. Because of that attitude, he'd lived exactly the devil-may-care life he'd wanted, circus, sexy resorts and all. I'd had no business criticizing him, because I was finally doing exactly what *I* wanted over my family's objections.

Arsen rubbed his head, playing the fool, and I caught myself smiling. No wonder Arsen and I had stayed friends since childhood, even if he had disappeared from my life for all those years.

My smile slipped. He hadn't ever played the fool with me, had he?

Was I as blind as those deputies?

Agent Manaj strode to me. "You can leave. I know where to find you if I have more questions."

"And Arsen?"

The dark-haired deputy clapped him on the back.

Her nose wrinkled. "Him too."

"Thanks." I hustled to Arsen's Jeep and waited while he shook hands with the deputies.

He returned, grinning, to the car. "You okay?"

"Yeah. You?"

His eyes glinted. "They bought it." He opened the door for me.

Relieved and unaccountably annoyed, I climbed inside the Jeep, which had reached volcanic temperatures. I rolled down the window and fanned myself. "Did they say anything about Ethan?" I asked.

He looked at me blankly. "Ethan?"

"That guy you're supposed to be watching? The one who's in jail?"

"Nah. I'll bail him out tomorrow. By the way, Manaj suspects a link between Davin and Tanner's deaths."

I nodded. It was the only reason she'd be here. "Did she say anything?"

"She didn't have to."

I fiddled with the seatbelt, looked up.

On the far side of the parking lot, where Manaj had interrogated me, stood a lean figure in big glasses. A camouflage-print scarf covered her hair. For a moment my vision blurred, and I thought she was the woman from the park. (I was beginning to think of her as *Madame X*). But this mystery woman was taller and slimmer. She turned and strode athletically down the street.

"What's she doing here?" I asked.

"Who?" Arsen peered through the windshield.

"There was a woman right..." But she'd disappeared around the corner. "No one." A shiver raised the flesh on my bare arms. Was I being followed by a gang of women in scarves and big glasses?

"Hey." He touched my hand. "I'm sorry. You must be shaken up after seeing Davin's body."

I was, but I was more shaken by my growing paranoia. Or is it paranoia after you've found two murder victims? "It's a strange feeling. There's someone nearby, in Doyle, who cares so little about people's lives that he's willing to kill."

"Maybe," he said shortly. "But no one's going to hurt you, Sue. I'll make sure of it."

"I don't see how anyone can."

He started the Jeep. "I'll figure out who's doing this." A pulse beat in his jaw. "I promise."

I braced my elbow on the window frame and scrunched my hair, my fingers against my scalp. As an ex circus performer and scuba instructor, Arsen was uniquely *un*qualified to find the killer. I didn't need him getting into more trouble on my behalf. "Maybe it is time we let the police handle things," I said. "It's not as if our investigations have been going well."

His brows drew together, and for a long moment, he didn't speak. "You're probably right. It's best if we drop it."

He drove me home. Bailey met us at the front door and made little jumps of happiness around my ankles.

Arsen walked through the kitchen, the sitting room, my bedroom, checking the windows. Assured that Dixie and I were safe, he warned us to keep the doors locked and drove off.

I retrieved a doggy treat from the top of the refrigerator and tossed it to Bailey. The beagle caught it mid-air and trotted to the rag rug beneath the sink to devour it.

Dixie plunked into a chair at the kitchen table and propped her head on one fist. "I heard you found another body."

I straightened. "How did you find out so fast? Do you have a radio stashed away in here too?"

"Connections."

"What sort of connections? I'm starting to think maybe there is a conspiracy going on."

"A conspiracy?" Dixie rolled her eyes. "Seriously?"

"Two people are dead, and the FBI is investigating. They don't show up for a run-of-the-mill murder."

"Yeah, but a conspiracy? That's a little out there."

Coming from a woman who had an alien-hunting trailer, that seemed rich. But I've noticed that people with crazy obsessions are the first to discount your own crazy obsession. Not that mine was crazy. Or an obsession. I opened my mouth to protest.

A car crunched up the gravel driveway.

"That must be our guests." I hurried to the foyer and straightened the racks of UFO paraphernalia against the stairs.

Two thirty-something women lugging over-sized suitcases bumped through the screen door. Though one was blonde and the other brunette, one slender the other curvy, there was something about them that said they were family. They both grinned identical grins. Freckles spattered across the same pert noses. Both were gorgeous in a windblown, just-out-of-the-car sort of way.

Wagging his tail, Bailey came to sniff their high-heeled boots.

"Hi there!" The blonde bent and scratched Bailey's head, and I wasn't sure if she was talking to me or the dog. "We have a reservation? Buckles?"

"Yes," I said. "A room with two twins."

"We'd prefer queens, if you have them," the brunette said, taking her turn lavishing affection on Bailey.

I winced and motioned around the foyer. "Sorry. It's a Victorian. The rooms just aren't big enough for two queen beds."

The women looked at each other a long moment.

Reluctantly, the brunette nodded. "If that's all you have." Her mouth curled with distaste.

I slid behind the desk and took the blonde's credit card. "Where are you from?" I asked.

"Pennsylvania," the brunette said. "We're doing a road trip around the country and thought a UFO B&B sounded fun."

Arsen strolled inside. "Hey, Sue. I forgot to..." He noticed the women and trailed off.

The new guests eyed him appreciatively.

He smiled and stuck out his hand. "Arsen Holiday. Guide."

"Guide to what?" The brunette giggled.

"Whatever you need," he said.

"I'm Beryl." The brunette stepped close and took his hand.

"Heidi," the blonde said.

Oh, brother. I bent my head to the computer and tried not to make a face. But Arsen had every right to hustle business or... whatever.

He reached into the pocket of his khaki shorts and withdrew a crumpled card. "I lead hikes around the area and teach paddle boarding."

They squealed.

"I've always wanted to try paddle boarding," the blonde, Heidi, said. She clung to Arsen's hand longer than was strictly necessary.

My fist tightened on the pen.

Laughing, they made arrangements to meet Arsen after they'd "freshened up."

"Is it okay if I leave my T-bird in the driveway?" the brunette asked.

"That's yours?" Arsen whistled. "Nice."

"It was a splurge after we sold our company." Beryl hefted her suitcase.

He leapt to take it from her. "What sort of company?"

"A dating app," Heidi said.

My mouth crimped. It just had to be a dating app. Though if they were flush with tech funds, I was surprised they hadn't gotten two rooms. But maybe they were naturally frugal. After all, a T-bird isn't a Ferrari.

"I bought a Ferrari," Heidi said, "but it's not as comfortable on long drives."

Oh, for Heaven's sake! "Here are your keys," I sang out. "One for the room, and one for the front door. The room's upstairs and on the right."

"Here, let me take that," Arsen said, grabbing Heidi's suitcase.

"I can do that," I said quickly. I rose from my desk chair. "It's my job."

"I don't mind." Arsen led them up the stairs.

Bailey – the traitor – trotted after them.

Dixie propped one shoulder against the kitchen doorway and crossed her tanned legs. "Jealous much?"

"Not at all." I busied myself with their paperwork. "What's to be jealous of?"

She glanced at the brass chandelier. "Oh, I dunno. Maybe the Charlie's Angels upstairs with Arsen?"

"There were three Charlie's Angels."

She smiled crookedly. "You can fool some people all of the time, and all people some of the time, but you can't fool yourself forever."

"Be cryptic all you want. I need your help."

"Doing what?"

I winced, sheepish. "Breaking and entering?"

Chapter 18

Dixie straightened off the doorframe and dropped her arms to her sides. "Breaking and entering? Forget it. I'm not going back to jail."

"You don't need to go inside Manaj's room," I wheedled, guiding her into the kitchen. Afternoon sunlight gilded the linoleum floor. "All you need to do is get me past the chain. And then put it back on from the outside."

Expressionless, she leaned against the butcher-block counter. The hem of her men's t-shirt caught on a cupboard handle, and she untangled it. "I don't do that anymore."

This afternoon was an inconvenient time for her to stop. "Oh well. I guess I can go through the window again."

"You just found a dead body." She shifted her weight, her violet-tinted head brushing a spider plant on a low shelf. "Don't you think you should stay out of this?"

"Says the woman with the police scanner."

"I knew this would happen," she said.

"Knew what?"

"You broke into her room once, and now you've got a taste for the adrenaline rush."

"Give me a break." Rules exist for a reason, and I'd never been one to flout them. Dixie had done enough flouting for the both of us. But this was different.

"Denial ain't just a river in Egypt. Crime is a slippery slope, Susan."

"Stop mashing up metaphors and help me."

She rubbed her chin. "I really don't think I should encourage you."

"I have every right to be in that room. It says so in the room contract. She's in breach by having set up a way to lock me out."

Her gaze flicked to the kitchen ceiling. "Fine. I'll do it. But I'm not going inside."

"That's okay, you can be lookout."

But we didn't get a chance. The new guests took their time getting ready, and when they left with Arsen, a businessman without a reservation showed up. I couldn't turn him away, not with all those empty weekday rooms. Then Manaj returned, and Dixie left, and I was out of luck.

Giving up, I sat on the gazebo steps and threw the octopus thing to Bailey. The sun was lowering, hovering above the peaks to the west. It would be another two hours until it dropped behind the mountains, but the light already had a sideways, soft quality. The pink roses twining up the gazebo's lattice scented the twilight air, and my frustration eased.

"You really knew what you were doing when you planted these," I said to the roses, though I was really speaking to Gran.

The B&B phone rang in my pocket. "Hi, this is Wits' End, Susan speaking."

"Susan, this is Professor Green."

My throat tightened. Ethan hadn't been my problem. Why did I feel guilty? "Professor Green! I didn't think you could get cell reception where you are."

"I got lucky - though I don't know how long it will last. This call could drop any second. How's Ethan?"

Bailey dropped the blue octopus at my feet.

I chucked it to the other end of the yard, and it landed beneath a rose bush.

Bailey raced after it, his ears flapping.

"Ethan?" I parroted.

"Yes, Ethan. My son. Have you seen him lately?"

"Oh. Right," I said, sweating. "I saw him yesterday."

"Where? What was he doing?"

"He was at Arsen's. There was some talk of swimming, but then he and Arsen returned to Wits' End instead." Separately, but they'd returned.

"Swimming! Ethan's not a strong swimmer. He should stay away from the water unless there's a lifeguard present. What's he doing now?"

How does one spend one's time in jail? "I don't know. Have you tried calling Arsen?"

Bailey dropped the fuzzy octopus at the base of the gazebo steps.

"I just did," she said. "He didn't answer my call. I left a voicemail."

If Arsen had recognized her number, it was little wonder he hadn't picked up.

My scalp prickled. I hoped that was the only reason. But of course, it was the only reason. Arsen was with two sexy Pennsylvanians at the lake.

The professor's voice turned icy. "The point, Ms. Witsend, was that Ethan should not be left alone."

Bailey gave a short yip of impatience.

I reached between my legs, grabbed the toy, and threw it to the opposite end of the yard. It bounced beneath a pink tea rose. The dog raced away.

"I'm sure Ethan's not alone." I wiped my upper lip. You're never truly alone in jail, are you? Not with all those guards and fellow prisoners.

"*Really?*"

I tried to inject confidence into my voice. "Really. Is there anything you'd like me to tell him when I see him next?" I said, desperate to change the subject.

"When do you plan to see him next?"

"I don't have any firm plans, but I'll probably see him Monday." Because I'd make sure Arsen bailed Ethan out tomorrow.

"Very well," she said, and the call ended.

I wasn't sure if we'd gotten cut off or if she'd hung up, but a feeling of unease descended. Had I imagined something *off* about that call?

Now I really was getting paranoid.

Octopus between his teeth, Bailey plopped to the ground at my feet. He cocked his head, daring me to wrestle it away.

I accepted the challenge, and he mock growled as I lightly tugged on two of the octopus's dangly legs. I released the toy.

He trotted away, his head raised, victorious.

A warm breeze shivered the rose petals.

I glanced at them and smiled. "Did you have to deal with this craziness when you were in charge?"

The roses didn't answer. But then again, I hadn't really been talking to them.

Feeling eyes on me, I glanced up.

Agent Manaj lounged at the top of the exterior stairs. She raised a wine goblet in a mock toast and walked inside.

I switched phones and called Arsen.

"Hey," he said. In the background, women shrieked with laughter. There was a splash.

My brow puckered. "I just got a call from Professor Green."

His voice rose a full octave. "Did you answer it?"

"It was on the B&B phone. Of course, I answered it." I always answered that phone.

"What did you tell her?"

"Nothing."

He blew out his breath. "Thanks. You're the best."

"But I got the feeling she knew something was up."

"How could she? The professor's on top of a mountain somewhere."

"I don't know, I just..." I sucked in a quick breath. That woman lurking in the hotel parking lot had been the same age and build as the professor. *That* was who she'd reminded me of. The professor was supposed to be deep in the Sierras, but what if she wasn't?

"What's wrong?" he asked.

"Nothing." If I told Arsen my suspicion, he'd either think I was crazy or decide to investigate. "You are going to get him out of jail tomorrow, aren't you?"

"The professor's not getting back until Friday. I figured a couple more days—"

"Arsen!"

"Fine. I'll bail him out tomorrow."

"Promise?"

"Yeah, yeah," he grumped. "I promise."

"Maybe a couple nights in jail will have mellowed him."

"And you call yourself a student of human nature," he said gloomily.

We hung up, and Bailey and I returned inside.

The beagle trotted to the fluffy white sitting room rug, turned around three times, and lay down, shutting his eyes.

There are times I'm jealous of that dog. I never fell asleep that easily.

I paced, picking up books and putting them down. The FBI agent's footfalls were soft in her room. Above me, a chair scraped against the floor.

Finally, at seven o'clock exactly, Manaj departed — for dinner, I presumed.

I phoned Dixie. My cousin materialized in my kitchen ten minutes later.

"When did she leave?" Dixie asked.

"Right before I called you."

She opened the junk drawer and pulled out a thick, rubber band. "For safety's sake, let's assume we've got twenty minutes."

It was a surprisingly cautious proposal from my violet-haired cousin, and I nodded. Besides, Manaj's wasn't that big of a room.

We tiptoed upstairs, and I unlocked Manaj's door. The security chain stretched across the narrow gap, blocking our access.

"How does she do that?" I muttered.

"Watch and learn." Dixie looped the fat rubber band over the chain and tugged, wiggling it sideways.

The chain dropped, clattering against the wooden door.

"That's genius," I said.

She smiled modestly. "I didn't invent the trick."

I hurried inside the room, my pulse hammering. Manaj had

returned the UFO photos to the walls. The bed was made. Her briefcase sat on top of the desk beside her laptop.

Movements jerky, I depressed the latches on the black leather briefcase.

Nothing happened.

"It's locked," I said, disappointed.

Dixie huffed out a breath and strode inside. "Let me see." She pulled a violet skull hairpin from her hair and fiddled with the lock. It popped open.

I gaped, marveling. "You're amazing. Will you teach me?"

"No." She opened the laptop and booted it up.

"That's got to be password protected."

She grunted. "I'd hope so."

I riffled through the papers in Manaj's wastepaper basket – brochures for restaurants and descriptions of local sites and trails.

"Gross," Dixie said. "What are you doing?"

"Searching her trash. What does it look like I'm doing?" I uncrumpled a sheet of paper. On it was a rough drawing of a flying saucer. A band of light shot from the UFO's base, and a cow floated in the beam. "Obsessed much?" I muttered.

Dixie glanced at the drawing. "Not bad."

"It's not good either." Not that I could do much better.

"Keep it for Mr. Sorenson. He'll see it as proof she's a Man in Black. She isn't, but he doesn't need to know that."

"Why are you so sure?"

"Because she tried to *find* The Disappeared, not hide the truth about what happened. That's why she nearly lost her job. I'm in."

"What?"

"I'm in her computer." She scooted her chair away from the desk.

"Wasn't there a password?"

She stood and stretched. "Of course, there was a password."

"Then how'd you get in?"

"I took some computer classes in juvie. Another inmate – a hacker – took the class with me. She taught me a few things."

"Not the education the State of California had in mind."

My cousin angled the laptop toward me. "There's a file labeled *McCourt*."

A door banged open downstairs.

We stared at each other, wide eyed.

Dixie raced from the room.

"Arsen!" she called out. "Where've you been?"

Footsteps stomped up the stairs, and she shut the door behind her. I glanced at the clock on the computer. Dixie had said twenty minutes, and I figured we'd used ten.

Breath quick, I opened the computer file and started reading. There was a file on the sheriff - notes of interviews and encounters, as well as none-too-flattering observations by Manaj.

Laughter in the hallway outside. A door slamming.

"What are you doing here?" Arsen's voice floated through the closed door.

"I was looking for Sue," Dixie said. "Have you seen her?"

I clicked open a crime scene file — Tanner McCourt's neck had been broken and his room searched — most likely by his killer.

So, the person who'd picked up the phone when I'd called Tanner *had* been his killer. I'd suspected as much, but the confirmation chilled me.

An electronic file on Davin Markarian. It contained a rap sheet and legal records I didn't have time to understand. I opened the file dated to his murder — crime scene pics of Davin coiled in the garbage bin. I closed those quickly.

I opened a file of notes she'd typed today... Davin's neck had been broken as well. So probably the same killer.

There were also files on the Greens. I opened the professor's. Okay, she was a real professor, which I'd kind of already figured out. Divorced. Yeah, I'd picked up on that too...

I frowned. The name of her husband - Montel DiCostanzo — looked familiar. Where had I seen it before?

Minimizing the file, I scanned the screen. A file labeled *DiCostanzo* sat in the lower right corner.

The door popped open, and I jumped, biting back a shriek.

"Time's up," Dixie said.

I opened the DiCostanzo file and sucked in my breath. Guido Valducci. Federal witness. Mob racketeering. *Whoa.*

Dixie leaned over me and shut the computer down. "I said, *time's up.* Do I need to spell it out?"

"Dixie—"

"Manaj is parking her car."

I swore. Hastily, I returned the photos to the manila file and slid it in her briefcase, locked it.

Dixie bounced on her heels. "Come on, come on, come on."

I shut the laptop, returned the chair to its place. Snatching a tissue off the box on the desk, I wiped laptop and briefcase. I hurried into the hall.

"Stall her!" Dixie shoved me toward the foyer stairs.

I jogged to the staircase and glanced over my shoulder. Dixie had the door mostly closed and fiddled with the chain lock.

The front door opened. Manaj, in her trademark black suit, strode into the foyer.

I clattered down the stairs. "Agent Manaj! There's something I need to talk to you about."

"I'm exhausted. Can it wait?" She stepped past me, and I edged in front of her.

"Aliens," I ad-libbed.

She blinked.

"What?"

"My UFO presentation, I mean." I glanced at the brass hanging lamp. "I'd love to include your take on The Disappeared."

"You've heard my take. There are no such thing as aliens."

"Then why are there so many UFO sightings and strangeness here, around Doyle?"

"There aren't."

"But many scientists believe aliens live among us. In 2014, Canada's defense minister said he thought there were as many as eighty different alien species on Earth."

"He's military. They're probably trying to cover up their own secret tests, make people think the lights in the sky are UFOs."

"There's another theory that the government keeps the existence of aliens hidden," I rambled on, face hot. "They don't want to create panic among civilian populations."

"Right," she said. "Excuse me." She edged toward the stairs.

I maneuvered in front of her. "And there's another theory that the government is working with aliens. The whole misinformation campaign is a double blind."

"That is the stupidest thing I've ever heard."

Dixie sauntered down the steps. "Hey, you're the one who booked a room in a UFO B&B. What did you expect?"

"Peace and quiet, for starters," the agent said.

"So how do you explain The Disappeared?" my cousin asked.

"Gas leak. Mass hysteria."

"That's exactly what a Man in Black would say," Dixie said.

"I'm here to solve two murders," Manaj said, "not spread disinformation."

"So, you admit that's what a Man in Black would do," Dixie said.

"Admit what? You two are nuts." She brushed past me and up the stairs.

"She knows more than she's saying," Dixie said. "And she knows what a Man in Black is. You know what that means."

"Yeah." I scrubbed my hands across my face. "It means we've pissed off an FBI agent."

Chapter 19

I returned the morning's breakfast dishes to their place in the sky-blue cupboards. Cool morning air wafted through the open kitchen window, stirring the blue curtains. Birds twittered on pine branches gleaming with dew. It was the sort of scene that normally filled me with a sense of peace. But peace evaded me this morning.

My personal cell phone rang, and I snatched it off the butcher-block counter. "Hello?"

"Why did you call me five times last night?" the sheriff asked.

I winced. Five might have been a *teensy* excessive. "Because I've learned something important," I whispered, glancing at the ceiling. Agent Manaj moved about in the room above, her footfalls light.

"And?"

"And I don't feel comfortable talking about it here. Can we meet?"

She blew out her breath. "Fine. Whatever. Antoine's. Thirty minutes."

I blinked. "The bar?" At this hour? It was only ten o'clock.

"They have cheap coffee." She hung up.

Obviously, I still had a lot to learn about Doyle.

Already dressed in loose, linen slacks and a slouchy blue t-shirt, I grabbed my purse off the kitchen table, ready to roll.

Bailey woofed quietly.

"All right, you can come." After a quick search, I unearthed his leash, and we strolled from the B&B.

I loved these moments of freedom. No one was checking out today. My breakfast duties were done. I'd already cleaned all the rooms but Manaj's, which I'd been locked out of.

Bailey and I walked down looping roads lined with old Victorians and barns and mysterious stone houses. A morning breeze, promising afternoon heat, tossed my hair.

Bailey stopped at every tree and mailbox to sniff, slowing our progress. In spite of that, we arrived at Antoine's early. There was no dog bowl in front of its batwing doors (the secret signal dogs were welcome). I tied his leash to the hitching post and walked inside.

The antique western chandeliers were unlit. Sunlight streamed through the tall windows. It illuminated the sawdust-covered floor, the round tables, and the wooden booths. I walked to the long, curving bar.

Antoine, an older, African-American man, stood behind it and polished a coffee mug. His hair was the color of old ivory, and he wore an apron over his rounded stomach. "Anything I can get you?" he asked.

"A cup of coffee, please."

He grunted and ambled to the coffee pot, poured a cup, and returned, setting it on the bar in front of me.

I took a sip and winced, feeling the lining peeling off my stomach. Setting the cracked mug aside, I examined the mix of initials and misshapen hearts carved into the wooden bar.

The batwing doors creaked open.

Looking sporty in sneakers, yoga pants, and a burgundy, zip-up jacket, the sheriff strode to the bar. She sat beside me and nodded at Antoine.

Wordlessly, he poured a cup of coffee and set it in front of her. Antoine walked down the bar and disappeared into a back room.

She took a gulp of coffee, winced, and set it down. "So?"

"Manaj is really here because of a federal crime. One of the FBI's informants against the mob was killed."

"What does that have to do with me?"

I pulled my day planner from my purse and consulted my notes. "The informant who was killed was Montel DiCostanzo. He spilled the beans on a mobster named Guido Valducci."

"And?"

"And Montel was married to Professor Green. He's Ethan's father."

"Still not getting the connection."

Now she was just being obtuse. "DiCostanzo was cellmates with your, er, with Tanner," I said, my speech rushed. "He was killed in his cell two days after Tanner was released. What if their deaths are somehow connected?"

"That's a leap."

"Is it? Tanner gets out of jail. His cellmate is murdered. His cellmate's ex-wife and son turn up here, then Tanner is killed. It's a pretty weird coincidence."

The sheriff stared for a long time at the bottles lining the mirrored wall. "When did the Greens make their reservation?"

"A week before they arrived — and about a week after DiCostanzo was killed. Normally, they wouldn't have gotten in — our summer weekends are booked well in advance — but we had a cancellation."

"But Manaj let the professor go on her jaunt into the mountains anyway. That's... interesting."

143

"Maybe Manaj figured because Ethan was here, the professor would have to return to Doyle?"

The sheriff sipped her coffee and made a noncommittal noise.

"What other reason could she have?" I asked.

The sheriff took another sip. "What else did you learn about DiCostanzo?"

Ha! So, she *was* interested. "Not much. Her files said he was a CPA." As a former accountant, I found his abuse of the double-entry bookkeeping system offensive.

"That's not surprising." She unzipped her burgundy yoga jacket.

"Why?"

"Tanner was in a low-security prison for white collar criminals. His cellmate would have to be another white-collar criminal, like an accountant." She sipped the coffee. "This mob accountant, DiCostanzo, was an informant against Guido Valducci, you say?"

I nodded.

"I heard about that case. Valducci was a nasty piece of work. So, Ethan's father, DiCostanzo, cut a deal with the feds — probably got a nicer jail cell in exchange for ratting out his employers. And if Valducci found out what he'd done..."

"From Tanner? You think he told Valducci that DiCostanzo was the rat?"

"That's gotta be what Manaj suspects." She blew out her breath. "And I wouldn't put it past him. Tanner was broke when he got out, desperate. If he thought giving up DiCostanzo was worth something, he'd do it."

"But if Tanner took a payoff from the mob," I said, "then why didn't he have the money to pay me?"

She laughed shortly. "Who says he didn't?"

"But he didn't..." I trailed off. "Oh." Why pay for a perfectly good room when the owner/manager is a sucker?

She clapped me on the shoulder and rose, scraping back her barstool. Its legs left tracks in the sawdust. "All right. That intel wasn't totally useless."

Not totally?

"Anything else?"

"No, just a drawing of a UFO she'd sketched."

She gulped the last of her coffee and thunked the mug on the bar. "What do you care what she draws? Your B&B attracts nutjobs by design."

I crossed my arms. "People interested in the unexplainable aren't nutjobs."

"Keep telling yourself that." She laid two dollars on the counter and strode out the swinging doors.

I looked at my nearly full coffee cup. A suspicious film had formed around its rim.

Adding some bills to the sheriff's contribution, I departed.

Outside, Bailey sat beside the brick wall, his tail thumping on the plank walk. A toddler in a red-and-yellow striped shirt patted his head. His mother, in a skirt and sunhat, beamed.

"Hello." I smiled and untied Bailey's leash.

"What a sweet dog," the woman said. "Is he a purebred beagle?"

"I'm not sure about purebred, but he's a beagle." I'd inherited him with the B&B and had nothing to do with his cuteness or sweet disposition. Pride warmed my heart anyway.

We said our goodbyes. Bailey and I crossed Main Street and walked to Ground. I needed to get the taste of Antoine's coffee out of my mouth, and I wanted to talk to Cherie again. She'd had strong opinions on Davin Markarian. Had they changed since he'd died?

A dog bowl sat beside the chalkboard stand outside Ground's red-painted front door. I paused for Bailey to lap water, and we walked inside.

The scent of roasting coffee beans filled the air. A long line formed along the black granite counter. Cherie and Jayce moved at light speed pouring drinks, making change.

I scanned the coffee shop for empty tables and did a double-take.

Arsen lounged on a sofa beside a front window and perused a newspaper, his clean-cut profile serious. His foot nudged the low table, rattling his espresso.

Bailey lunged for him, and I let the dog tug me along.

"Hi, Arsen."

He dropped the paper in an untidy heap on the table and smiled, his teeth brilliant white against his tanned skin. "Hey, Sue. What's up?" Bending to scratch Bailey, his khaki tee strained against his muscular back.

"I was just walking Bailey. Where's Ethan?"

He leaned back and rested one ankle on his opposite knee. Dirt drifted from the treads of his hiking boot and onto his gray hiking slacks. "Same place he was last night."

"You mean they wouldn't let him out?" I asked, aghast.

"I mean I haven't been to the courthouse yet. It's only..." He glanced at his dive watch. "Eleven o'clock."

"But the courthouse opens at nine."

"What's a few hours?"

"To a man in jail? It's a little mean, isn't it? Leaving him there?"

"Sue, do you know what happened last night after I returned those two ladies safe and sound to your B&B?"

My lips flattened. Did I want to know? I'd heard them get in after eleven, giggling their way up the stairs. "I think I'd prefer not—"

"I went home. I relaxed on my deck and listened to fish jump in the pond. And then I went to bed. It was heaven."

"I know Ethan's a challenge," I said weakly. "But jail—"

"I look on it as a character-building experience."

"Funny." I planted my arms akimbo. "I thought the same thing about Ethan staying with you."

"That it would build his character?"

Bailey looked anxiously at the two of us.

"That it would build yours," I said. "I don't know much about how the courts work, but I suspect you can't show up at four-fifty-five in the afternoon to get him out at five. There are procedures. Processes. If you wait, he might get stuck in jail another night."

Arsen angled his head. His expression said that wasn't such a bad thing.

"I get that he's a pain," I said. "If you don't have the energy to get him out, I will."

He sighed. "I'll do it."

"When?"

"When I finish my espresso."

"I can wait." I sat beside him on the sofa and pulled my day planner from my purse.

He paled. "What do you mean, you'll wait?"

"I'll go with you," I said sweetly. "For moral support." Because I knew that as soon as I left Ground, Arsen would order another espresso and dawdle away the afternoon. I penciled the word, *courthouse*, into my planner.

"You don't have to do that."

"But I want to. I've got free time, and I'm curious about how the whole process works. I've never bailed anyone out of jail before. It'll be interesting."

"It'll be boring."

"I'll bet there are all sorts of characters getting bailed out today."

"It's not a good place for you."

I batted my eyelashes. "What do you mean?"

He laughed. "Fine. We'll go now." His hazel eyes narrowed with cunning. "Though I don't think they let dogs inside the courthouse."

"I'm sure we'll be able to work something out." As long as I got Arsen inside the courthouse, I was *fairly* certain he'd go through with it and bail Ethan out.

Arsen finished his espresso. We strolled down Main Street, making frequent stops for Arsen to greet people he knew. He knew a lot of people.

"What are you doing on Tuesday evening?" he asked.

"Are you going to make me look in my planner?"

"Want to come to the Xavier Ultra book signing?"

My heart gave a funny jump. "Why not?"

"Great. If we step up to his table together, it will look like there are two of us getting a book signed, and I can talk to him longer."

I stumbled on a curb. "It's a small bookstore. I don't think you're going to have any trouble talking to him."

"Xavier Ultra is legendary. The bookstore's going to be packed."

"Mm hm," I said, doubtful.

Ethan was being held in the town rather than the county jail. I wasn't sure why or what the difference was (Arsen tried to explain it to me and failed). But the town jail was at the end of Main Street, housed in the basement of the old courthouse, a brick building fronted by Greek columns.

We paused at the edge of its small garden, planted with drought-resistant lavender. I craned my neck at the bell tower atop its peaked roof.

"Susan!" My chiropractor, Zack Harwell, strode toward us, his long arms swinging at his sides. "What are you doing here?"

Arsen's brows drew downward. For some reason, he'd never liked my chiropractor. "What are *you* doing here?" he asked.

"Parking ticket." Zack's handsome face twisted in a comic grimace. "Can you believe it?"

"We're meeting someone," I said and squeezed my day planner against my chest. It didn't seem right to tell him we were bailing Ethan out of jail. I couldn't guess how Ethan felt, but if I ever got arrested, I'd prefer to keep it quiet.

"Ah." The chiropractor's expression turned knowing. "It has something to do with the murders, doesn't it?"

Arsen scowled. "What do you know about them?"

"Only what I read in the papers," he said. "But you know what it's like in a small town. Everyone's somehow connected to the players – me through Susan."

A stellar jay skimmed a juniper bush and landed in the courthouse garden. It pecked at something beneath a lavender bush.

"Not only through me," I said. "Davin was a client of yours."

"Davin." He put his hands on his hips and stared at his loafers. "I can't believe he's dead. Do the police have any idea who killed him?"

"They're not talking to us," Arsen said.

The chiropractor gazed earnestly at me. "But Susan's friends with the sheriff."

"Hardly," I said.

Arsen stared at me.

I squirmed beneath their combined gazes. "She treats me like a suspect." Badly.

The chiropractor's warm eyes crinkled with concern. "How are you holding up? The paper said there was a break-in?"

"She's fine," Arsen said.

"The only thing stolen was my grandmother's recipe book."

Zack's pale brows lifted. "A recipe book? What were they after? Your grandmother's secret sauce?"

I laughed, startling the jay. It fluttered into the nearby pines.

Zack's freckled face turned serious. "Sorry, I shouldn't joke. Not with two men dead." He shook his head. "Now I wish I'd gotten to know Davin better. But once he was on the table, it was just the usual chiropractor-patient banter."

"About what?" I asked.

The chiropractor rubbed his chin. "Well, he wasn't a huge fan of his job, but I got the impression it was the best he could do in Doyle. I was surprised he returned here after his troubles."

I frowned. They'd all come back — Cherie too. And this being a small town, it wasn't the best place for a fresh start. Everyone knew Davin and Cherie's sins. Tanner's too. Why had they returned? "That's a good point. Did Davin ever tell you why he came back?"

"He said it was home."

"Did Davin have family here?" I asked.

"No," Arsen said, surprising me. "He didn't."

"It does seem odd," I said. "I wonder..." Could Davin, Cherie and Tanner have returned because they expected some sort of payoff? Hidden money or a scheme that wasn't quite complete?

"What?" Zack asked.

I shook my head, pausing at the base of the courthouse steps. "Nothing."

"Well, you two have a good day." Zack tipped an imaginary hat and jogged up the steps.

"I really don't like that guy," Arsen muttered.

"Why?"

"He reminds me of..."

"Prince Harry?"

His expression flickered, and for a moment he looked almost haggard. Then his face cleared, and he was good-time Arsen Holiday again. "Yeah, that must be it."

"What have you got against the royals?" I asked, knowing he was lying. Why did it feel like I was missing something with Arsen, something important? I smoothed the front of my blue tee. "Gran swore by him for fixing her back problems."

"Nobody's perfect, not even your grandmother."

"Zack brought up a good point though," I said, changing the subject. "Why did all three of our local hoodlums return to the scene of the crime?"

"They were white-collar criminals, not hoodlums, but yeah. If I'd been in their shoes, Doyle would be the last place I'd come."

"No wonder Tanner chose Wits' End," I said, glum. "I was the only person in Doyle who didn't know he was a deadbeat."

"No one knew until he got arrested five years ago."

"Zack did. He told me Tanner welshed on a bet between the two of them."

"Did he?" Arsen looked thoughtfully at the tall courthouse doors.

"It was only five hundred dollars — enough to hurt, but not enough to kill over."

"I wonder if the sheriff knew?"

"A hint her husband wasn't playing it straight, you mean? You can't blame her for not knowing he was a crook. He was her husband. She was in love."

"How do you know?"

I folded my arms and stared up at him.

"What?" he asked.

I tilted my head toward the brick courthouse.

"Fine, I'll get Ethan," Arsen said. "You can even watch me go inside."

I opened my mouth to retort that I'd do just that. But a gnarled, female figure in movie-star glasses and a filmy head scarf strode around the corner of the courthouse. The woman from the park, Madame X, cut through the lavender. She clutched a shiny black handbag in one hand.

"Okay, I trust you," I said quickly, patting him on the arm. I hurried after her.

For her age, the woman was fast, striding purposefully down Main Street. She nodded to passersby but didn't stop to chat. No fiddle-faddling around for Lady X.

Bailey whined as I tugged him away from a particularly interesting lamp post.

But I couldn't lose her. The woman knew something, and my successful burglary of Agent Manaj's room had given me a burst of confidence. I thought of Davin Markarian, and my enthusiasm dimmed, my steps slowing. This wasn't a contest with a prize at the end. Two people were dead.

The woman darted into an alley.

Bailey and I jogged after her.

We turned the corner into the alley, shady and narrow and empty.

Chapter 20

Jamming my hands on my hips, I scanned the narrow, brick alley for signs of old ladies. Had Madame X seen me following and sprinted around the far corner? Or had she disappeared through one of the doors lining the buildings?

We stepped into the shaded alley, and the temperature dropped. I rattled the handle of the wooden door on my left. Locked.

Bailey and I crossed to the next door, metal with flecked blue paint. Also locked. The third door, painted pink, opened easily. A dog bowl sat outside it.

"You're in luck," I said to Bailey.

We stepped inside, and a wave of chemical odors assailed me.

Bailey sneezed, the sound drowned beneath the roar of hair dryers.

Eyes watering, I continued down a narrow hallway piled with cardboard boxes of beauty supplies.

We passed through a pink curtain and emerged inside a salon. Two women sat beneath hair dryers. A third was tilted back in a chair, black poncho around her neck, getting her hair washed.

A young woman in a pink apron hurried toward us. The tag pinned to her apron strap read: *Rita*. "What an adorable dog! Is it a beagle?"

Bring a beagle, and everyone's nice to you. "Yes, his name's Bailey."

"What a sweetie!" She patted his head and straightened. "Do you have an appointment?"

"Um, no. I was looking for a friend, but I don't see her."

A hair stylist levered the third woman's chair up and swiveled her to face the mirror. *Madame X!* She'd tied her filmy scarf around a handle on the shiny black handbag in her lap.

Madame X was one cool customer. She gave no sign of recognition when our gazes met in the mirror. X and the stylist spoke to each other, then the stylist adjusted the chair and drew a pair of scissors from a metal bin.

There is an etiquette to the hair salon. While it can be a hotbed for gossip, one does not simply interrupt a haircut. And I figured Madame X would be more likely to talk if I kept things covert instead of demanding answers in front of the entire salon. Besides, I could use a trim.

"Have you got any appointments available now?" I asked.

"You're in luck." Rita leaned forward and nodded. "The beauty school's got a free spot." She motioned to the chair next to Madame X's. "Would you like a cut?"

I gulped. *Beauty school? Students with scissors?* "How about a wash and blow out?"

"Or I could give you highlights!"

"Just a wash and blow out," I said firmly. Highlights were expensive, and I wasn't letting a future beauty school dropout anywhere near me with bleach.

Her shoulders slumped. "If that's all you want..."

"It is."

She led me to the chair beside X and pointed to the dog bed in the corner. Bailey took the hint and curled up on top.

I smiled down at the older woman. "Hi. Haven't we met?"

"I don't think so," X graveled.

Ha! I'd recognize that smokers' voice anywhere.

I sat in the swivel chair, and the student stylist snapped a poncho around my neck. "I think you may have known my grandmother," I said, "Harriet Witsend?"

She stared straight into the mirror. "No. Cindy, please use larger rollers this time. Last week I looked like a French poodle."

Rita swiveled me around and levered my chair toward the curved sink. Hot water hit my scalp, and I winced.

"Too hot?" Rita asked.

I gasped. "Just a little."

A blow-dryer whirred to my right.

She adjusted the temperature. "Sorry. I should have tested it on my arm. I always forget."

"It's okay. No harm done." And soon I was lost in the nirvana of someone else shampooing my hair. Why does it always feel so good when someone else is doing it, and so perfunctory when I shampoo my own hair? I snapped back to reality. I had no business blissing out when I had Madame X to interrogate.

Rita slathered on conditioner, and round two began.

Too soon, she cranked my chair upright.

The chair beside mine was empty. Frantic, I looked around the salon.

X gripped her purse beneath a sky-blue hairdryer.

Rita leaned forward, hands clutched to her chest. "Just a blowout?"

"Just a blowout," I said. What could go wrong with a blowout? Besides, I'd finish before Madame X, so she wouldn't get another chance to slip away.

Face crunched in concentration, Rita got to work, rubbing styling gel into my hair and clamping it into sections. Out came the blow-dryer. She rotated my chair, the dryer roaring in my ears. I tried to study Madame X whenever my chair turned toward her, but the top half of her head was hidden beneath the alien-looking dryer.

Smiling, Rita shut off the blow-dryer and swiveled me to face the mirror. "What do you think?"

I thought I looked like a nineteen-eighties country star. My hair was massive. "Um. I'm not sure this is the right look for daytime," I said, meek.

Her face fell. "Oh. Let me get my instructor." She hurried to the aproned woman who'd been working on Madame X. The instructor nodded and strode to my chair.

She stared at me and frowned. "You started the curls too high. There's too much volume. She looks like she's going to a cut-rate beauty pageant. But it's fixable."

I shifted, angling the chair so I could observe Madame X in the mirror.

She adjusted the dryer, pulling it lower over her head.

The instructor shifted my chair, removing Madame X from the frame. She rubbed serum into her hands and ran it through my hair. Taking a paddle brush from a round, metal container, she swiped it through the curls. "This stretches them out, so they're more relaxed. See?"

I strained my eyeballs, but couldn't see Madame X.

"Thanks," Rita chirped. "What if we—"

"It looks great," I said, turning the chair with my heel. "Thanks."

Madame X sat parked beneath the dryer, and I blew out a relieved breath.

I made my way to the cash register. If I left now and waited outside, Madame X might escape via the other entrance. Slowly, I dug bills from my wallet and added a generous tip. The hair might not have been quite right, but I didn't want to discourage a student. "Do you mind if I look at some of your magazines before I go?" I asked, stalling. "I'm looking for a new hairstyle."

"Of course," Rita said. "And be sure to ask for me when you come back."

Collecting Bailey, I settled into an uncomfortable, iron-backed chair beside the counter. I took a tattered magazine from the rack and snapped it open. X wouldn't escape this time. Keeping one eye on her, I flipped through the magazine. You'd need a professional stylist to pull off these hairstyles. And who has one of those on call?

Finally, Madame X strode to the counter. She ignored me and paid.

I returned the magazine to its rack and followed her out the front door, which opened onto a small parking lot.

She stopped, not looking at me. "Not here." Her lips barely moved. "Then where?"

"Meet me on the creek path, by the waterwheel. Fifteen minutes." She strode ahead, vanishing around the corner of a weathered, 19th-century wood building. I waited five minutes in the building's shade and pretended to fool around on my phone.

My head jerked up. What if she'd just said that to ditch me?

I trotted down the alley to Main Street.

The day was already getting too hot to handle, so we kept to the shade. Bailey and I hustled down Main Street to the low, stone bridge. A narrow set of steps, partially hidden by blackberry bushes, led to a dirt path along the creek. We hurried down the flagstone steps and into the coolness of the gully. Shade trees arched over the creek, forming a green and gold tunnel of foliage and sunlight, dappling the water.

Bailey strained toward the creek.

"I know you're not thirsty." He'd lapped plenty of water at the salon. "And no swimming today."

Making a rattling sound, a car drove over the bridge above us.

I sped up, rounding the bend. On the opposite bank was a brick patio with two Adirondack chairs and a miniature red waterwheel.

Madame X waited on a tree stump and smoked an e-cigarette.

My muscles relaxed. She hadn't ditched me after all.

I found a leafy spot on the bank and sat, watching the waterwheel revolve. "What's going on?"

"You tell me."

I gnawed my bottom lip. "You heard about Davin Markarian?" I asked, turning.

"I heard," she said grimly. "And don't look at me! No one can know we're talking."

"Why?"

"Why doesn't matter. You want to talk? Face front."

Reluctant, I turned to the stream. A trio of fallen leaves, gold and brown, drifted past. "What can you tell me? What do you know? Why are you leaving me notes and cryptic warnings?"

"One note. One warning."

"Who *are* you?" I asked, exasperated.

She sighed. "Tanner McCourt had his irons in a lot of fires, and to mix my metaphors, he got burned."

"What other fires?"

"Let's just say there are a lot of ways to scam the welfare system," she said, "and he knew them all. But when the county finally figured out what he was up to, they didn't catch everyone involved in his schemes."

"And Tanner didn't give them up?"

"He gave up the small fry — Davin Markarian, Cherie Cavalier. But the big kahuna is still out there."

"And who's that?" I asked.

Bailey snuffled near my feet.

"Do you know who really makes out on disability fraud? It's not the peon who fakes a back injury. It's the service providers, the lawyers, and the government officials. They take their cut to grease the wheels or look the other way."

"Was there someone higher up in the government involved? Like the sheriff?"

"You're asking dangerous questions, Susan."

I jiggled my foot. "Two people are dead. It would be more dangerous not to know."

She exhaled heavily, and I imagined her blowing out a stream of smoke. "Are you sure about that?"

"I don't believe McCourt's involved. I *like* the sheriff."

"I like a lot of people, but that doesn't mean I trust them."

"Do you have any actual evidence she's involved?"

"Some people say she knew what he was up to and was ordered to keep quiet about it. Some people say she kept quiet because she was profiting from it too."

I tossed a leaf into the creek. That wasn't evidence. It was supposition.

Bailey perked up, his ears twitching.

"Someone broke into my house the other day," I said.

"I know. You need to leave this alone, or yours might be the next body they find."

Bailey's leash dug into my palm. "Is that a threat?" I asked.

"I'm no threat to you," she said wearily. "Consider it a commonsense warning."

Okay, forget that line of questioning. But she knew *something*. "So, Tanner didn't rat out some of his more important associates in Doyle. Are you saying one of them killed him to make sure he stayed quiet?"

"It sure looks that way."

"Why?"

"Think about it."

I did. "Tanner needed money," I said. "Was he blackmailing someone for their part in the welfare scheme?" Someone like the sheriff?

"I suspect so. There were rumors he was blackmailing someone before he went to prison."

"But Tanner would have been as vulnerable as the person he was blackmailing," I said. "How could he have gotten away with it, when they each had something on the other?"

"Now you're asking the right questions."

Bailey nosed a clump of ivy.

"Who was he blackmailing?" I asked.

"No idea. But there's no reason to think he'd given it up after he was released."

"Who are you?" I motioned with my hands, jerking Bailey's leash.

He shot me a reproachful look.

"You said you were a friend of my grandmother," I continued.

"And that's the only reason I'm helping you. Let's just say I work for the government and leave it at that."

To know so much about our small town's shenanigans, she had to be local government. Plus, I'd seen her near the courthouse.

"So why kill Davin?"

She didn't respond.

"Hello?" I twisted on the creekbank.

She was gone.

Chapter 21

Cursing, I looked up and down the empty trail. If I couldn't even keep tabs on a little old lady... Well, what *could* I do?

I decided to cheer myself up with food. Bailey and I trudged up the stone steps to Main Street. We crossed the low bridge, keeping to the shade of the elms and the shop balconies.

My favorite Doyle restaurant, Alchemy, was a white-painted corner building, opposite a stone barn. Couples lounged with their dogs on the front patio. We walked past them and inside the cool, red-tiled interior.

The hostess looked up from her stand. "Hi. Table for one or are you meeting someone?"

"For one." Hey, I'm a modern woman, and if I want to sip iced tea and eat panini alone, who's to stop me? "And I have a dog."

"Right this way." She grabbed a menu from the stand and led me through the crowded restaurant to the patio. White canvas curtains framed the outdoor area. A tall, black fan whirred in a corner.

"Susan?" Jayce looked up from a nearby table. Her blonde sister, Lenore, sat beside her. Two men sat opposite them: the Hispanic, dark-haired detective and a broad-shouldered man with unruly ebony hair and wearing a paramedic's uniform.

I smiled. "Hi, Jayce."

"Hi! This is Brayden." She twined her fingers inside the dark-haired man's. "And Connor." She nodded to the uniformed detective beside Lenore.

"We've met," I said.

The waitress shifted her weight.

"Of course," Jayce said, "the murders. Are you here alone?"

"Just me and my dog." I raised the leash.

Bailey's ears perked, and he strained toward the trio.

"What a cutie! Why don't the two of you join us?" She flipped a lock of long, mahogany hair over the shoulder of her burgundy tank top. "We just sat down and haven't had a chance to order."

"Thanks," I said, pleased. I liked Jayce, even if I didn't know her that well, and this gave me the chance to subtly ask the deputy about the murders.

They scooted their chairs aside to add a fifth. I sat between Jayce and her sister and slung my big purse over the back of the chair. My knee bumped the dark-haired deputy's, and my face heated. "Sorry." I looped Bailey's leash around my chair arm, and the beagle sprawled on the tile floor.

"I don't mind." Connor bent to scratch Bailey's head.

"I hear you have a celebrity coming to your bookstore?" I asked Lenore.

Her pale face pinked, and she plucked at the collar of her simple white shift. "Xavier Ultra. Every wilderness fanatic within fifty miles is calling my shop. But it's good for business."

"A friend of mine is planning to go to the signing."

"Let me guess." Lenore braced her slim elbows on the ivory tablecloth. "Arsen?"

"You know him?" I asked.

"Everyone knows him." She smiled. "It's a small town."

A twinge of jealousy rippled through me. Not that I was jealous romantically. But I guess a part of me liked to think of Arsen as *my* friend, as if I could hoard his friendship. And that was wrong and ridiculous.

We ordered and made small talk. I tried to figure out a way to segue into murder talk. Fortunately, I didn't have to. Jayce did it for me.

"How are you holding up after the McCourt murder?" She sipped her iced tea. "Has it affected your business?"

"Not yet," I said. "I know it sounds ghoulish, but I think the UFO hunters find it intriguing. But..." The breeze from the fan tickled the back of my neck, and a chill descended on the patio.

"What?" She sipped from her water glass, the ice cubes tinkling.

"Wits' End is more than a business," I said. "It's my house, and someone was murdered inside it." And then there'd been the break-in. Would the B&B ever feel normal again?

She sobered. "It leaves a stain, doesn't it? The feeling of your home being invaded by a dark presence."

"Not a presence, a person," the paramedic corrected.

Jayce shook herself and smiled. "Of course. Unless the Doyle PD thinks aliens committed the crime?"

Connor laughed. "We've got plenty of suspects right here on the ground."

"Or under it," Jayce muttered.

"Because that man, Davin Markarian, is dead now?" Lenore asked quickly. She frowned at her sister.

I pleated my cloth napkin. "Davin's murder doesn't make sense. I was sure he'd killed Tanner. I guess I was wrong." But Davin *had* pushed that air conditioner out the window. No one else could have done it.

Connor's dark brows drew downward. "What do you know about Davin and Tanner McCourt?"

"It's no secret that Tanner gave up both him and Cherie when he got caught embezzling." I ran my fingers along the cool side of my water glass.

Jayce shifted in the iron-backed chair and stared at her boyfriend. "Cherie made a mistake, but she's paid her dues. She's trying to get her life on track. And she's been a great employee." She looked to me as if for backup.

"There's a rumor that there were others — or at least one other person — that Tanner didn't give up," I said.

Connor pinioned me with his dark-eyed gaze. "Where did you hear that?"

"I overheard some people talking," I said vaguely.

"Which people, exactly?"

"I'm not sure. Some older... women." Why not tell them about the mysterious Madame X? Maybe they knew who she was. Maybe she was the local crazy everyone but me knew about, because I wasn't quite a local yet? But something held my tongue. "It was just something I overheard."

"Well if you overhear anything else," Connor said shortly, "let me know."

"So, what's the word on that FBI agent who's staying with you?" Jayce asked. "You two looked like buddies at Antoine's the other night."

"We're not."

"Is it true she's obsessed with UFOs?"

I fiddled with my water glass. A bead of moisture snaked down the side. "She says she isn't." It was one thing to tell the sheriff I worried about the FBI agent. But Manaj was staying at my B&B. I felt protective of guests and their UFO foibles. "Even so, Agent Manaj has become something of an attraction herself. A few of my guests think she's a Man in Black." I laughed.

The others glanced at each other.

"Because she always wears black," I explained feebly. "You know, a secret agent tasked with keeping the UFOs secret?" Or with spreading misinformation, if Dixie was to be believed.

"Agent Manaj is an interesting character," Connor said. "And for now, she's our boss."

Jayce bit her bottom lip and tilted her chin down, as if repentant, but her green eyes danced, mischievous. "I think we've just crossed the blue line," she said to me. "No gossip about fellow law enforcement. But of course Susan and Lenore and I are interested. There's a killer in Doyle, someone who's killed twice, and since this is such a small town, it's got to be someone we know. How could we not be worried?"

"Especially after someone tried to drop that air conditioner on me," I said.

A gust of wind rustled the canvas curtains, and Bailey started to his feet.

"Right," Jayce said. "And the best defense is knowledge." She looked at the white ceiling. "Wow. I never thought I'd say that."

"I'm glad I never know what you'll say. There are worlds inside you." Brayden leaned toward her and kissed her, long and slow.

Connor grinned at Lenore. "Don't mind us."

"Embarrassment is good for the soul," Jayce said when she came up for air.

I met Connor's gaze. "Did you learn anything about that air conditioner?"

Connor's face tightened.

"She should know," Lenore said quietly. "It's her life that's at risk."

The detective hesitated, then, "The screws bolting the unit into place seemed to have all come loose at the same time."

"So, it wasn't an accident," I said, an unpleasant, prickly feeling swelling in my stomach. "Someone tampered with it."

Connor nodded. "More than likely, especially after the break-in at Wits' End. Has anything happened at the B&B that you haven't told me?"

"No. I don't have any secret knowledge about Tanner's death or Davin's or anything else." I frowned, thinking. Something wasn't right.

"What?" Jayce asked.

"I was just wondering," I said, "why did the intruder break in at all? If it had been to hurt me, he didn't try very hard. And if he'd been looking for something — some evidence he'd left behind — why did he go downstairs, to my rooms? The murder happened upstairs. And the only reason I can imagine he would take my Gran's recipe book was because he thought it was my planner."

"Why would he want your planner?" Connor asked.

"Maybe he thought there was guest information in it," I said.

"Or something else?" Connor's voice hardened.

"Connor." Lenore laid her pale hand atop his larger one.

The waitress arrived with our food, Bailey became more interested in everyone, and the conversation shifted. The next winery concert, the upcoming bike race, last summer's fire in the valley.

I suspected I'd given Connor more information than I'd received. But then Jayce made a joke and a feeling of contentment spread through me. He was with the police, and all would be well.

*****

No wiser, Bailey and I left the restaurant and ambled down the wide sidewalk. I might not have gleaned any intel, but it had been... *nice* hanging out with Jayce and the deputies. Maybe I was becoming a part of Doyle after all.

I stopped short beside the window of a t-shirt shop, and Bailey sniffed a nearby elm. Or had the deputy invited me to join them so they could pump me for information? I twisted Bailey's leather leash more firmly around my hand. No. Jayce had invited me to their table, not Connor. And even if they'd had ulterior motives, I didn't think I'd given anything away the sheriff wouldn't want me to.

But why shouldn't I have told them what little I knew? I bit the inside of my cheek. They were the good guys, right?

The good guys who'd hauled Dixie in for questioning.

Bailey and I crossed the stone bridge. A trickle of sweat dampened my neck, and I peeled my blue t-shirt from my back.

Heat shimmered in waves off Main Street. A pickup drove past, and I winced at the sunlight glinting off its bumper.

On impulse, I veered left, down the steps to the creekside path. The temperature dropped in the shade, trees arcing over the small creek, and I breathed a sigh of relief. I loved Doyle, but the summers could be broiling.

We strolled down the path, enjoying the occasional splash of water from the creek beneath. Doyle's woods were a wonderland of ferns and moss-covered logs. Civilization was out of sight beyond the top of the slope. For a moment, I allowed myself to fantasize that the narrow mushrooms sprouting from a tree stump were fairy homes and that maybe, just maybe, UFOs did exist.

The bushes rustled above us, and I glanced up quickly.

Bailey growled.

My gaze searched the ivy-covered bank. Tiny insects swarmed in an erratic cloud beneath a wall of trees at its crest.

Tugging Bailey forward, I shrugged and hurried on. It had only been a bird or small animal — best not to think about what kind of small animal. The woods were populated with more than squirrels and chipmunks. Rats lived here too. Big rats.

A shadow moved swiftly across the path, and I glanced upward, into the tangle of branches.

Bailey stopped and stared at the hill sloping upward on our right. He gave a short, angry bark.

"There's nothing there. Come on." I lengthened my strides.

Brown eyes worried, Bailey trotted onward.

We rounded a corner, and a crumbling brick wall arose at the top of the hill. I tried to place our location. The wall had to belong to a building, or a parking lot, but I couldn't remember seeing it before. Cherubs perched on the top of the wall at regular intervals. The nearest cherub's bare bottom was shiny white and dimpled with age. I should have noticed something like that in Doyle, but I didn't recognize any of it.

I stopped and looked back the way we'd come. Above us, leaves rustled.

We continued on. There was only one path along the creek. I couldn't have gotten lost on the secluded trail, but it now seemed cut off from civilization. Just fifteen feet above us would be people, cars, but all I could hear was the sound of my own footsteps and Bailey's panting.

I quickened my pace. The brick wall stretched on, revealing more decaying cupids. At some point, the path had to branch up the slope, into the park, and I'd be back in civilization.

A groan. A crash.

I whirled toward the noise. A blur of white and green tumbled toward us.

I leapt forward. Something clipped my heel, and I yelped with pain.

A crack. A splash.

Howling, Bailey bolted up the hill.

A concrete cherub, its features blurred by moss, lay face-up in the creek.

Chapter 22

Clouds of mud plumed in the creek, billowed around the cherub's broken wings. An earth-colored stripe carved the ivy on the hill above and marked the cherub's fall from the corner of the crumbling wall.

I stared, frozen.

It hadn't been an accident.

Bailey raced to the creek bank and barked hysterically at the cherub.

A tremor shook my frame. Someone had pushed that cherub.

And I hadn't heard any running footsteps. Which meant they were still there, on the other side of the wall.

I held my breath and listened.

My heartbeat thrashed in my ears. The creek babbled past. Bailey barked on and on.

From behind the wall, came a faint scraping sound.

I bolted, my purse banging against my thighs. I've never been much of a runner, but terror drove me forward, my feet skimming the dirt trail.

Bailey howled, his stubby legs a blur beside me.

Behind us, something crashed, floundering down the hillside.

I lengthened my strides, careening, heedless, around a sharp bend in the path.

The trail fork rose before us, the top of the bandstand cresting the tree-lined bank. I didn't slow, veering right and up the trail.

We burst from the trees and hurtled into the park.

Near the bandstand, two mothers gossiped on a bench and watched their children play tag on the lawn. The women looked up at me, their eyes widening.

I slowed, and Bailey reduced his speed to match mine. Gasping, I glanced over my shoulder.

No one followed.

I braced my hands on the knees of my linen slacks. A hot stitch of pain flared in my side. My right ankle burned. I twisted to check the damage. A thick fold of skin had pleated sideways, leaving a patch of pink and bloody skin. The cherub must have clipped my heel.

Bailey stared at the trees behind the bandstand and half-whimpered, half-growled.

"It's fine," I rasped. "We're okay." I wanted to write the incident off as my imagination, as an accident. But I couldn't. And whoever had pushed that cherub might still be nearby.

I straightened. "Let's go."

We crossed the park and strode toward home.

I stopped to scan behind us. A mail truck sat beside a crooked Victorian, the mailman stuffing envelopes inside its box.

Bailey tugged me onward. We approached an elderly lady walking her cat. Bailey growled. The cat hissed. Trying not to stare at the cat's rhinestone-studded leash, I exchanged strained pleasantries with the woman and walked on.

I was safe. Totally safe. If someone had been following me, they weren't now. And why bother following me, when everyone knew where I lived?

A frightened laugh burst from me, and I clapped my hands to my mouth. Cell phone. Surely no one would attempt to murder me while I was talking to someone on my phone? I called the sheriff.

"What now?"

"I think someone tried to kill me." I hiccupped and hurried past a ranch-style house set back from the road.

"Are you drunk?"

"No. I was walking along the creek path—"

"Alone? Are you stupid?"

"I didn't think—"

"That much is obvious."

"And someone pushed one of those cherubs off that brick wall, and it nearly hit me."

"It wouldn't have killed you unless you were right beneath it. And there's no part of that path which runs right alongside that wall. It was an accident. Unless someone was trying to lame you so they could kill you more easily," she mused. "Did you see anyone?"

"No, but—"

"So, it might have been an accident."

"I heard someone chasing after me."

"And you didn't turn around and look?"

"There wasn't time!" Turning would have meant slowing, and slowing might have meant getting caught.

"Where are you now?"

The B&B's gabled rooftop rose above the pines. The scent of roses trailed in the wind. "Just outside my house."

"So, let me get this straight. You're safe at home — or almost there. You weren't hurt. You didn't see anyone. You have no evidence this was anything but an accident. Am I supposed to come over and hold your hand?"

"Maybe there's evidence of foul play at the wall," I said, chagrined. It did sound stupid when she put it that way.

She grunted. "Foul play. Fine. I'll check the wall. Happy?"

Not really, but I was alive and home. My footsteps crunched on the gravel driveway of Wits' End. "Thanks."

She hung up.

"I don't think she likes me," I told Bailey.

He whuffed in agreement.

I let him off the leash, and he raced into the backyard.

The phone rang, and I answered without thinking. "Did you change your mind about the wall?"

"What wall?" Arsen said.

"Oh." I winced. "Sorry, I thought it was someone else." The business with the falling cupid really did have me rattled if I'd thought the sheriff would get back to me that fast.

"I'm calling to let you know I'm with Ethan."

"Who?"

"Jailbird Ethan. The professor's kid? Are you all right?"

I wasn't all right, and suddenly I wanted to see Arsen. He knew how to put problems in perspective – distant perspective. "Where are you two?"

"Angels Camp."

"Angels Camp?" I sputtered. "But that's forty miles away!"

"But that's where his lawyer's office is."

"Lawyer? Ethan needs a lawyer?"

"It's complicated."

I walked up the porch steps. "Wait, is this the same lawyer who helped Dixie? I need to pay him." My stomach clenched. And I hadn't seen a bill yet. I wasn't sure I wanted to.

"Yeah, it's Nick," he said.

I gripped the screen door. "See what he has to say about her case, will you?"

"I doubt he'll tell me anything. Client confidentiality and all that stuff."

"Will you try?" I walked onto the screened porch.

He sighed. "I'll try. Are you sure you're okay? You sound funny."

"I scraped my heel and haven't had time to bandage it." And it really stung. "Are you going to be around later?"

"Unless Ethan drags me into another disaster. Why? Do you want to meet up?"

I took a deep, hopeful breath. "Maybe the two of you would like to come over for dinner?" I walked into the foyer and shut the door behind me.

"Sure. I'll check with Ethan. Oh, hey, I've gotta go. Talk to you soon." He hung up.

Disappointed, I wandered into the sitting room and sank onto the velvety ebony couch. I dropped my purse onto the cushion beside me.

Okay, I was still a little freaked out by the near miss with the statuary. But I needed to get a grip.

I drew my planner from my purse and flipped to the project pages. *Goad the murderer into trying to kill me* was not on my task list. With a sigh, I made notes on my conversation with Madame X and the deputies. I hesitated, then jotted down the time and location of the falling cherub.

I drummed my fingers on the page. I'd succeeded in interviewing all my suspects. But I'd made a rookie planner's mistake — I hadn't set goals for the interviews. I drew a line beneath Ethan's name and added:

- *Where was everyone when the A/C and cherub dropped?*

At least Ethan couldn't have been involved in the statue incident. He'd been with Arsen, and he'd been in jail when Davin was killed.

My pen tapped the page. But what if Ethan had a co-conspirator... like his mother, who'd been suspiciously out of touch? How could I be sure she was really roughing it on the mountain peaks? It seemed a little coincidental that they'd both been in my B&B when the man who'd shared a cell with Ethan's father was staying here as well. Something was definitely up.

I added two more bullets:

- *What did Ethan and Prof. G know about Tanner and DiCostanzo?*

- *Why was Ethan's father killed?*

I studied the page. I needed to talk to Cherie again. Next time, with goals.

Dixie, in shorts and a purple tank, wandered into the kitchen. "Hey. Anyone try to kill you recently?"

"Thirty minutes ago." My voice didn't wobble, so that was something.

She blinked. "Seriously?"

"Another near miss - this time falling statuary."

"Seriously?"

"Ask Bailey if you don't believe me."

Her eyes widened. "Oh, no! Was Bailey hurt?"

"No, and I'm fine too," I said tartly.

"I can see you're okay. What happened?"

I told her about the creek path, and my theories about Ethan and his mother. I didn't tell her about the sheriff. All Madame X had given me was unfounded gossip. It didn't seem right to spread it around.

My cousin tugged on a lock of her violet hair. "So, you think this was a revenge killing? And Ethan and his mom are in it together? I dunno. She didn't seem revenge-y."

"The word is *vengeful*, and it isn't as if we had any deep talks about her husband."

She pursed her lips.

"Why?" I lifted my brows. "Did you?"

"No-o."

"But?"

"But she was acting kind of weird."

"Define weird in a UFO B&B."

Dixie folded her arms over her tank top. "She lurked."

"Where?"

"Upstairs and in the side garden. Professor Green spent a lot of time in the breakfast room supposedly reviewing her research. She always sat with her back to the windows."

"I fail to see the relevance of her seating arrangements."

She rolled her eyes. "So she could watch the front stairs, duh!"

And make sure Tanner didn't come down them? I eyed her. "You've spent time with Ethan. What do you think about him?"

"He's naive. I could totally see him getting caught up in some weird quest for vengeance. He'd think it was noble."

"Does Ethan do noble?" I asked, surprised.

"I said *think* he was noble, not that he actually was." She turned on her heel and sashayed through the door to the side porch. The screen door banged shut.

I drummed my fingers on my planner. The afternoon was getting eaten away, and I didn't want to return to town after my recent near miss. But there were other ways of getting information.

I called Ground.

"Ground, this is Jayce."

"Hi, Jayce. It's Susan Witsend."

"Oh, hi! What's going on?"

"Um, is Cherie there?" I rose and walked to the kitchen windows, sliding them open. One of the windows stuck, scraping against the frame.

"Yeah. Do you want to speak to her?"

"Yes, please," I said, "but first, was she there all day?"

"She started at noon."

"Did she have any breaks?" I opened the door to the side porch and let it hang wide. A breeze flowed into the kitchen, tossed the rose bushes in the yard.

"Susan, what's going on?"

"Something weird happened after I left you. I was walking back along the creek path — you know, the one that starts by the bridge on Main?"

"Yeah."

"A statue from that long brick wall sort of fell on me—"

"What?"

"I mean, not *on* me, but it did clip my ankle, and I think it might have been pushed."

She blew out her breath. "And you want to know if she could have done it."

"I'm not accusing anyone." I walked onto the porch and sat on the wooden bannister. "I'm just trying to figure things out."

There was a long pause. Then, "She was just getting back from break when I returned to Ground."

"Which was when?" I asked.

"Not long after lunch."

Which was about the time I'd narrowly avoided the stupid statue. Cherie couldn't have done it. There wouldn't have been time.

"Look," she said in a rush, "I know what you're thinking, and I'm not going to say you're crazy for thinking it. I know about her past. But I get feelings about people, and they've never been wrong. At least, not really wrong. And I'm telling you, she's not the person who did this. But if you accuse her, it's going to hurt her. A lot."

My hand tightened on the phone. "I won't. I don't think Cherie killed anyone."

"Why not?"

"Tanner's neck was broken, and Davin was dumped in a garbage bin. Cherie is well-muscled, but I don't think she's *that* strong."

"So, what do you want from Cherie?"

"I just want to ask her some questions about Davin."

"What questions?" she asked, her voice laced with suspicion. "She's getting her life together. It's been hard enough for her dealing with the police. If people around town start bugging her, it's going to be even harder."

"About Davin's past and his relationship with Tanner. That's all."

Another long pause. "All right. I'll get her. Hold on."

The clatter of the phone being put down. A murmur of voices.

Clinging to the support beam, I turned and looked down at the broken rose bush. I didn't have my Gran's gardening skills, but at least I could prune the broken branches.

"Hello?" Cherie asked.

I straightened on the bannister. "Hi, Cherie, this is Susan Witsend, from Wits' End."

"What do you want?"

"I'm sorry to bother you with this, but do you know if Davin or Tanner had any other schemes going with someone? Someone who might not have gotten caught all those years ago?"

Her voice grew shrill. "Why are you asking me?"

"You're the only person who might know. And someone's been harassing me. I've had two near misses — things that looked like accidents but might not have been. And someone broke into the B&B the other night."

"What's that to do with me?" she asked.

"I'm afraid someone thinks I know more than I do. I'm worried that same person killed Tanner and Davin. And if they think I know something — and trust me, I don't — then they might think—"

"That I know too much," she whispered.

"You're the only one left from the, er, gang, or at least the only one anyone knows of. Unless there was someone else?"

"There was no one else. But..."

"But what?"

"Hold on," she said.

In the background, a metal door slammed.

"Is everything okay?" I asked.

"If we're going to talk about this," she said in a low voice, "I needed to step outside, where it's more private."

My stomach quivered with unease. "Maybe privacy isn't such a good thing for you right now."

"It's okay. I'm just outside the kitchen door."

"You were saying?" I asked, wishing she was inside and safe.

"I always had the feeling that Davin and Tanner had something else going on the side, something they were keeping from me." Her laugh was bitter. "Can you believe I was jealous? God, back then I was such an idiot."

"Do you have any idea what they might have had going?"

"No, but at the time, I thought it was bigger than what we were doing. I guess that was why I was jealous. They wanted me to help them with the small stuff, but they didn't value me enough to bring me in for the big money."

"Why did you think that?"

Bailey trotted up the porch steps and sat at my feet.

I ruffled his fur.

She sighed. "Just... little things they'd say. Or not say. The way they'd go quiet when I walked into the room, like I'd interrupted something." She hesitated. "I remember one time they were talking about setting up a clinic. I'm pretty sure I'd have known if that had happened though."

"Why?"

"Clinics are public, even if where the money flows isn't."

"You mean the money would have been siphoned off?"

She laughed shortly. "Big time. But Tanner never had the heft to pull something like that off."

"Would that be the sort of thing the mob might get involved in?"

"One clinic? I don't know."

"What if there were more than one?" I asked.

"Maybe."

I extended my legs. "If you don't mind my asking, how exactly were you three, um, running your operation?"

"False welfare claims," she said. "It was easy, since we were all working in different departments. We could pass the claims from one person to the next, signing off on them, and no one was the wiser. Until Tanner got caught."

"How were the claims falsified?" I slipped from the railing and closed the screen door to the kitchen. The front porch was screened. This one was not.

"The people who were supposed to receive the benefits didn't exist."

"How did you three figure all this out?" I asked.

"The thing is, we didn't. Tanner said he got the idea from someone else."

"Who?"

"I asked, and he wouldn't say. There was something, well, smug about him when I asked. Like he had a big secret he was dying to share. But I think whoever gave him the idea, he or she was local."

"Why?" I asked, bending to ruffle Bailey's fur.

"Because Tanner saw him on a regular basis. He'd boast about going to meet his golden goose." She gasped.

My chest squeezed. "What's wrong?"

"Nothing. I thought I saw... Nothing. I'm just freaking myself out. Look, I'm going to go inside. There's nothing more I can tell you."

I glanced sidelong at the door to the kitchen. "You've told me more than I could have hoped for. Thanks. And take care of yourself."

"They say confession is good for the soul. I can't hide what I did. Not in a tiny place like Doyle. So, I might as well talk." She hung up.

But why had Cherie returned to a place like Doyle at all?

Chapter 23

Arsen shifted the basket of garlic bread, and I set the lasagna on the kitchen table. Dixie and Ethan leaned forward and inhaled, eyes closed. Through the open kitchen windows, twilight deepened over purple mountains.

"Your grandmother's recipe?" Arsen had changed into jeans and a fresh, olive-green tee, and he smelled of soap.

"Of course," I said. My grandmother had tossed whatever vegetables she'd had on hand into the lasagna sauce and it was always wonderful. I'd watched her one evening and carefully measured and copied her ingredients onto a recipe card. My version might not be as spontaneous, but it was delicious.

"Your grandmother made the best." Dixie adjusted the strap of her purple tank. "She *was* the best." She glanced up at me and grinned. "Have I already told you this joke?"

Arsen chuckled.

"What joke?" Ethan asked. He looked none the worse for wear after his stint in the Doyle jail. For once he was out of his board shorts and in jeans and a plain white t-shirt.

I laughed, my heart squeezing at the memory. "My grandma. She had this thing."

"She'd go up to strangers and ask if she'd told them this joke," Dixie said. "It totally confused them because, a) they'd never met her before, and b) she hadn't told them a joke yet."

"And then what?" Ethan asked.

"Then she'd tell 'em a joke," Arsen said. "They were never very good, but everyone laughed because the whole situation was so off beat."

"Why would she do that?" Ethan asked.

"She liked to shake things up," I said. "And make people laugh." I really missed my grandmother.

Ethan stared at the food on the table. "Is it vegetarian?"

"No," I said.

"Good." He straightened and tore a slice of garlic bread from the loaf. "Time in the pen changes one's perspective on food. You gotta eat for fuel, you know? To *survive*."

Biting back a laugh, I sat and passed the green salad to Arsen. One corner of his mouth quivered.

"We're glad you made it out in one piece," I said, somber.

Ethan gnawed on the bread, scattering buttery crumbs across the blue tablecloth. "You're not in control, you know? It makes you realize how small you are and what really counts."

Zero control? Going to jail was my new worst nightmare.

Dixie's expression shifted.

"Like family," Ethan said. "You both talk about your grandmother a lot." He motioned around the table toward Dixie and myself.

"She wasn't my grandmother," Dixie said. "But she was cool."

"I thought you two were related?" Ethan asked.

"Different grandparents," I said. Ethan making polite conversation? I ventured a questioning glance at Arsen.

He shook his head slightly.

Had jail changed Ethan? He hadn't checked his cell phone all evening.

"Aside from cooking," Arsen said, "what have you been up to today?" He dropped a few token leaves on his plate, then cut a monster-sized slice of lasagna.

"I heard Tanner and Davin might have been running another scam on the side." Even though I didn't consider Ethan much of a suspect, I didn't want to mention Cherie's name in front of him. Just in case.

Arsen nodded, his hazel eyes thoughtful. "Any hint it might have been blackmail?"

Ethan's shoulders jerked.

"Blackmail?" I asked. "Why do you think that?"

"I've been doing more digging." Arsen shoveled lasagna into his mouth and swallowed. "There are rumors going around Doyle that Tanner was blackmailing someone."

"Who?" I asked.

"No idea yet."

"I suppose it's possible," I said. "Cherie said he acted like he had a big secret, and that he'd been smug about it." I winced. I hadn't meant to say anything about her.

"What's wrong?" Arsen asked.

"Nothing," I said. "I thought Tanner might have had a new, more profitable scam. But I guess it could have been blackmail."

Arsen poked a lettuce leaf with his fork and frowned, unimpressed. "It's the simplest answer." He braced his elbows on the table and interlaced his calloused fingers. "Maybe he found out about someone else's fraud or embezzlement and blackmailed him or her. Later, he copied their scheme and started his own welfare scam at the county."

"That's simple?" I asked. "What if...?"

The curtains at the open window breathed gently. In the dimming light, the pine trees were jagged teeth lining the mountain tops.

"What?" he asked.

"What if Tanner wasn't blackmailing this person back then," I said, "before he went to jail? Madame X said he was covering for someone — a bigger fish. What if—"

"Madame X?" Dixie quirked a brow. "Who's that?"

My cheeks warmed. "That's just the name I gave her. She's the woman who put the tape cassette in my car."

"Tape cassette?" Arsen frowned. "What are you talking about?"

I explained.

Arsen dropped his fork with a clatter. "And you went to meet her alone? What the hell were you thinking?"

Ethan glanced up.

"She was thinking anyone who still used tape cassettes had to be ancient," Dixie said sharply. "And she was right."

"Old doesn't mean harmless." Arsen's face reddened. "Why didn't you ask me to go with you?"

"She said to come alone," I said.

"When people tell you to come alone," Arsen said, "you never come alone. Sue, this is not okay."

"Nothing happened," I said.

"Aside from someone trying to drop that statue on you today," Dixie pointed out.

I ground my teeth. I never should have told my cousin about that cherub. But I wasn't going to let good garlic bread and conversation go to waste. It was time Ethan talked, even if I had to give up a little information to get some.

"Statue?" Arsen's gaze ping-ponged between Dixie and me. "What statue?"

"What's important about the statue incident," I said, "is that Ethan couldn't have been involved, because he was with you."

Ethan blinked. "Me? You think I did something?"

"What statue?" A pulse beat in Arsen's jaw.

"You couldn't have pushed the statue off the wall," I said to Ethan. "You were with Arsen."

"One of the cherubs on that old brick wall by the creek path," Dixie said.

Arsen put his head in his hands and groaned. "You were alone on that path?"

"I had Bailey."

He shot me a pitying look.

"Why did you think I killed Tanner?" Ethan asked.

"I didn't," I said, "not really. But with your father—"

Ethan sucked in his cheeks. "What do you know about my father?"

"I know that he shared a cell with Tanner McCourt."

Ethan's mouth slackened. He slumped in his chair. "So that was why."

I grimaced. He hadn't known? Ethan shouldn't have heard it like this, and I felt like a slug.

"That was why what?" Dixie asked quietly.

His hands fisted on the table. "Why my mom insisted on coming here. She must have known..." He shook his head. "My mom didn't kill Tanner either. And she's been in the mountains all week."

I wasn't so sure, but I nodded and rose to turn on the kitchen lights.

"I never met him," Ethan said, his voice flat. "Mom didn't talk about him much. But sometimes she'd get a letter and would sneak off to read it." He laughed shortly. "The old man wasn't much for tech. He wrote letters, and my mom kept every one. I found them all. Then she got a phone call. I knew something was up and listened in. It was the prison. He was dead. She didn't tell me about that either." He pushed a piece of lasagna around the plate with his fork. "I thought when she brought me here, she'd finally tell me the truth."

I sat, the wooden chair squeaking on the linoleum. "I'm very sorry for your loss."

"Thanks, but it was almost a relief," he said bitterly. "He never bothered to try to contact me."

"Families are complicated," Arsen said, gruff.

"So, you didn't know Tanner was connected to your father?" I asked.

"If I'd known," Ethan said, "I would have run the other way. I don't want anything to do with my father. Or his friends."

"Cellmates aren't necessarily friends," Dixie said.

Ethan pressed his hand to his chest, rumpling his white tee. "My mother didn't do this. She didn't! What about that sheriff, the dead guy's wife?"

Arsen rubbed his chin. "She had reason to kill him. And she discovered the body."

"Did you hear or see anything the afternoon Tanner was killed?" I asked.

"No," Ethan said.

"What about the door to room seven?" I asked. "Do you remember if it was open or shut?"

"All the doors in the hall were shut," he said.

But it was unlocked when the sheriff arrived. Well, duh. Someone had picked up the phone when I'd called. Then they'd left out the back door.

Unless Professor Green was the killer.

Nails clicking on the floor, Bailey trotted into the kitchen. He leaned against Arsen's leg. Arsen – the weak link when it came to Bailey's begging – picked a piece of ground beef off his plate and fed it to the beagle.

"Sheriff McCourt's strong too," Dixie said. "I once saw her jam a guy up against a car. She's got some impressive moves."

My stomach twisted. I didn't want it to be McCourt. So, she was a little short tempered. After what she'd been through, she had good cause.

Did she believe it was cause to kill?

"So, the sheriff could have done it too," Ethan said.

"It's possible," I said and looked away from Ethan. His mother had looked strong as well. I'd watched her easily heft luggage I would have struggled with. "But is the sheriff strong enough to break a man's neck?".

"Breaking a neck isn't only about strength." Arsen's gaze lost focus. "It's also about speed and skill. And there are women out there who have that."

"But to heft Davin into a garbage bin?" I shook my head. "That's some serious lifting."

"I could do it." Dixie bit into a piece of garlic bread, dribbling crumbs on her plate.

We stared at her.

She shrugged. "Fireman's carry. I learned it in hapkido. Or use something for leverage. No problem."

I opened my mouth to ask her about neck breaking, and couldn't. Suddenly, I didn't want to know.

"Tell me about this Madame X," Arsen said.

"She told me she works for the government," I said. "I think she meant the local government, because that would explain how she knew so much about what Tanner was up to. I don't know who she is, but she's probably in her eighties and likes to wear scarves over her head."

Arsen snorted. "That doesn't exactly narrow it down."

"I'd think someone at her age in local government would have been forced into retirement by now," I said.

He angled his head and squinted. "Not necessarily. This is a small town, and a lot of things run on relationships. I could easily see the mayor or town council deciding to let a nice old lady stay on —

especially if she was getting the job done."

And Arsen knew all about the machinations of bossy old ladies. He was at the mercy of his aunts.

A car's tires crunched in the driveway, and we fell silent.

"Those must be our guests," I said, uneasy, "back from dinner."

"Do you have any other murder suspects?" Dixie asked.

"No," I said. "Unless you think an old, five-hundred-dollar debt is worth killing over."

Footsteps sounded on the porch, and the front door creaked open.

I pushed back my chair and stood. "I'd better see who it is."

Arsen's mouth tightened. "You never explained why you were interrogating your chiropractor about Tanner."

I edged toward the door to the foyer. "Because I saw Davin in Zack's office," I said. Sheesh, Arsen was acting like he was jealous, but if he was, it was only because I'd gone sleuthing without him. Did it make me a bad person that the thought depressed me?

Agent Manaj and Deputies Hernandez and Denton trooped into the kitchen. The deputies, in their official windbreakers, wore grim expressions. The FBI agent looked as impassive as ever.

"Hi." I rubbed my palms on the thighs of my linen slacks. "Is everything all right?"

"No." The FBI agent brushed back one side of her black jacket, exposing her holstered gun. "Dixie Knoll, you're under arrest."

Chapter 24

I gaped at the FBI agent and the two uniformed deputies. At the kitchen table, Arsen, Dixie, and Ethan sat in a frozen tableau – the *Last Supper* plus lasagna, minus apostles.

"Under arrest?" I asked, shrill. "What for?"

"For the murder of Tanner McCourt." Agent Manaj adjusted the lapel of her sleek black blazer.

Deputies Hernandez and Denton didn't meet my gaze. They were focused on Dixie, pale in her chair.

"But that's crazy," I said. "Why would she kill anyone?" She wouldn't! She couldn't!

Arsen stood and placed a hand on my arm. "Sue, it's okay."

"It's not okay!"

The two deputies walked around the kitchen table and half-lifted Dixie from her chair.

Bailey leapt to his feet and snarled. Arsen grabbed his collar, calming him.

The deputies turned my cousin, unresisting, and snapped cuffs onto her wrists.

"I'll call Nick." Arsen pulled his phone from the pocket of his jeans. "I'm sure it's a mistake."

"It has to be a mistake," I said, "because Dixie didn't kill anyone. Tell them, Dix."

Dixie's mouth clamped shut. She shook her head and gave me a warning look.

"Agent Manaj," I pleaded, "this can't be right. You know this makes no sense."

"Dixie will get a chance to explain herself at the station." She and Hernandez took Dixie's arm and led her through the kitchen door.

Denton hesitated in the doorway, his boyish face serious. "Sorry about this. If it's a mistake, we'll figure it out." He hurried after them.

If? I looked to Arsen, but he was turned toward the sink, his head bent, and murmured into his phone.

"Whoa," Ethan said. "Did that just happen?"

"Ethan," I growled, "if you know anything—"

"I don't! Dixie's cool. If I knew anything that would help, don't you think I'd say something?"

Bailey whined.

I knelt on the linoleum floor and stroked his warm fur.

Arsen turned and braced himself against the sink. "Nick's on his way to the station. Don't worry. He'll sort this out." He set the phone on the butcher-block counter.

"He was supposed to sort it out last time!" I shook myself. "Sorry. That was unfair. Nick did get her out. Something new must have happened to make them think..." I trailed off and stood. What the hell could have happened? And Manaj didn't say they were arresting her for Davin Markarian's murder. The two deaths had to be connected, didn't they? I turned, my hip bumping the table, rattling the water glasses.

Arsen rubbed my shoulder. "Do you want me to drive you to the station?"

"I can't go," I said, tasting something sour. "I have guests out for dinner and don't know when they'll return." They had keys, but I made a point of being here around this hour for their return. Besides, the best I could do for Dix was to get her a lawyer, and Arsen had already done that.

"Do you want me to go to the station?" he asked.

"I'll come with you," Ethan said.

All right, be logical. "If the lawyer's on his way, I'm not sure what any of us can do for her at the station."

"That's not the point," Arsen said. "Ethan and I will go."

Relieved, I pressed my palms to my eyes. It was irrational, but I hated to think of Dixie on her own – not that she would be on her own with her lawyer there. The lawyer whose bill I still hadn't received. My stomach quivered. I couldn't think about that now. There would be some way to pay him. Maybe I could take out a second mortgage on the second mortgage.

"Dixie didn't do this." Arsen pulled me into a one-armed hug and quickly released me. "She'll be all right. Come on, Ethan."

Bailey and I walked them to the door. We stood on the porch while Arsen's Jeep backed away, his headlights illuminating the driveway in stark grays. When his taillights had disappeared around the bend, I hurried into the foyer and called the sheriff.

"What now?" McCourt asked, voice resigned.

"Manaj arrested Dixie for Tanner's murder." I walked behind the front desk and plopped into the rolling chair. It zipped backward, banging into the built-in bookcase. A flying saucer keychain slid from a shelf and dropped to the floor.

Bailey pressed against my leg. I retrieved the keychain and rubbed his back.

There was a long silence. "Interesting."

"Interesting?" I braced my elbows on the scarred wooden desk. "It's a disaster! It doesn't make any sense. Dixie had no reason to kill him. Just because she had a little trouble with the law when she was younger—"

The sheriff snorted.

"—doesn't mean she's a killer," I said, raising my voice. I dropped the keychain into a desk drawer. "Look, do you know anything about this?"

"I know the sheriff's department executed a search of your cousin's trailer."

"That... But..." They hadn't even searched the B&B that hard, and it was a crime scene. "Why?"

"Because she's a suspect."

"She's not the only one." I stared blindly at the lit computer screen. "She's not even the most likely suspect. Why Dixie?"

"Is this an existential quest...?" She trailed off.

"What? What are you thinking?"

Bailey wriggled past my legs and beneath the wooden desk.

"It's a good question," she said. "Dixie isn't the strongest suspect. The judge doesn't give out search warrants without good reason. Why does Dixie work for you?" she asked abruptly.

"Why not work for me?"

Bailey whimpered, and I bent, petting him, my chin low to the desk.

"I mean, why did you hire her?"

"Well, I didn't. She helped Gran with the cleaning when I wasn't around, and it didn't seem fair to let her go when I took over." Plus, my parents had told me I'd never be able to manage my cousin, and I'd had to prove them wrong. And I had. Dixie and I were doing just fine. Mostly.

"Even though you can manage cleaning those rooms on your own."

It was true, I *could* have done it on my own. "It's a lot easier if I don't have to."

"And more expensive. Tell the truth, with Dixie's salary, how much are you making on this B&B?"

Heat flushed through my veins. "Enough." Thanks to the summer and ski seasons, we were profitable, but barely. "What does this have to do with Dixie being arrested?"

"It calls into question her real reason for being in that B&B, and why you keep her on."

"But it's my decision to keep her on. It isn't as if she insinuated herself into the B&B on the off chance your ex-husband might decide to stay here."

"But with an ex-con in the house, it diverts any suspicion from you."

"From me?" I sputtered. "Why would anyone be suspicious of me?"

"Tanner owed you money—"

"We've been over this! Yes, he owed me money, but it's not the last time I'll get stiffed." Though it had been the first. "I'm not going to murder every deadbeat who shows up on my doorstep. And I certainly didn't hire Dixie as a scapegoat in case I decided to commit a crime."

"I'll call you back." She hung up.

Furious, I stared at the phone. Seriously? That was so rude! I frowned. Though this *was* the first time she'd offered to call me back.

The front door creaked open. My new guest, a silver-haired hiking enthusiast from Los Angeles, strolled into the foyer.

I forced a smile. "Hi! How was your dinner?"

"Wonderful." The tanned skin around his eyes crinkled. "Thanks for the recommendation."

Bailey crawled forward, low to the floor, and stuck his nose from beneath the desk.

"Are you in for the night?" I asked.

"Yep."

"In that case," I said. "I'll lock the doors."

He waved cheerily and jogged up the stairs, taking them two at a time.

I locked the front door, then walked up the stairs after him and locked the rear door to the exterior stairs.

Duty done, I returned to the kitchen and cleaned up. But I couldn't stop worrying about Dixie. Gran had believed in Dixie enough to ask me to take care of her. It was one of the last things she'd said to me. I had the sinking feeling I'd let her down.

Drying my hands on the dish towel, I walked into my sitting room.

Bailey nosed at a spot on the fluffy white throw rug.

I dropped the towel on the coffee table and my butt on the black sofa.

Bailey hopped to the cushion beside me, and I didn't scold him.

Think. My day planner lay open on the coffee table, and I flipped the pages to my current project lists. I added a new header: *PAY LAWYER.*

Empty lines cascaded beneath it. How to pay Dixie's lawyer? *Step one... Step one...* I tapped my pencil on the page.

Okay, I'd come back to that later. I ground the tip of my pencil into the page beside my crime solving list. Which I hadn't gotten anywhere on.

I flipped to the three and five-year goals pages. I'd never gotten around to filling them out, because I hadn't been able to think that far ahead. Inheriting the B&B hadn't been part of the plan. But lately, nothing had been going according to plan.

Slumping on the couch, I ground the heels of my hands into my eyes. Why had I believed I could help the sheriff or Dixie or anyone? It wasn't as if my organizational skills had gotten me this B&B. I'd earned nothing and deserved nothing. And I gave Arsen a hard time for being a spoiled rich kid. What a hypocrite.

Bailey snorted.

I rubbed his back. Brown and black fur drifted onto the couch.

Sitting forward, I flipped to the notes pages. Enough self-pity. I scanned the color-coded murder notes.

I needed more.

Bailey laid his head on my lap, his weight and warmth comforting.

My cell phone rang, and I checked the number. *Arsen.*

"Hey," he said. "I'm at the station."

I gripped Bailey. "Are they letting her go?"

"No. The lawyer told me they found something in her trailer, something that belonged to Tanner McCourt."

"What?" I released the dog, and he snuggled closer on the velvety couch.

"They won't say, but they seem to think she got it from his room."

My insides hollowed out. "Okay," I said dully. "Thanks."

"Do you want me to come over?"

My eyes burned. I cleared my throat. "No, thanks. You've got Ethan."

"Are you sure? I can drop him at my place."

"No, it's okay," I said. "I'll be fine."

"All right. I'll come by tomorrow morning."

"Great. Thanks. For everything. Bye."

We hung up.

The phone dangled, limp, from my hand.

There was no reason for Dixie to have been in Tanner's room. She couldn't have gotten inside when he was alive, because he'd never left.

Unless...

My cousin was hiding something.

Chapter 25

My heart wasn't in making breakfast that morning — it was too full of worry for Dixie. I went through the motions – eggs, bacon, yogurt, fruit. But the food was ash in my mouth. I hoped it tasted better to my weekday guest.

Despite the morning's coolness, sunlight streamed through the screens and promised another hot mountain afternoon. My neck ached as I swept the front porch, the broom making scritching noises across the floorboards. I'd thought it was getting better, but Dixie's arrest had ratcheted up the tension. All those years of my cousin hanging around in the shadows, and now this... I didn't want to believe she was guilty, but doubt gnawed me.

I filled the plastic watering can and watered the ferns dangling from the ceiling and grouped beside the wicker table and chairs. Dixie would have made fun of my green top and white shorts, which matched their cushions.

But Dixie wasn't here.

Arsen's ginormous Jeep rolled into the driveway. He and Ethan stepped out and walked up the porch steps.

I opened the screen door. "Hey."

Arsen pulled me into a hug, and the watering can bumped against his thigh.

Briefly, I rested my head on his broad chest. I'd never paid much attention before to how muscular he'd become, but now I felt the hard planes of his muscles beneath his microfiber tee.

I stepped from his embrace. "There's still breakfast on the table."

"Thanks," Arsen said. "How are you holding up?"

"I'm fine," I said.

"Dixie didn't do this." Ethan's brown hair fell into his eyes, and he pushed it away with an impatient gesture. His plain black tee bagged over the top of his army green cargo shorts. "She's being framed."

My jaw clenched. Isn't that what every jailed criminal claimed? But there was no good reason for Dix to have something from Tanner's room. And it was a stretch to say she'd had a good reason to be at Wits' End the afternoon I'd found his body. "Did the lawyer tell you anything else?"

Arsen angled his head toward the foyer door. "Ethan, you mind giving us a minute?"

He hitched up his shorts. "Privacy. That's another thing you don't see in Club Fed. I get the need." He slouched inside, letting the screen door bang shut.

"He's not going to be able to resist telling his mother about jail, is he?" And she'd tell Arsen's aunts, and auntly fury would rain from the heavens.

Arsen grimaced. "Forget about Ethan. How are you doing, really?"

"I can't believe Dixie did this." But I was starting to doubt, the suspicion a black tar, weighting my gut.

He laid a roughened hand on my shoulder. "Nick's a great lawyer. If anyone can get her out, he can."

"Yeah," I said, doubtful.

"It'll be okay," he said. "You'll see."

I twisted my mouth into a smile. "Did you learn anything else?"

He shook his head. "Only what I told you last night."

"Did Nick say what sort of evidence the police had discovered? What had she taken?"

"Tanner's wallet."

"So, it was a simple robbery after all," I said, my voice dull. The sheriff had never said anything to me about a stolen wallet. Had she known? She must have. Otherwise, why would she have focused on Dixie from the start? "What does Dixie have to say?"

"She didn't say anything when she was in custody. Beyond that, any conversations between Dixie and Nick are confidential."

Of course. Dixie'd had enough experience with Johnny Law to know to keep her mouth shut.

Arsen squeezed my shoulder. "This isn't over."

"Right." There would be a trial. How much would that cost? Paying for a few hours legal consulting was one thing, but trials could go on for weeks — months. And there was all sorts of prep work involved...

A wave of nausea sickened me. I'd have to sell Wits' End. The B&B was a gift from Gran, and if I had to lose it to help my cousin, well, that was what Gran would have wanted.

I blinked rapidly and pushed open the screen door. "Breakfast is getting cold."

Leaving him with Ethan in the breakfast room, I hurried to the kitchen and blotted my eyes on a paper towel.

The front screen doors banged shut, and I frowned. Manaj had already left, and I hadn't heard my other guests come downstairs.

A feminine shout. A raised male voice.

I followed the angry voices into the breakfast room, scented with bacon.

"Jail!" Professor Green braced her hands on the white tablecloth and glared at Arsen. "How could you?" Her white hiking shirt rumpled around the hips of her sand-colored slacks. Mud crusted her boots, and she'd left tracks on the hardwood floor.

He stammered. "It wasn't my idea—"

"Your aunts assured me you'd take care of him. I will let them know exactly what you led my poor son to. And leaving him there for the entire weekend, while you two galivanted about swimming and doing what all! Shameless!"

Arsen paled.

She spun toward her son. "My poor baby. Thank God I returned early. I knew I shouldn't have left you alone with that reprobate."

Ethan shrank in his chair. "But—"

"Don't worry," she said. "I won't make that mistake again."

She slammed her hand on the table, and the plates and glasses jumped. The professor pointed a shaking finger at Arsen. "And don't think I'll stop at your aunts. When your clients learn how reckless, how depraved you are! Leaving my son to take the blame for what you did!"

Arsen blinked. "Wait. What?"

"No one will believe for a moment that my son initiated any of this."

"But he did," I said.

She whirled on me. "Stop trying to protect your boyfriend."

My cheeks warmed. "He's not— that's not the point."

Behind her back, Ethan shook his head frantically.

"Your son got himself arrested all on his own," I said.

"And why was he on his own?" she asked. "Because that... that man didn't do his job."

Arsen cleared his throat. "Sue—"

I banged shut the lid on a warming tray. "That isn't fair."

"Ethan would have never gotten himself into trouble if it weren't for that person's influence," she said.

Ethan shot me a pleading gaze, and guilt twanged through me. It wasn't entirely his fault if he'd gone off the rails once free of his helicopter parent. I'd be mad if my kid had been in jail too, but Ethan seemed okay. Better, even. He wasn't constantly focused on his phone anymore. There had to be a way to defuse this without throwing him under the bus.

"Ethan knew exactly what he was doing," I said.

She crossed her arms. "You would say that. It's obvious you and

Mr. Holiday have a thing going. Can't he speak for himself?"

Ethan gripped his phone, his knuckles whitening.

"Professor Green—" Arsen began.

"Ethan did it intentionally," I said, more determined.

She gaped at me. "He went to jail on purpose? That is the most ridiculous thing I've ever heard."

"It was a..." I glanced at Ethan, clutching his phone like a security blanket. "...radical tech detox."

Her salt-and-pepper brows skyrocketed. "What?"

Arsen's jaw slackened.

"You must have noticed his problem," I said. "He could barely interact with the real world, he was so involved with his phone. But now, look." I waved at Ethan, his back to a tall window. "He hasn't been on the phone all morning."

She frowned. "What are you talking about?"

"He knew he couldn't control himself," I said. "So, he got himself thrown in jail, so he'd be separated from his phone for a few days. Why do you think he got arrested on a Friday night, when he'd be stuck in jail all weekend? He knew the courts wouldn't be open for bail hearings until Monday."

"And it worked," Ethan said. "My phone's not even on." He brandished the blank screen at his mother.

"That's..." She drew back her shoulders. "I don't believe it."

Ethan's eyes widened. "Mom, would I lie to you?"

"Well, no, of course not." Her mouth worked soundlessly. "But... jail?"

"Arsen has some friends who are cops," he said. "They took real good care of me."

"Is this true?" she asked Arsen.

He colored. "Ah—"

"Of course, it's true," I said. "And it was successful. Ethan's a changed man. We had dinner last night, and he didn't check his phone once."

"I learned a lot." Ethan nodded like a dashboard bobblehead.

"The point is," I said, "it was a controlled environment, and Ethan made the decision to do this on his own. Didn't you Ethan?"

He nodded, his coffee-colored hair flopping into his eyes. "Arsen didn't even know what I had planned."

"Ethan's going to write a blog article on the experience," I said.

He nodded vigorously. "Right. You know. To help others."

"So," I said, motioning to the sideboard, loaded with food, "can I offer you breakfast? We're low on eggs, but I'd be happy to cook more."

She blinked. "No, no. I already... Ethan, you really did this?"

He lowered his head.

"Well." She swallowed. "Well. That may be, but I don't like you staying in this environment. I understand that girl who worked here was arrested."

My muscles tensed. I'd had more than enough. "And I understand that the man who was murdered was cellmates with Ethan's father," I said hotly.

Her mouth fell open. "That's—" She looked from me to Ethan.

"It's okay, Mom," he said. "I know about my dad. It's not your fault."

"But it is quite a coincidence," I said, "you and Ethan turning up at the same B&B where Tanner McCourt was staying."

Beneath her white top, her shoulders hunched. "I don't think that's any of your business."

"Maybe not," I said, "but I'm sure the police and FBI will be interested. Should I get Agent Manaj so you can tell her?" The FBI agent wasn't here, but I didn't think the professor knew that.

A muscle pulsed in her jaw. "I didn't kill him."

"But you did know Tanner's relationship to your husband."

"Ex-husband."

"Did he invite you here," I continued, "or did you come on your own?"

Abruptly, she pulled out a chair and sat. "He called."

"Why?" Ethan asked.

She stared at her hands, lying limp on the white tablecloth. "McCourt said he had information about Montel — Ethan's father — but he wouldn't tell me over the phone."

"What information?" Arsen asked.

"There wasn't any," she said. "It was all an excuse. McCourt wanted money."

"Money for what?" Ethan asked.

"Money not to tell the world about your father."

"Did you give it to him?" I asked.

"Some." She plucked at the tablecloth. "Enough to keep him quiet while I figured out what to do. I knew one payment wouldn't be the end of it. But then he died, and I didn't have to worry about it anymore. But I didn't kill him!"

"And your trek into the mountains?" I asked.

"I needed some excuse to come here." She shot Ethan a pleading look. "I didn't want you to be hurt. I didn't know—"

"That I already knew my father was in jail." Ethan brought his feet up on the chair and clutched his legs.

"I just wanted to protect you," she whispered, and my heart lurched. No wonder she'd been over protective.

"How did you find out?" she asked him.

Ethan shrugged. "Little things. I dunno. I just knew."

"We should talk," she said.

Her son stared at his empty plate. "Yeah."

She cleared her throat. "Have you got two rooms available? We'll need a place to stay tonight."

"Um, yeah," I said. "I'll get you keys." I walked to the front desk and unlocked the top drawer.

Arsen slipped from the breakfast room and into the foyer. He leaned over my desk. "A radical social media cure?" he whispered.

"I had to say something," I muttered. "I know your aunts."

He laughed softly. "I didn't think you had it in you."

I grabbed the room keys from the drawer and made a note in my guest book. "Nice to know I can still surprise you."

"The women in your family never stop surprising me."

I thought of Dixie, and my gut wrenched. Not all our surprises were good ones.

Chapter 26

I settled Ethan and his mother in their rooms. By the time I'd finished, Arsen had left, so I got to the business of cleaning.

Gingham curtains fluttered at the bedroom's open window. I tucked a sheet into a neat, hospital corner and straightened, looking around the L.A. hiker's room. Hot pain flared in my neck. This afternoon's appointment with the chiropractor couldn't come soon enough. And Zack was more than a chiropractor. He was becoming a friend.

I whisked my duster across the wall's UFO photos. The sheriff had been right. Most days, I could manage without Dixie. I paused, staring at a blurry black-and-white photo of a triangular object in the sky. But I'd rather have her here.

Piling my arms with cleaning supplies and damp towels, I pushed open the door to the hall with my hip. My foot caught on something soft and there was a low yelp. Towels cascaded to the green carpet.

Bailey turned sorrowful eyes on me.

I winced. "Sorry, Bailey."

He whined, his tail thumping the carpet.

"Talk about mixed messages." Kneeling, I rubbed his back. "I'm not happy about this situation either. But don't worry, we'll get Dixie back."

I carted Bailey downstairs, then returned to the second floor and picked up the fallen towels.

Bailey at my heels, I squeezed through the door to the laundry room downstairs. My grandmother had installed an industrial-sized washer and dryer. They took up so much space that the dryer door banged the wall whenever I opened it. I dropped the towels in the to-be-washed basket.

Bailey whimpered.

"Let's check your food."

He followed me into the kitchen, and we both examined his bowls. Neither were empty.

"Do you want to go outside?"

His tail wagged, a perpetual motion machine. I opened the screen door to the side porch. The beagle trotted outside then sat on the wood-plank porch and gazed at me.

Life would be so much easier if I spoke Dog. "Walk?" I asked.

He woofed gently.

I unhooked his leash from beside the door and clipped it to his collar.

At the top of the steps, he looked up at me and whined.

"Someday, you're going to get over this fear of going down stairs." I picked him up and set him down on the lawn. He tugged me forward. But instead of running for the street, the beagle stopped in front of my grandmother's spirit house. He looked over his shoulder.

"What?" I asked, reaching to unhook his leash. Clearly, I'd misread the signals, and he wanted to play in the yard.

He barked, a sharp yip.

I glanced over my shoulder. No one was there. The rose bush I'd fallen into didn't look too bad from this angle, but I needed to prune the branches I'd broken.

Bailey gave another, lone bark.

I turned to the dog. "Is Timmy in the well? What's with you?"

He pawed at the wooden post that held the spirit house.

Thinking something might have died behind it, I moved forward, cautious. I hadn't had the heart to light incense in it today. A cone of gray ash stood, lopsided, on the miniature house's front "porch." I brushed the ash to the ground, leaving a mercury streak on the side of my hand.

I drew in a quick breath.

A small, white envelope, the kind a florist would use, was wedged behind the spirit house's open door.

I retrieved the envelope and pulled out the card — Victorian roses on the front, a message on the back: *Eleven o'clock, bandstand.*

The clock on my phone said it was nearly noon. I'd missed the meeting. If Madame X knew my morning routine, she'd have expected I'd have come to the spirit house to light the incense in time.

It was more than a little creepy that she knew about that routine.

An ache rose in the back of my throat. The woman's vague hints hadn't helped my cousin. But if she knew something, maybe she could. She'd said she'd known my grandmother. If that was true, she would have known how much Dixie meant to her.

I looked from the spirit house to the old Victorian. "Let's go, Bailey."

We started into town on what was likely a wild goose chase. I was already late, so the odds were Madame X wouldn't be waiting at the bandstand. But it was a fine day. The sun was shining, the birds chirping. And though we were approaching the noon hour, the summer heat hadn't reached its zenith. A walk into town would do me good. Maybe I'd stop in Ground and get a cup of coffee. Or go to the cupcake shop and get something more dangerous.

Since nothing at the cupcake shop was low-calorie, I stepped up the pace. We hurried past decaying Victorians and overgrown gardens.

Bailey got into the spirit and bounded ahead, straining at the leash.

We rounded the corner and approached the park.

A trio of young mothers sat on a bench beside the bandstand and watched their toddlers race around the lawn.

I didn't see any veiled old ladies loitering about, but Bailey and I climbed the bandstand steps.

He sniffed an uninteresting-looking vertical beam.

I lounged against the white-painted banister and scanned the park.

"You're late."

I jumped, yelped, turned.

Madame X scowled in a saggy black dress and sensible shoes. A zebra-patterned scarf draped over her gray hair.

I looked around wildly. Bailey had moved on to examine another post. "How did you—? Where—?"

She shook a lime green e-cigarette at me. "Things are getting serious, young lady. I expect you to be prompt."

"I only just found your note." My neck corded, the aches from my fall reasserting themselves. "Dixie's been arrested."

"What a convenient fall guy she made."

"The police don't think so," I said. "They found evidence in her trailer."

Her white brows rose. "Evidence can be planted."

"This is Doyle, not Moscow."

She slowly shook her head. "I'm glad your grandmother isn't here to see this."

"I know." I sagged against the wooden railing. "She was certain Dixie had given up her life of crime." So sure, that I'd believed it too. Dixie was no killer. But was she a petty thief? The thought sickened me.

"Not to see Dixie's arrest, to see your lack of gumption."

My stomach hardened, tightening. "And how would my grandmother have felt about you? About all your vague hints rather than hard facts? About you following me around like some stalker—"

"Following you? I haven't been following you."

"I saw you watching Arsen and me when we found Davin Markarian's body."

She lifted her chin. "I did no such thing. When I wanted to meet, I scheduled a meeting. It was all perfectly proper."

"Wait. Really? You weren't there? Because I saw a woman in a scarf watching us."

She tapped her sensibly-shod foot. "I assure you, it wasn't me."

"Then who...?" I trailed off. Professor Green had been suspiciously well informed about my weekend activities. How had she known Arsen and I had gone swimming, unless she'd seen us? Could she have stayed in town instead of going up to the mountains, like she'd claimed? My scalp prickled. If she'd been here the whole time, she was a suspect in Davin's death.

"Who what?" Madame X asked.

"Never mind. You wanted to meet. We're meeting. What did you want to talk about?"

She took a step closer, and I smelled peppermint on her breath. Peppermint schnapps. "This isn't over. The police and that daffy FBI agent might have the answers they want, but they don't have the truth."

"And what is the truth?"

"They think Dixie used her martial arts skills to break those men's necks. That she left Wits' End after you and Arsen Holiday, found Davin at the hotel, and killed him."

"Well, I guess, but how can we prove she didn't?"

"Oh, she left Wits' End that day, but she didn't go to the hotel."

"What? How do you know this?"

"Because Dixie's not stupid, and she's no killer. You need to find out where she really went."

"But how?"

"Seek and ye shall find, Susan. Seek and ye shall find." She trotted down the stairs.

"That's not very helpful," I shouted after her.

She vanished around a corner of the bandstand.

I crossed my arms. I was *not* chasing after her.

Bailey woofed.

"Well," I said to him, "it *isn't* helpful." I should have stuck with my first instinct — the woman was nuts. And not a good nuts, like my gran. Madame X had passed the Eccentricity exit and was well on her way to Crazy Town.

I gnawed my bottom lip. *Had* Professor Green been lurking in Doyle the entire time? I shook my head. Didn't matter. There was probably an innocent explanation. Maybe she'd just been keeping watch on her son. But if that were true, she would have witnessed his bad behavior and...

I swallowed. It didn't matter. The police had found evidence, real evidence, in Dixie's trailer. Was X saying the police had planted the evidence? But why...? I sucked in my breath.

Not the sheriff? She'd certainly acted surprised to learn of Dixie's arrest. But she'd known about Dixie's sexual harassment claim against Tanner, about the firing. She'd known Dixie would make the perfect fall guy. And her deputies had searched Dixie's trailer.

Picking up Bailey, I carried him down the stairs and set him on the lawn.

We walked up the green slope to Main Street. There seemed to be more tourists than usual for a Tuesday. Visitors ambled down the shaded, plank sidewalks. They paused to gaze into shop windows filled with t-shirts and artisanal honey and hiking guides.

"Witsend!"

In front of the cupcake shop, I stopped and turned, stiffening.

The sheriff barreled down the sidewalk. Magically, tourists parted before her. "With me." She pointed past the cupcake shop and kept walking.

Wary, I followed her around the corner to a cozy, parklike area where a small, round stone building stood. With its green door, it looked like an elf house. But it was our tourist information center and closed on Tuesdays, its metal shutters shut fast over its single window.

The sheriff moved deeper into the shady area behind the round building and sat on a bench beside the fountain.

I remained standing. "What's up? Are you off leave now Dixie's been arrested?" A bead of sweat trickled down the side of my face. This was a mistake. What if the sheriff really was the killer? What if she'd been the one to frame Dixie? Here, we were hidden from street view, and there was little chance anyone would stumble across us. You had to be headed inside the information center to notice the small garden.

"It was an anonymous tip that sent my deputies to your cousin's trailer. And you didn't hear that from me."

Carefully, I edged toward the street and pondered her words. "I see."

"I start work tomorrow." The sheriff looked at me intently.

"Congratulations. That's good news."

Bailey yipped an agreement.

Her blue-eyed gaze bored into mine. "Tomorrow, you understand?"

"Ye-es. I get it."

"Do you?"

"Not really." I tried to swallow but couldn't. "Unless you're saying Manaj is certain she's got her killer." I smiled, fleeting and false. "I don't blame her. They found your ex's wallet in Dixie's trailer."

She snorted. "I didn't think you were the type to give up so easily. And why are you looking at me like I'm about to shoot you?"

"You wouldn't shoot me," I said, shrill. "Everyone would hear you on the street. Just because we're kind of hidden here, doesn't mean you'd get away with it. Besides, you're not armed. Are you?" Confused, I crossed my arms. "And I'm not giving up on my cousin. I'm facing reality."

"Are you sure about that?" She rose and strode away.

A monarch butterfly fluttered erratically past. It landed, tentative, on a yellow, bell-shaped flower bobbing from the vines on the stone building.

The sheriff could have tipped off the cops, but then why tell me about it? Was I wrong about her? Had someone else set Dixie up? If it was an honest tip, the anonymous caller would have been someone who'd witnessed Dixie at the B&B the night of the murder. Or had Dixie blabbed to someone? I frowned. Dixie wasn't the blabbing type.

And why had the sheriff come to me with this information? She hadn't been big on keeping me in the loop before. Unless...

Evidence can be planted.

Unless the sheriff really believed that justice had not been done with Dixie's arrest. And maybe the leads I'd turned up hadn't been so useless after all.

Chapter 27

Boxed cupcakes dangling from my fingertips, I walked Bailey toward Wits' End. Now I didn't mind his frequent stops to sniff tree trunks, bushes, and mail boxes. I had some hard thinking to do.

If there had been a witness who'd put Dixie at the scene of Tanner's murder, who was it? Since Wits End was on a cul-de-sac, we didn't get a lot of stray walkers. Theoretically, someone hiking in the woods behind the B&B could have seen something, but it didn't seem likely. That left my neighbors.

We rounded the leafy corner to Grizzly Court, and I scanned the street.

Across from Wits' End, a ranch house with flecking green paint hid behind a tangle of juniper bushes. They blocked a half-dozen battered cars in the overgrown yard.

My neighbor on the left was a neat A-frame cabin, inhabited by a gruff, older man and his wife. And on the right, a family of four jammed into a tumble-down Victorian cottage with a tricycle in the front garden.

I crossed into the B&B's gravel driveway and let Bailey off the leash. He scampered into the backyard.

My stomach rumbled as I let myself into the B&B with the cupcakes. One of Gran's UFO booklets sat atop the blotter on the reception desk. How did that get out there? I made to put it away, then opened the slim paperback to the dedication page: *For Susan and Dixie. May you never be bored.*

Blinking rapidly, I closed the booklet and hurried to the kitchen, where I put away the cupcakes minus a red velvet.

I gobbled the cupcake, licking cream cheese frosting off my fingers. Then I grabbed my day planner and walked across the street.

The ranch house was silent, its orange curtains drawn.

I waded through the weeds to the front door. Knocked, waited, knocked again. My nose wrinkled at the scent of marijuana.

A shuffling sound emerged from behind the warped orange door, like a body being dragged. I stepped backwards.

The door opened, and a skinny, bleary-eyed twenty-something in sweat pants and nothing else blinked at me. "Yeah?" His blond hair fell lank about his shoulders.

"Hi, I'm your neighbor across the street, Susan."

He rubbed his eyes and yawned. "Yeah?"

"Were the police here a few days ago, asking if you'd seen anything at Wits' End?"

"Yeah."

"What did you tell them?"

He leaned against the doorframe. "Didn't see nothing."

Double negatives irritated me, but I ignored it. "Did anyone else in your house see anything?"

"Nope."

Pain flared in my neck, and I massaged a spot beneath my skull. "It's just that my cousin Dixie was arrested, so it's important we know what everyone saw. For the lawyer."

His brown eyes warmed. "Dixie? She's cool."

"That's why I need to know what people saw the afternoon Tanner McCourt was killed."

He scratched his arm pit. "Like I said, we didn't see nothing."

"Okay." I hitched my purse up on my shoulder. "Well, if you think of anything..." I trailed off. This dude hadn't thought of anything for a long time. "Bye."

I stopped on the sidewalk and made a note of the conversation in my day planner. Snapping it shut, I hurried across the street to the Victorian cottage.

A child's wail drifted through the garden, cluttered with toys. Beside the front porch, a plastic swing set stood at an awkward angle.

Determined, I climbed the steps and rang the bell.

The door popped open, and a frazzled-looking woman with a toddler on her hip looked out at me and frowned. "Susan?"

"Hi, Carol. Sorry to bother you, but I was wondering if you or Frank saw anything at Wits' End the afternoon Tanner McCourt died?"

She shifted her grip on the toddler, gnawing a baby carrot. "The police asked us the same thing. Perry had a cold." She glanced at the toddler. "And we were so busy, we barely even noticed the police had arrived. Why?"

"So, you didn't see anything?"

"No." She stepped backward, angling the toddler on her hip away from me. "Why?"

"I'm just trying to figure out what happened."

Her brows lifted. "Isn't that what the police are for?"

"Yeah." I rubbed my forearm. "Except you may have heard they arrested Dixie."

Her lips flattened. "I heard. I'm sorry. I don't know what I can tell you."

"Well, thanks anyway." I trotted down the steps and into the street. In front of Wits' End, I stopped and made notes in my planner – time, date, subject, interview result (nothing).

Feet dragging, I walked to the A-frame cabin on the other side of Wits' End and climbed the steps to the front door. Mr. Fitzgerald wasn't exactly mean, but he and his wife liked to be left alone. A NO SOLICITORS sign hung above his doorbell.

I drew a deep breath and knocked on the door. Waited.

The door swung open, and Mr. Fitzgerald glared beneath his bushy gray eyebrows. His face could have been carved of wood, it was so gnarled and brown from the sun. "What do you want?"

"Hi, Mr. Fitzgerald. I'm Susan from—"

"I know who you are. What do you want?"

"Did you see anyone around Wits' End the day of Tanner McCourt's death?"

"The day of his murder, you mean."

I wilted. "Right."

"I don't gossip. And you shouldn't either." He began to shut the door.

"It's not gossip if it's about my house and I'm asking," I said hastily.

He paused, his steel-colored eyes narrowing. "Don't you have better things to do, young lady? Because I know I do."

"Anything you might have told the police would be a big help."

He rubbed his bristly chin. "What I told the police is between me and the police."

"But they think Dixie might have been involved!"

"Is that so surprising?" he asked, gruff. "She's been involved in a lot in her short life."

Wind soughed in the pines beside the A-frame. The trees bent, their branches tossing.

"But not murder," I said. "They've arrested her, but I know she couldn't have done it. They're on the wrong track."

His expression softened. "I don't peg her for a killer either, and that's what I told the cops."

I felt a rush of gratitude. "So, did you see anyone? Or anything odd?"

"Nothing *odd*."

"But you saw someone?" My breath bottled in my lungs. Not Dixie. It couldn't be Dixie.

"I saw what looked like one of those delivery boys coming down the back steps that afternoon."

"Do you remember what time?"

"Fifteen minutes before the cops showed up, and then they came to bother me about it that night."

"Did you notice the uniform?" I asked, excited.

He shook his head. "It was too dark. The only reason I noticed is because I think you're a damn fool to leave those doors unlocked. Your grandmother did the same thing. I told her and told her she couldn't trust—"

"But it was definitely a man?"

"I couldn't say. Too dark. Too far away. The face was hidden by a cap. He or she was wearing a windbreaker."

"Thanks. And you told the police this when they came around the evening of the murder?"

"What kind of damn fool question is that? When else would I tell 'em?" He slammed the door shut.

Buoyant, I returned to Wits' End and recorded the conversation in my day planner. I paced the sunlit kitchen.

So, Mr. Fitzgerald *had* seen something. And Dixie had been near Wits' End the afternoon of the murder. The cops could have put those two together and pegged her for the crime.

But Mr. Fitzgerald hadn't called in the anonymous tip that had sent the police to Dixie's trailer.

I yanked open the microwave and pulled out the rose-colored cupcake box. How quickly would those calories go to my hips? Because I was seeing Zack for my chiropractor's appointment soon. And though you never look your best with your face mushed into a paper mat, I had some standards.

I shook my head. Nope, sacrifices would have to be made, and I needed more calories to figure this out. So, I lifted a yellow-frosted lemon poppy seed cupcake from my dwindling supply and sat at the kitchen table.

Tanner had almost never left his room. He'd used delivery people to bring him food and even do his laundry. He'd even set his garbage bins outside his door for me to empty. Someone could have come up the back stairs dressed as a delivery person and killed Tanner. But Tanner was cunning. He wouldn't have opened the door unless he was expecting an actual delivery or he knew whoever it was.

Bailey trotted into the kitchen and sat on the linoleum floor. He gazed at me with a mournful expression.

"Forget it. Dogs shouldn't eat cupcakes." I retrieved a treat from the top of the refrigerator and tossed him the tidbit.

He ignored it and laid down, setting his head on his paws.

I rubbed the back of my neck. I didn't remember seeing any take-out on Tanner's desk when the sheriff and I had found his body. If someone posing as a delivery man had killed him, surely Tanner wouldn't have had time to eat the food and throw out the remains?

Thumbing through my day planner, I reviewed my notes. No mention of takeout boxes in the trash. If only I'd had a chance to take pictures!

Bailey set his paw on my foot.

"I said, no cupcakes." In Bailey's defense, his begging never went much beyond giving me the sad eye. And it occasionally worked, especially when Arsen was dining in. But I wasn't feeding him lemon cupcake, and I was pretty sure poppy seeds were toxic to dogs. I liked Bailey too much for that, and I sure couldn't afford a vet bill on top of Dixie's legal fees.

I sat up straighter.

Wait a minute.

I flipped the notes pages in my day planner, scanned what I'd written.

Wait a minute!

I leapt up and paced. Could it be that simple?

Maybe, just maybe. And if I was right, then Dixie really was innocent.

And I'd failed her.

Chapter 28

Arsen had a sixth sense when it came to food. He'd turned up at the B&B just as I was putting the cupcake box in the microwave.

He grabbed a chocolate-peanut butter from the box. "I talked to the lawyer, Nick."

"What did he say?" I grabbed my keys from the butcher-block counter.

"He said we shouldn't give up hope. Are you going somewhere?"

"The chiropractor's."

His expression became a careful blank. "Are you hurt?"

"My neck is still bothering me."

"I'm not surprised. There's a lot of evidence that chiropractic is a sham."

"It makes the pain go away, and that's all I care about."

"If you're in pain," he said, bending to scratch Bailey, "maybe I should drive you to the chiropractor."

"You don't have to." I couldn't explain why, but I didn't want Arsen and Zack in the same room together, at least, not while I was there.

"It's no problem." He tossed his keys in the air and caught them one handed. "Let's go."

"No, really," I trotted after him. "I can drive myself."

But somehow, I ended up on the passenger side of Arsen's Jeep, and we drove into Doyle.

He pulled into the chiropractor's empty lot and parked the Jeep.

Arsen leapt from the car and strode around to my door before I could unbuckle. He helped me from the high seat, his broad hands gentle on mine.

"Thanks," I said, feeling suddenly awkward.

"No problem. I didn't know you were in so much pain."

Heat suffused my face. My neck pain had dropped to the occasional dull throb. But Witsends didn't cancel appointments at the last minute - not when there was a cancellation fee. Besides, I had a question that only the chiropractor could answer.

Arsen and I strolled into the office's green-painted waiting room. I glanced through the open reception window to the small office. It was empty.

We settled in the cheerful blue-and-green checked chairs. I grabbed the local paper, and Arsen flipped through a hiking magazine.

"How'd you hurt your neck anyway?" he asked.

"I tripped." Over a shingle and off the roof. All things considered, I was lucky a sore neck was my only problem.

"You should try yoga. It's great for balance."

An image of Arsen, bare chested in yoga pants and high on a granite mountain, flashed into my mind, and my face warmed again. "I didn't know you did yoga."

"Tried it once, but I got bored with it, though it's a great stretch. I prefer Tai Chi, which is also good for balance."

"Then why didn't you recommend Tai Chi?"

He grinned. "Because you'd get bored with it. Come to think of it, you wouldn't like yoga either."

"I might."

He gave me a look. "Are you kidding? All that time in silence, just thinking? It would make you crazy."

"Tai chi looks fun." Another image popped into my head – of Arsen guiding my hips into a Tai Chi pose. *Stop it, stop it, stop it!*

Down the hallway, the door to the chiropractor's room opened. Zack led Agent Manaj (black jeans, black t-shirt, black boots) to the reception window.

The chiropractor's tawny eyes warmed. "Hi, Susan. I'll be right with you." He ducked his head and walked through the door into his small office.

What was the FBI agent doing here? Manaj was in jeans, so... off duty? My nostrils flared. Why not? She'd caught her so-called murderer. Why look any further?

"Down girl," Arsen said beneath his breath.

I sat back and folded my arms, more angry at myself than at the agent.

At the reception window, Manaj turned to face us. Impassive, she nodded to me and strode outside.

The chiropractor beamed and ambled into the reception area. "Hi, Susan." He rolled up the sleeves of his dress shirt, exposing the fine, coppery hair on his arms, and tilted his head toward his consulting room off the hallway.

I followed him inside.

He shut the door. "How are you feeling today?"

"My neck's a little sore." I stepped onto the metal plates and leaned forward against the near-vertical table. My face pressed into the paper-lined pillow.

"I'm sorry to hear it, but I'm not surprised. You really wrenched it. Have you been icing it?"

"Um..."

He laughed. "In other words, *no*. Let's take a look."

The table hummed, lifting my feet and reclining me so I lay on my stomach. I pulled my hair over one shoulder.

He lifted my right foot, bending one knee at a ninety-degree angle, then the other. A gentle push on this muscle, a gentle prod on that.

"Yep, you've done something." His hands explored the hollows of my back, and I forced myself to relax. This was Zack. We were only friends.

He thunked a spot beneath my shoulder blade with his spring-loaded adjustor.

"What was that FBI agent doing here?" I asked.

"A consult, like any other patient."

"Now that she's wrapped up the case, I didn't think she'd be staying in Doyle."

"I guess arresting someone isn't the end of it." He made another adjustment.

My jaw clenched. "I'll bet she has a great medical plan, working with the government."

"Probably," he said absently. "Relax."

"You know what it's like," I said, "being self-employed. Every time I get my insurance bill it's like a knife to the gut."

"Tell me about it."

The table droned, and he raised me to standing. I stepped off the metal plate and onto the carpet.

He motioned to a low examination table covered in a blue, faux-leather cushion. "Why don't you have a seat?"

I sat, insides jangling, and he walked behind me.

"Just relax." He raised my right arm over my head and prodded the joint with his thumb. Zack moved my hair over one shoulder, and his fingers brushed the back of my neck.

I shivered and closed my eyes. "I guess Davin had insurance with his employer?"

"Not a very good policy," he said and stilled, one hand on my shoulder. "You're wondering where he got his money."

I sighed. "I'm wondering about a lot." Like how do I get out of this office without making a fool of myself?

"The thing is," Zack said, "I've been wondering that too. A few weeks ago, I spotted Davin in Angels Camp at that new French restaurant. The expensive one."

"Was he alone?"

"He was with that barista from Ground."

"Cherie?" I asked. Now that was interesting. And disturbing.

"I think that's her name. The tall blonde? I wondered how they could afford the place, because I sure can't."

"Me neither. I wanted to ask, since you're a chiropractor... Could a woman break a man's neck?"

He walked around to the front of the table and arched a reddish brow. "Because I'm a chiropractor?"

"You know more about bones and joints than me."

He rubbed his square jaw. "Well, yes. I suppose they could under the right conditions, if they knew what they were doing." He patted my shoulder. "Go home. And this time, put some ice on it. You know the drill."

We walked into the reception area.

Arsen dropped his magazine on the end table and rose from his chair.

Zack walked behind the reception window, and we scheduled another appointment. I noted it in my day planner.

"That's some organizer," Zack said. "You ever go anywhere without it?"

"Never," Arsen joked. "If Sue wasn't organized, the rest of us would have to be."

I snapped the thick leather book shut. "Laugh all you want, but there's something powerful in writing things down. It helps me figure things out, get stuff done."

I paid the bill, and Arsen and I left.

"How are you feeling?" he asked, helping me into the sweltering Jeep.

His hand lingered on mine, and my breath hitched.

I shook myself. What was wrong with me? "Worried." Releasing his hand, I strapped the seatbelt across my chest. I sat gingerly on the hot seat, making sure not to touch anything with my bare skin.

"About Dixie?" He rested one hand on the open door. "She's got a great lawyer, and we both know she didn't do this."

My stomach twisted with guilt. Arsen had never doubted, but I had. I leaned closer to him and the air flowing through the open door.

"And who knows?" he asked. "Maybe it's a good sign that the FBI agent is still hanging around. She might not be a hundred percent convinced Dixie did it either."

"Maybe."

"I've been thinking. Maybe we should hire a private investigator?"

"We?" I asked. "She's my cousin. Let's talk to that lawyer about it, but if she needs someone, I'll take care of it."

"Dixie's my friend. I've got a stake in this too."

"Arsen, did you know I haven't received any bills from Nick yet?"

He shifted his weight, crossed his arms over his broad chest. "It's still early days."

I shifted on the blistering seat. "Is that the only reason?"

He grimaced. "I might have told him to send the bills to me."

"Arsen! Dixie's my cousin. This is my responsibility."

At the edge of the parking lot, a trio of Aspen trees rustled in the warm breeze. He shut my door and walked to the drivers' side.

I snapped open the planner and made notes about what Zack had told me.

When he got into the car, I didn't look up. "Arsen, I do not want you paying for Dixie's lawyer. I mean it."

"What's the harm?" He started the Jeep and the air conditioning. "I've got plenty of money."

"That's not the point."

He turned in his seat. "You don't have to take care of everyone, you know. And you can't be in control of everything."

"I'm not trying to take care of everyone." I stared out the window at the small parking lot. "Just Dixie." And I wasn't controlling. I made sure I wasn't controlling. All I wanted was to control my own life. Was that so much to ask? But my life was filling with people I cared about, and when bad things happened to them... It wasn't controlling to want to help.

"And you want to take care of me, and to take care of your grandmother, when she was alive."

"Is that such a bad thing? We're family. And you're my closest friend. But this is more than that. You're trying to pay for lawyers, offering to hire private investigators...."

He leaned his head on the rest. "Yeah. I guess it does look like more."

We sat in silence, the air conditioner humming.

"Did you learn anything else from the lawyer?" I finally asked.

"What?" He straightened. "No. Why?"

"Desperation. Madame X told me that Dixie left the B&B while we were at the lake. If the FBI knows about it, well, no wonder they picked her up. She has to tell her lawyer where she really went."

"I'll let Nick know about this, but Dixie's not in the sharing mood."

"What about Professor Green?" I asked.

"What about her?"

"I was wondering if she really did go into the mountains last week, like she'd claimed. She seemed to know a lot about what we were up to. And she was so controlling of her son."

"I still can't believe she gave me a babysitting list," he said.

"It wouldn't surprise me if she'd really stuck around to keep track of him." I leaned closer to the air vents, my hair ruffling in the cool air.

"She didn't do a very good job then," he said.

"I think I saw Professor Green watching us when we found Davin Markarian's body."

His jaw tightened. "She was there? If you're right, and she's been here all along, she could have killed them both. She's certainly got the motive."

The chiropractor emerged from his front door and stared at us, idling in the lot.

I shut my day planner and waved it in farewell. "But why kill Davin?"

"Maybe he knew the truth about why she wanted Tanner dead. She said Tanner was trying to blackmail her, but maybe Davin was, too, after she'd killed Tanner."

"Tanner and Davin both had broken necks. I asked Zack if a woman could have done that. He said, yes. What do you think?"

He hesitated. "It's possible. When we went hiking together, I could see the professor was fit. If she knew what she was doing, if she surprised Tanner and Davin... She could have done it."

I blew out my breath. "So, what are we saying? She killed Tanner to stop the blackmail? Or maybe Tanner was somehow involved in his cellmate's death, and she killed him out of revenge?" My insides churned. And now she was staying in my home.

He shifted to one hip and pulled his cell phone from his back pocket.

"What are you doing?" I asked.

"Checking the Internet."

"For what?"

"To see if your chiropractor's right... Damn. He is." He leaned across the seat and held out the phone. A video of a muscular woman demonstrating neck breaks played, her voice tinny. He handed me the phone and pulled onto the street.

"But if the Professor could break a man's neck, that explains why the cops think Dixie could have too." They probably thought she'd learned the technique in juvie.

His expression turned somber. "I hadn't thought of that."

"What do you know about Cherie Cavalier?"

"The woman who works at Ground? She's nice. Friendly. Pretty."

I rolled my eyes. "That wasn't what I meant."

"I know what you meant. I don't know much about her."

"But she was tangled up with Davin and Tanner. She couldn't have killed them – she wouldn't have had the time and I doubt she had the capability. But she's tangled up in this somehow."

He turned the Jeep onto Main Street, and we rolled past the frontier-style buildings.

"Do you want me to talk to her?" he asked.

"No," I said quickly. Though if anyone could charm her out of information, it would be Arsen. So why didn't I want him to? Was I jealous? I fiddled with the air vents. "I don't want anyone to know we're interested. I'm worried Cherie might be in danger."

"I hope you're wrong, but I'm afraid you're right. Now that Davin and Tanner are gone, she's all that's left."

"That we know of."

"Have you spoken to the sheriff about this?" he asked. "Because if you haven't, I will. Cherie needs protecting."

"The last time we talked, it was about Dixie. I don't know what the sheriff knows."

A woman in a floppy hat strolled across the street, and Arsen braked.

"What about this Madame X?" he asked. "Do you think she'll talk to Dixie's lawyer?"

"I don't even know who she is or how to find her," I said. "Though I did spot her outside town hall. Since she seems to know so much about local government shenanigans, maybe she works there?"

"If she does, I'll find her. You said she was past retirement age?"

"She looked that way."

"There are only three old ladies working in that place," he said. "No one has the nerve to force them to retire. I'll get their pictures."

"How?"

His smile was smug. "I've got my sources."

"Let me guess — a woman who works there?"

"How'd you know?"

I sighed and looked out the window. False fronts and colorful shop windows rolled past. "Just a stab in the dark."

"Once I have the photos, you can identify your mystery woman, and Nick can question her. There's another option you might not have considered. What if Ethan and his mother were working together?"

A trio of boys in karate uniforms bounded from the martial arts studio, and Arsen slowed again.

"You mean they conspired to kill Tanner and Davin? No way. You've seen what Ethan's like." But I gnawed my bottom lip. Ethan had been in the habit of doing what he was told. If his mother had asked for his help, demanded his silence...

"We've seen what he wants us to see. The whole helpless Ethan thing is a little over the top, don't you think?"

"Not with that mother." Professor Green was almost as controlling as my own parents, though I was starting to see her instincts as protectiveness rather than... whatever had motivated my parents.

He turned left, driving past the park.

I glanced at the bandstand. No women in headscarves lurked nearby.

"Think about it," Arsen said. "He gives himself an alibi for Davin's murder by getting himself thrown in jail. And the professor's supposedly off in the mountains, giving herself an alibi too. And then they alibi each other for Tanner's murder."

Great. Two murder suspects at my B&B tonight. I shrank against my seat.

"Come with me to the book signing tonight," Arsen said. "I want to keep an eye on you. There's already been one break-in at Wits' End, and I'm not a fan of your security system."

"Yeah, I got that."

"So?"

"So, I'm thinking."

"I'll let you make me dinner afterward," he said.

"Wow. What a treat. For you."

"Ethan cleaned me out with that bachelorette party." His blue eyes widened with sorrow. "My cupboard is bare."

I laughed. "You win. I'll come." Because the pieces were clicking into place. And I had a feeling having Arsen around might not be such a bad idea after all.

Chapter 29

Arsen and I walked home from the bookstore in a muggy and silent twilight. No breeze rustled the pine branches. Even the birds in their high roosts were mute, drooping, disinterested.

For the book signing, Arsen had changed into a fresh khaki tee and hiking slacks. Xavier Ultra's grinning mug beamed from the new hardback that swung from his hand. Arsen and the adventure writer had babbled about zero days and vitamin I, blue blazing and pack explosions. Xavier had invited us both to try our hands at photographing the stars tonight. By the desperate gleam in Arsen's eye, I could see he really wanted to.

"I shouldn't go on Xavier's hike," Arsen said for the third time. He whacked the book against the top of a juniper bush. "Not with everything that's happening."

"You're not spending the night at Wits' End," I said, impatient. "Go on the night hike." A bead of sweat trickled down my neck, and I flapped the hem of my green t-shirt to let some air in.

"Then come with me," Arsen said.

"I have to get up early to cook breakfast. I'm not staying out hiking until three A.M."

"That's okay." He kicked a loose stone, and it rattled into the center of the road. "I don't need to go."

I stopped in front of the signpost to Grizzly Court and slapped a mosquito from my bare leg. "Go. You're dying to talk mountain survival with the guy. And you've got that fancy camera you've never used. Now's your chance."

"I dunno." He scratched the back of his neck.

"Go! I'll keep the doors locked. No one will bother me. I'll be fine."

"Are you sure?"

I rolled my eyes. "I'm sure."

"Okay, but tomorrow I'm looking into getting you better security."

I threw up my hands. "Fine!"

We walked the rest of the way to Wits' End. Bailey, wriggling ecstatically, met us at the front door.

I baked cornbread with the kitchen windows open and the overhead fan spinning lazily. Near the spirit house, Arsen flipped steaks, sizzling on the grill. I'd marinated the meat that afternoon in garlic, balsamic vinegar, and brown sugar, but I couldn't smell any of that over the smoke.

Hopeful, Bailey pranced around the grill.

Arsen, the back of his khaki tee damp with sweat, laughed, knelt, and fed Bailey a sliver of beef.

Keeping an eye on them through the window, I retrieved my phone and called the sheriff.

"What now?" she snapped.

"Dixie didn't kill your ex-husband." I opened the oven and poked the corn bread. It sprang back to the touch, and I removed it from the heat.

"Good luck proving that."

"I can't. But I think I know who did kill Tanner. And I think something might happen. Tonight."

"What do you mean, *something might happen*?"

There was a knock on the kitchen door, and Professor Green strode inside. Ethan trailed behind her.

"I'll call you back," I said, and hung up. The kitchen was off limits to guests, something I hadn't posted, because it seemed obvious. I forced a smile. "Hi, what can I do for you?"

"I wanted to let you know that we'll be checking out tomorrow morning," the professor said. She'd changed into a blue, button-up hiking shirt and khaki shorts.

"Okay," I said, "I'll have your invoice ready."

"I don't want to go," Ethan said.

She glared at her son. "You have to go. I've arranged that internship for you, and it starts on Monday."

"But I'm not interested in environmental—"

"You don't know what you're interested in. This internship will be good for you."

His shoulders collapsed. "Whatever." Ethan drew his phone from the pocket of his baggy shorts.

I sucked in my breath.

He hesitated, put it back.

I smothered my disappointment. It had been stupid to think I could help Ethan in just a few short days. We barely knew each other. But maybe there was hope. Maybe Ethan really *had* broken free of some of his old patterns. But when would he finally break free of his mother?

"Come," his mother said. "Let's get dinner."

Mouth set in a taut line, he followed her from the kitchen.

Carrying a plate of steaks and foil-wrapped potatoes, Arsen

nudged open the screen door with his hip. Bailey, ever hopeful, danced at his heels. The scent of the marinated steaks filled the kitchen, and my mouth watered. I loved this sweet and garlicky marinade, with just a hint of kick from Cajun spice and sriracha sauce.

"What's with the Greens?" he asked.

"They're checking out tomorrow." I rubbed my temple. "Let's eat."

He set the plate on the table, and Bailey greedily tracked the motion. "It'll be a relief when they're gone," he said.

"You have no idea." They weren't bad. I had some sympathy for the professor. But they were too harsh a reminder of what I'd barely escaped.

He grinned. "Oh, yes I do."

We ate dinner, Arsen sneaking scraps to Bailey beneath the kitchen table and raving about Xavier's lecture. The adventure writer had seemed pompous to me, but he was Arsen's hero, not mine.

But my thoughts kept returning to the murders, and to Dixie, innocent and in jail.

We finished eating, and I took the dishes to the sink.

"Nick will get Dixie out." Arsen rose from his chair and came to join me at the sink. "We'll fix this. Don't worry."

I scraped the plates. "I know he will." Because I'd make sure of it.

Panting, Bailey stretched out his legs beneath the kitchen table. His eyelids lowered.

Arsen took the plate from me and turned me to face him. "I don't have to go on that hike, you know."

"If you don't, I'll be seriously angry."

Arsen pulled me into a hug. I relaxed into it, enjoying the feel of his muscular arms around me. Enjoying his warmth. His strength. I wanted this moment to last, this mirage that everything would be all right.

"I'm not afraid to be here alone," I said. "I'm just afraid..."

"Afraid of what?"

Outside the window, the moon seemed to wink at me high above the mountains. I couldn't tell him the truth. I stepped away.

He grasped my hand, keeping me close.

"What if we can't get her out of jail?" I asked.

"Don't think that way. And don't think you have to fix everything on your own. You're not alone and neither is Dixie." Even if he was sometimes feckless and unpredictable, he was also a loyal and good man. He'd always be there for me. My heart seemed to break open, as if I were truly seeing him for the first time, and understanding...

I gasped, releasing his hand.

What was wrong with me? We were best friends. Just friends.

"Is something wrong?" His brow furrowed.

"No. Um. I just..."

"Just?"

"I'm glad you're in my life," I said finally.

"How glad?" His voice dropped to a low rumble.

My heartbeat skyrocketed. "I can't imagine Doyle without you," I said quickly. "We've known each other for so long. And now..."

He closed the space between us, his gaze as soft as a caress. "Now...?" He put his hand beneath my chin and angled my head up, so I couldn't avoid his gaze. We were close, so close, and something flared inside me, between us, a dizzying current.

He was going to kiss me. And I wanted him to. I leaned closer.

He brushed a wisp of hair behind my ears. "Sue—"

The kitchen door slammed against the wall, and we leapt apart.

The sheriff strode inside. "What's going on?"

"Nothing." I jammed my hands into the pockets of my white shorts.

She looked from me to Arsen, and her eyes narrowed.

Arsen cleared his throat. "I'll take Bailey for a walk."

Bailey scrambled from beneath the round table. "Walk" was one word he understood.

We watched the two leave the kitchen, and the sheriff turned to me. "So? You said you thought you knew who killed Tanner."

A moth fluttered against the screened window.

"Yes. Um, you said you're back at work tomorrow, but are you still on leave tonight?"

"Yeah. Why?"

I bit the inside of cheek. "But if you had to arrest someone, could you?"

"If I saw someone committing a crime," she said, "I could act. But if you think you know who killed Tanner, I can't just go and arrest them."

"It's just... Someone told me Tanner's scheme was bigger than the police knew. That there were bigger fish involved."

She crossed her arms, wrinkling her freshly pressed khaki blouse. "It's possible. I always thought there were others involved when he got caught years ago, but I had no proof."

"And proof would be tough to get with people covering for each other. What you need is one person — the killer — to come clean."

"If I had the killer in custody, he'd talk."

"Tanner didn't."

She gazed past me, out the dark window. "What's your point?"

"Are you sure you can trust everyone in your department?"

She opened her mouth, closed it. Her lips compressed. "No. Again, what's your point?"

I grabbed my day planner off the butcher-block counter. "My point is, I have a plan to prove Dixie's innocence."

"No. No plans. No schemes. No cockamamie ideas."

"But—"

"Leave it, Witsend." She strode to the door.

"Give me five minutes to explain. Two minutes," I amended hastily.

She rubbed her jaw. "One minute."

I explained.

She ended up giving me five.

The sheriff shook her head. "That's not evidence. It's conjecture."

"But that's why—"

"No. Now that the *bad* ideas are out of the way, have you got anything that makes sense?"

"But someone has to act."

"No, *someone* doesn't. You're guessing."

I brandished my day planner. "It's all in here," I said, my desperation growing.

"Forget it."

"But—"

"No."

But this time, I couldn't take *no* for an answer.

Chapter 30

A full moon hung low and pendulous above the jagged mountains. It was bright enough I didn't need the flashlight in the pocket of my black hoodie. The moonlight cast long shadows through the stand of aspens.

Clumsily, I tiptoed around the back of the low building. Bushes rustled, and I imagined bears and police officers lurking.

My palms grew damp in my gloves, and I tightened my grip on the tire iron. How had Dixie ever managed the stress of lawbreaking?

Breaking into a guest's room, where I had a legal right to be, was one thing. Breaking into a place where I had no right to be was quite another.

Sweat stung my right eye. Roughly, I dashed it away with the back of my hand. I wouldn't let Dixie down again. This case couldn't go to trial. If it did, the jury would be blinded by Dixie's past rather than seeing her present. They'd come to the same conclusion the cops had — guilty.

A branch cracked.

I froze, my heart pounding in my ears. Slowly, I reached my free hand into my hoodie for the flashlight Arsen had given me last Christmas. I held my breath.

In the distance, tires whooshed over pavement. The aspen leaves rustled, a warm, night breeze raising the hair on the back of my neck.

Quaking in my yoga pants, I crept through the bracken and squeezed the tire iron.

Another branch snapped.

I whirled, turning on the flashlight.

"Hey!" Arsen stood, pale and blinking in the glare. He turned away, rubbing his eyes.

"Arsen," I whispered and willed my heart not to beat its way out of my chest. "What are you doing here? You're supposed to be at that Xavier Ultra hike."

"What are *you* doing here?" He yanked up the zipper on his lightweight hiking jacket. A backpack was slung over one shoulder.

"I'm just... out for a walk."

"Here?" He raised a skeptical brow and motioned toward the low building. "And without Bailey?"

"Were you following me?"

"Of course, I followed you. It's not often I see you creeping around Doyle after midnight." He grinned. "Not since we were teenagers."

He'd given up a hike with his hero for me? "But you've been looking forward to meeting him all week. This was your chance for some quality time with Xavier."

It was impossible to tell in the darkness, but I could have sworn he flushed.

"Why are you carrying a tire iron?" he asked.

I looked down at my gloved hand, surprised. "Oh. That."

"And why are you all in black? Are you planning on breaking in?" He jerked his chin toward the squat building.

"What?" I laughed, high and false. "No!"

"You think there's evidence that will prove Dixie's innocence in there, don't you?"

"I don't know what you're talking about."

"Because you might be right."

I gaped. "What?"

"I've been suspicious of this setup too. And it's the big fish that get the most out of these welfare schemes. I'm just surprised because..." He shifted his weight. "You know."

A weight lifted from my shoulders. He believed me. "I don't know where else to look," I said rapidly, "but there must be records. I thought the computer...?"

He nodded. "A quick smash and grab. Makes sense. Efficient and low risk."

Smash and grab? Had he and Dixie been comparing notes? "I don't know how quick it will be," I hedged.

"As quick as we can make it," he said, grim.

No. No, no, no. "Arsen, this was my idea. There's no sense in us both getting caught."

"You're right. I'll do it. You wait here."

The gray shadow of panic seized me by the throat. "What? No way! Besides, it's my tire iron." I clasped it to my chest. "And I brought gloves."

He walked to a small window beside the back door and set his backpack on the concrete landing. In a quick motion, he smashed it with his elbow.

I gasped. "What are you doing?"

He reached inside and unlocked the door. "Wait here."

"What? No." This was not going according to plan. Arsen wasn't supposed to be here! "Arsen, wait." I slipped in after him and shut the door.

The hallway was too dark to be able to see, but I could feel the closeness of its walls. "Arsen?" I whispered.

"Here," he said further down the hall.

I fumbled, my trembling hands finding a door, and eventually a knob. "I think we should check this store room."

"Isn't his computer up front?"

I edged into the room and turned on my flashlight, illuminating metal file cabinets in a windowless room. "He's got records here." I slid open a cabinet and scanned the files, which appeared to be patient records.

Arsen came to stand in the doorway. "We need the computer drive. Smash and grab, remember?"

"That was your idea, not mine." I hurried to the other side of the room and opened another cupboard. More patient files.

"What are you looking for?"

"He might not leave evidence on the front computer," I said. "Sometimes there's a receptionist working on it."

He grunted and joined me searching the files. "I don't see any billing records here."

I gave up. "Fine. Let's get the computer."

Since there were windows in the other open rooms along the hall, I switched off the flashlight. The odds were low a passerby would see my light and call the cops, but I didn't want to take the chance. Not with Arsen involved.

We slunk down the corridor. I jiggled the office doorknob. Locked.

"I got this." Catlike, Arsen swung through the open reception window and scrambled across the desk. Something clattered to the floor.

I winced.

"Whoops," he said. "Sorry. Just a pencil holder." He opened the door. "Got that flashlight?"

Looking nervously about the room, I handed it to him and strode to a metal cabinet beside a window. My gaze fell on the old pizza delivery hat. That must have been what he'd used to gain entry, and he'd kept it, even after I'd noticed it after the murder. Either he was crazy-arrogant or thought getting rid of it would be suspicious.

Arsen unplugged the computer drive beneath the desk.

"Maybe there's something in here." I opened another cabinet drawer. "Can I have the light?"

He rose, computer drive beneath his arm, and handed the flashlight to me. "Forget the cabinet. We need to get out of here."

I pulled out a file and flipped it open, shined the light inside. The flashlight beam wobbled. "Invoices!"

"Which would also be on the computer. Let's go."

"Don't worry," I said. "He doesn't have an alarm."

He frowned. "I doubt you'll find anything on paper—"

"We need to check the paper invoices against the computer records. Remember? I'm an accountant."

"You used to be," he said. "Now we're petty criminals. Come on, let's move. We can check the computer when we get back to my place."

"We're taking it to Wits' End. This is my burglary."

"With an FBI agent staying upstairs? I don't think so."

"But—"

"Let's argue about it somewhere else." He slipped into the reception area and vanished around the corner.

Flipping off the flashlight, I stumbled over a waste basket and made my way to the door. "Arsen, wait."

"We've already taken too much time." He opened the back door. Moonlight cascaded into the hallway.

"But Arsen—"

A beam of light blazed, haloing Arsen's head.

"Freeze, police!"

Chapter 31

"We're unarmed!" Hands in the air, heart in my throat, I hurried down the corridor toward Arsen and the blaze of light.

The sheriff ignored me. "Drop it," she barked at Arsen.

"Don't," a man shouted. "My entire business is on that drive."

I edged past Arsen and squinted.

The sheriff aimed her gun at Arsen. She was decked out in full uniform — jacket, utility belt, radio handset clipped to her collar.

Zack seemed less substantial beside her. His clothes and hair were rumpled as if he'd dressed hastily, his red hair gray in the moonlight.

"You." The sheriff's mouth twisted. "I should have guessed. Though I'm surprised about you, Holiday. You don't need the money. Are you breaking in for thrills?"

"Arsen has nothing to do with this," I said. Good God, what had I done?

"It doesn't look that way," she said. "Now put down that computer. Slowly."

"I'm setting down the computer." He lowered the computer to the cement landing. Arsen straightened, his hands in the air.

The sheriff pulled a pair of handcuffs from the back of her utility belt. She slapped a cuff on one of Arsen's wrists and locked the other cuff to the metal railing beside the door. "Talk."

"Zack Harwell killed Tanner and Davin," I said. My raised arms tingled, the blood flowing in the wrong direction. "The proof's on that computer."

Arsen rattled the handcuff. "Susan, no."

The chiropractor's eyes widened. "You think I..." He turned to the sheriff. "I give you permission to search that computer and my office. I had nothing to do with those deaths."

My heart sank. It had always been a longshot, but I'd hoped...

"It's not Susan's fault," Arsen said, tugging on the cuff. "She only came along to try to stop me."

"Is this true?" the sheriff asked me.

"No." I gave Arsen what I hoped was an *it's-okay* look. I should have given up this crazy plan as soon as he'd turned up. "Arsen only came to try and stop me."

"It looked more like he was helping you," the sheriff said. "Harwell, come with us. I need to get the extra pair of cuffs from my car." She grasped my elbow in a crushing grip and steered me toward the front parking lot.

Helplessly, I looked over my shoulder at Arsen, cuffed to the metal bar.

The sheriff dragged me to her official SUV. A second car, a Honda, sat parked near the office's front door.

"I can't believe you thought I was involved," the chiropractor said to me.

"You were way too interested in what I knew about the crime," I said. "And you had a pizza delivery hat! Sheriff, it's sitting right in his front office. He must have worn it when he came to kill Tanner, disguising himself as a delivery boy and coming up the back stairs so he wouldn't be noticed."

"Lots of people have those hats," Zack said.

"Unless there's Tanner's DNA on it," the sheriff said, "a hat's not evidence."

Zack laughed, a strained chuckle. "Why would his DNA be on it? It's my hat..."

She turned me around. "Put your hands on top of the car. Harwell, shout if this idiot moves."

I could barely reach the top of her SUV, but I did as she asked. "Sheriff, Arsen really isn't involved in this."

"He is now." The sheriff reached inside the front of the SUV. She fumbled a moment, grunted, and drew out a second pair of cuffs. Sheriff McCourt wrenched one of my arms behind me, snapped on the cuff, and then cuffed the other.

Opening the rear door, she helped me inside, protecting the top of my head with one hand. "Sit." She pointed. "Stay. Harwell, you stay here too. I'm going to get Holiday." She strode around the corner of the building.

"There will be evidence." My voice shook. "It might not be in your office, but it exists. You don't run a welfare fraud without a paper trail, even if it is a fraudulent one."

He raised a brow. "Welfare fraud? Is that what you think happened?"

The full moon sank lower behind the mountains, gilding their peaks.

"The real money in a fraud like that is made by the doctors and lawyers involved," I said. Madame X had tried to tell me. I only hoped we could find her and she had real evidence, because my shot at that was gone. "What did you do? Create false patients and bill the county for them? Did Tanner find out and demand his cut? Or were you partners from the beginning?"

He sighed and shook his head. "Why not tell you? No one will believe it, and I've been dying to tell someone. To answer your question, Tanner found out and wanted in. He made good money off me."

I was right? "Why didn't Tanner turn you in with his other partners when he got caught?"

"At the time, I expected he would." He rubbed his jaw. "His silence was a strange gift. But then he returned to Doyle and demanded more money for his silence."

"And so, you killed him."

An owl hooted, low and lonely.

He shrugged. "People underestimate me because, let's face it, I'm charming. But as a chiropractor, I understand the musculoskeletal system. I had no trouble breaking Tanner's neck."

"What were you looking for in his room? His proof that you were involved?"

"Yes, but I never found it, because it didn't exist. He was greedy and bluffing, and that got him killed."

"It must have been even easier for you to kill Davin," I said. "He was already seeing you as a chiropractor. Or was he really a patient?"

"He was always griping about his back. I offered him a quick adjustment. You shouldn't mind, after he dropped that air conditioner on you."

"Why did he?"

"You were asking too many questions," he said. "The idiot thought he was helping, now that he was my new partner." He put the last words in air quotes.

"Davin knew Tanner had another partner," I said. "He must have figured out – or maybe Tanner even told him – it was you. Did Davin try to carry on with Tanner's blackmail?"

"Tanner couldn't resist shooting his mouth off to his old partner." He stepped closer to the open SUV door. "Davin was just as greedy as McCourt. He had to die."

Horror curdled inside me, but I forced myself to keep talking. "And the cherub?"

"The what?"

"The statue of the boy with the wings."

He shrugged, the moonlight wavering across his handsome face. "Everyone knows they're unstable. I guess I got the idea from Davin."

"And you started getting worried. The questions I was asking were getting too close. Is that why you broke into the B&B and tried to steal my planner?"

"What can I say? I'm naturally curious."

He was naturally insane to take such a chance out of mere curiosity. I gulped. "And if I was figuring things out, the police might be too. And the five-hundred dollar bet Tanner owed you? Was that real?"

His face scrunched in disbelief. "Of course not. Do you think I'd be stupid enough to gamble with Tanner? But you knew there was a connection between us, so I threw you an innocent explanation."

"You stole Tanner's wallet when you killed him." The cuffs bit into my wrists, and I squirmed. "Maybe you took it to make the murder seem like a robbery. Maybe you were looking for something. But when you learned my cousin was a person of interest, you planted Tanner's wallet in her trailer. Then you called in an anonymous tip."

"For someone as paranoid as your cousin, she doesn't have very good security on that trailer."

The moon vanished behind the mountaintops, and the parking lot darkened. A branch creaked.

"And what about me?" My voice cracked. "Are you going to snap my neck as well?"

"Why would I? The police will never believe you. It's all supposition, and they have a suspect in custody. But if you do push this, I'll kill your friend, and then I'll kill you, and no one will think it was anything but an accident."

My breath quickened. I edged further from him, my yoga pants squeaking on the car seat. "My friend?"

"Arsen Holiday. You're left with an interesting choice. Keep trying to clear your cousin's name, or put your lover in danger."

Fury sparked inside my chest, and I raised my chin. "We're really just friends," I said, nails biting into my palms.

In a swift motion, he grabbed my neck. "Don't test me."

"Let go," I croaked.

Suddenly, the pressure released. The chiropractor flew backwards. A thud. A grunt.

I gasped, sucking in gulps of air.

Arsen's hands were around the chiropractor's throat. Zack, on his toes, made choking sounds. Arsen shook him like Bailey with the furry octopus in his teeth.

"That's enough!" The sheriff grasped Arsen's shoulder, and Zack tumbled to the pavement.

Swiftly, she rolled the chiropractor onto his stomach and cuffed him.

Arsen hurried to the open SUV. "Are you all right?" he asked me.

I nodded, swallowing.

He helped me slither awkwardly from the SUV.

"What are you doing?" Zack shouted. "Why'd you let him go? He assaulted me."

The sheriff pressed a button on the handset clipped to her collar.

Zack's voice floated from the radio. "*People underestimate me because, let's face it, I'm charming. But as a chiropractor, I understand the musculoskeletal system. I had no trouble breaking Tanner's neck.*"

She pressed the button again, and the recording clicked off.

Zack's eyes bulged. "You... you recorded me?"

The sheriff's smile was chill. "Do you really think I don't carry two pairs of handcuffs on my belt?" She maneuvered the chiropractor into the rear of the SUV and shut the door. "Turn around." She uncuffed me.

Blowing out my breath, I massaged my wrists. "Thanks."

Arsen wrapped an arm around my shoulders. "Nice job, Nancy Drew, but you could have told me what you were up to when we broke into the office."

"I almost did tell you," I said. "You were bent on getting out of the office quickly. But we needed to be inside for at least fifteen minutes. That gave the sheriff time to alert Zack his alarm had gone off and to get him there in time to arrest us. Though your presence gave her a reason to leave me alone with Zack."

Arsen frowned. "If the alarm went off, why aren't the other police here?"

"Trade secret." Sheriff McCourt walked to the front of the SUV. "I'll take your statement tomorrow, Susan."

We watched her drive off, her taillights vanishing around the corner.

"You and the sheriff put this whole thing together?"

"Yep." After he'd told me he'd seen Cherie and Davin together, I was sure Zack had been setting Cherie up to take the fall – or worse. We'd had to act fast. "Zack did too good a job covering his tracks. With Manaj in charge of the arrest, the sheriff didn't trust that she'd be able to get a warrant to examine Zack's finances. Plus, Tanner was her husband, even if he was a crook. Finding the real killer mattered."

He pulled me closer. "Are you sure you're all right?" he asked, his voice a low rumble.

My heart turned over. "Are you kidding me?" I hugged him. "Dixie's off the hook. We caught the real killer. I couldn't be better."

He kissed my forehead. "No, I guess you couldn't."

Chapter 32

Agent Manaj handed her credit card across the B&B's reception desk. "Here, take it."

Bailey panted on the rug in a patch of mid-morning sunlight. Dust motes floated like gold dust around his doggy head.

"How did you enjoy your stay?" I swiveled to face the glowing computer.

"You've got a nice place," she said, grudging. "I'd recommend it."

"Please do tell the other Men in Black," I joked. "I'd love their business."

The FBI agent stared down at me. Her brown eyes narrowed, her mouth a hard line.

My hand froze over the credit card reader. "I was only kidding," I stammered. "Because you wear black. Even though you're not a man."

Silence.

"You're not... I mean, I was kidding but..." Suspicion sprouted in my brain. Because if she wasn't a Man in Black, she'd been doing a good impression of one. "You're not a Man in Black, are you?" I whispered.

"I applied for the position," she said, expressionless. "But I'm still waiting to hear back."

I blinked. She'd made a joke!

Wait. That *was* a joke, wasn't it? I smiled uncertainly.

In yellow rubber gloves, a tank top and shorts, Dixie trotted down the stairs. The bucket of cleaning supplies swung from one hand. She spotted the agent and paused on the bottom step. "Oh. It's you."

"We had to arrest you after we found that wallet in your trailer," Manaj said. "It was nothing personal."

My cousin walked down the last step to the foyer and set the cleaning supplies near the desk. "Whatever."

"I had to go where the evidence took me." She met my cousin's angry gaze. "No matter what."

I handed Manaj her credit card and a receipt slip. "Here you go."

Dixie's nostrils flared. She strode into the kitchen, and Bailey whined, looking at me with concern.

The agent bent over the desk to sign, and her black hair cascaded forward. "By the way, I fixed the lock on your window. Your security is terrible."

"Oh. Um. Thanks?"

"It's funny though. I could have sworn someone got into my room again anyway."

"Really?" I squeaked.

She straightened, her gaze boring into mine. "It's a good thing I didn't catch them. Tampering with evidence is a felony."

"Good to know." A bead of sweat trickled down my neck. "I'm going to talk to someone about improving B&B security." Maybe the sheriff could give me some tips.

"You do that." She picked up her black suitcase and strode outside.

My muscles released. She might have guessed I'd done it, but I wasn't in handcuffs. Yet.

I bent to scratch Bailey behind the ears. "But all's well that ends well, right?"

Arsen, a clipboard beneath his muscular arm, sauntered through the front door. "Manaj checked out?"

My heart skipped a beat, and I forced myself to calm. Since our "moment" in the kitchen the other night, nothing had happened between us.

Nothing.

Had I imagined that moment?

My face warmed. Or had I messed the whole thing up by putting my best friend in harm's way? I'd thought I'd had everything under control, the perfect plan. I'd told myself Arsen could make his own decisions. I'd even had a sheriff in on the con. But I'd been arrogant. Arrogant and foolish. And a killer had threatened Arsen.

I cleared my throat. "Yep," I said. "The case is closed. Manaj has got no more reason to stay."

"She must be disappointed. The sheriff was the one who caught the real killer. And Manaj never really cracked the case of The Disappeared all those months ago."

"I'm not sure she was trying that hard." If she was a Man in Black... *Nah.* "And speaking of solving cases, did you find out from your source who Madame X is?"

He shifted. "About that...."

"What's wrong?"

"Nothing. Not really. But there's no old lady that fits your description at city hall. Or at the county government, for that matter."

"That's... weird." Then who was she?

"Maybe she used to work there," he said. "Or has friends who still do."

"Right. Maybe." This was going to bug me now. But I had a feeling I'd be seeing Madame X again. "What's with the clipboard?"

He glanced down, as if surprised to see it. "For your security upgrade."

"My upgrade?"

Bailey snorted at my feet.

"I'm thinking key cards on the guest rooms and front and rear doors. We can program them so you need a card to get in the main building after a certain hour. And the guest room doors need peepholes and safety locks. Plus, when's the last time you tested your emergency plan?"

"My plan is to pull the fire alarm. There's not much to test."

He shook his head. "CCTV coverage wouldn't be a bad idea either."

"What do you know about security?"

He raised the clipboard. "All answers are on the internet."

I groaned. "Key cards are a good idea, but I don't know when I'll be able to afford them. I haven't even got the lawyer's bill yet."

"Right, I almost forgot." He pulled a folded sheet of paper from the back pocket of his jeans and handed it across the desk. "Here."

Wary, I unfolded the invoice. My brow furrowed. The bill was surprisingly reasonable. "Is he sending me a second invoice?"

"No, that's everything."

"But..." I scanned the invoice. "He only charged two hundred dollars an hour." California lawyers, even in the foothills, billed a lot more than that.

"You got the friends and family discount."

"I barely know Nick Heathcoat." I braced my forearm on the wooden desk.

"Yeah, but I do."

"Arsen, I pay my own bills." My experience with lawyers was limited, but I didn't know any who gave discounts this big. And I couldn't take money from Arsen. Not after what I'd done.

"Right, and that's the bill."

"I don't want you pulling a fast one and paying for half, then telling me this is the entire bill."

"Are you complaining I got you a discount?"

"No, but—"

"So, let's talk security," he said.

"Let's talk about that move you pulled on the chiropractor the other night. Where'd you learn to do that?"

His expression turned bland. "What move?"

"The way you did... whatever you did to him."

"I don't know. Instinct, I guess."

I've known Arsen a long time, and I can tell when he's lying. But I let it go.

"Listen," he said, "I've got a buddy in the security biz. He can get you a great discount on the equipment, and I'll do the install."

"You." I raised a skeptical brow. "You will do the install."

"Sure, it will save money."

I rose and planted my hands on the desk. "Arsen, what's going on?"

"A killer snuck into your B&B disguised as an over-aged pizza delivery guy. You need to take care of this."

"Agreed," I said. "And I appreciate your help, but don't you have your own business to run?"

"You know how it is. Being a guide is weekend work. I'm thinking security could be a sideline."

"I thought you wanted to become a private investigator?"

"Do you have any idea what the licensing requirements are? It would take forever. Besides, I'm good with technology. Although..." He eyed me skeptically. "You're not really a tech person, are you?"

"What's that supposed to mean?"

"I *could* install the system, but then you'd have to manage it. You don't have the time to learn all that."

"I'm a fast learner. I understand technology. I can do technology!"

He grinned. "Great. I'm going to scope out the upstairs."

I watched him climb the steps to the second floor and sighed. He'd totally pulled the "you-can't-do-it" trick, knowing I'd insist on doing it.

Dixie emerged from the kitchen carrying a vase filled with Eden Roses. "Is she gone?"

"For now."

"I went ahead and pruned those broken branches. I figured I may as well cut some flowers. Where do you want 'em?"

"Why not right here?" I nodded to the desk.

She set them down and arranged the flowers. Dixie stepped back, studying them critically, then nodded.

"There is one thing I wanted to ask you," I said.

She rubbed her palms on her shorts. "What?"

"I heard you left the B&B the afternoon Davin was killed, and Arsen and I were at the lake. Where were you?"

"What, are you checking up on me? You don't own me. It's none of your business."

It was typical Dixie. Chaotic. Stubborn. Uncontrollable.

I wouldn't want her any other way.

"You look weird," she said. "Is everything okay?"

The scent of roses filled the foyer, and Bailey rested his head on my foot. I smiled. "Everything's perfect."

Gran's Coffee Cake

INGREDIENTS:
1 pkg active dry yeast
½ C tepid water
½ C soft butter + 1 T
1/3 C sugar
3 egg yolks
¾ C milk
¼ tsp salt
¼ tsp ground cardamom
3 C all-purpose flour
Chocolate streusel filling (recipe follows)
¾ C chopped pecans
Powdered sugar glaze (recipe follows)

DIRECTIONS:
Add yeast to tepid water and mix, dissolving yeast. Cream ½ C butter with an electric mixer until light, then beat in sugar and egg yolks. Add yeast/water mixture, salt and cardamom. Gradually mix in the flour until dough is soft and flour completely combined.

Knead dough on a board until the dough is smooth. Return the dough to your mixing bowl. Butter the top of the dough with the remaining 1 T of butter. Cover with a cloth and leave the dough to rise somewhere warm for approximately 1 ½ hours or until the dough has doubled.

Roll the dough out on a floured surface and flatten it into a long, rectangular shape, so the dough is approximately 8 inches wide by 54 inches long, and ¼" thick.

Evenly dust the chocolate streusel filling over the rolled out dough, leaving a 1-inch border around the edges. Sprinkle the filling evenly with the pecans. Roll the long edge like a jelly roll, so you end up with a long tube of dough, with the filling in the center. Pinch and seal the ends. Cut a three-inch piece off each end (one will be the beak, the other the feet).

Shape the duck into a figure-eight design, using 1/3rd of the dough for the top piece (the head) and 2/3rds for the bottom (the body). Set on a large buttered baking sheet. Pinch the back end of the "body" to make a tail. Press the 3" piece to the head for the bill and press the other 3" piece to the bottom to make feet. (See figure below).

Cover with a towel. Set in a warm place and allow to rise for 45 minutes, or until doubled. (At this point, you can put the dough in the refrigerator and leave overnight, if you wish to bake it the next morning).

Bake at 325 degrees (F) for 30-35 minutes until brown. While the coffee cake is warm, ice with the powdered sugar glaze. Serve warm.

CHOCOLATE STREUSAL FILLING: Mix ½ C sugar, ¼ C all-purpose flour, 2 T butter, 1 ½ tsp cocoa powder, ½ tsp cinnamon. Mixture should be crumbly.

POWDERED SUGAR GLAZE: Whisk 1 C powdered sugar with 4 tsp milk and ½ tsp vanilla.

Arsen's Waffle Biscuits

INGREDIENTS:
3 eggs
1/4 C shredded sharp cheddar cheese
1 tube refrigerated biscuit dough
salt and pepper, to taste

DIRECTIONS:
Over medium-low heat, warm a non-stick skillet. Whisk the eggs. Scramble the eggs in the skillet, but don't let them dry out. While the eggs are cooking, heat a waffle iron.

Stir the shredded cheese into the eggs. Remove the skillet from the stove.

Spray the waffle iron with the non-stick cooking spray of your choice (Arsen prefers butter flavor). Separate the biscuits and split them with a sharp knife, but DON'T COMPLETELY SPLIT THE BISCUITS IN HALF. They should fold open but still be connected at one end.

Make a sandwich, putting some egg and cheese mixture inside a biscuit.

Place a biscuit in the waffle iron. Let the lid close gently, but don't smash the biscuit flat or force the lid to close completely.

After one minute, fully close the waffle iron, flattening the biscuit. Cook for two more minutes.

Remove the waffle biscuit from the waffle iron and repeat with the rest of the biscuits and cheesy eggs.

About the Author

Kirsten Weiss authors genre-bending stories of mystery, suspense, and enchantment.

She worked overseas for over fourteen years, in the fringes of the former USSR and deep in the Afghan war zone. Her experiences abroad not only gave her glimpses into the darker side of human nature, but also sparked an interest in the effects of mysticism and mythology, and how both are woven into our daily lives.

Now based in San Mateo, CA, she writes paranormal mysteries, blending her experiences and imagination to create a vivid world of magic and mayhem.

Kirsten has never met a dessert she didn't like, and her guilty pleasures are watching Ghost Whisperer reruns and drinking good wine.

You can connect with Kirsten through the social media sites below, and if the mood strikes you, send her an e-mail at kweiss2001@kirstenweiss.com.

Follow her on Twitter: @KirstenWeiss

Check out her story world boards on Pinterest: www.pinterest.com/kirstenweiss/

Sign up for her newsletter for cool free stuff and book updates at: kirstenweiss.com

If you post a picture of this book to Instagram, you can tag her @kirstenweissauthor

Made in the USA
Monee, IL
02 March 2023

29040451R10134